P9-CRH-925

MUSIC TO MURDER BY . . .

Putting down her cup and taking in her surroundings she saw—good gracious, what a coincidence—the gentleman who had hummed at London airport. She smiled and nodded. Unknowing and out of key she began to hum "Song of India."

Mantoni glowered. *Allora*, so she derided him in public with all her friends of the *polizia*. She wished him to understand that she knew what he was doing—what he had done—and that she found him ridiculous and was only awaiting her opportunity. *Allora*—so. He got up. This was now personal. This was vendetta. He would go at once to the dealer he knew of and when he had his pistol—and its silencer—she would find that it would be he, he who would be making the opportunities.

PRAISE FOR MISS SEETON

"A most beguiling protagonist."—*New York Times*

"Miss Seeton is a star."—*Detroit News*

"Light, zany, this novel is peopled by several genuine human beings you hate to see go."—*Houston Post*

Berkley books by Heron Carvic

MISS SEETON SINGS
WITCH MISS SEETON

MISS SEETON SINGS
HERON CARVIC

BERKLEY BOOKS, NEW YORK

This Berkley book contains the complete
text of the original hardcover edition.
It has been completely reset in a typeface
designed for easy reading and was printed
from new film.

MISS SEETON SINGS

A Berkley Book / published by arrangement with
the author

PRINTING HISTORY
Peter Davies edition published 1973
Berkley edition / April 1988

ISBN: 0-425-10714-0

A BERKLEY BOOK ® TM 757,375
Berkley Books are published by The Berkley Publishing Group,
200 Madison Avenue, New York, New York 10016.
The name "BERKLEY" and the "B" logo
are trademarks belonging to Berkley Publishing Corporation.

PRINTED IN THE UNITED STATES OF AMERICA

10 9 8 7 6 5 4 3 2 1

For
Pamela
with
love and gratitude

MISS SEETON SINGS

London

THE WORDS—what were the words? Jewels—*i diamanti*—yes, that was it. Tentatively he began to sing under his breath: *"Les diamants chez nous sont inn— sont inn—"*

What was the French for *innumerevole?* He began to sweat.

Why, why, why, if he must indulge in this foolishness of singing the words of a song to establish recognition, must the tune be Russian and the words French? When anyone knew that Italian was the only language in which to sing. When anyone understood that Italian composers were superior. And that he—that he—should sing foreign words to strange music must at once raise question in people's minds as to his nationality—or his taste.

Elio Mantoni appraised himself as an artist, pure and simple. The adjectives were flights of fancy, for by nature he was impure and devious. He could overpaint an old master or underpaint a modern student with equal facility and reasonable ability. He could, and did, produce an efficient facsimile of any picture he was asked to copy. He could upon demand produce ghost replicas of genuine old canvases which, discovered in some attic, had been borrowed to determine their authenticity. Should such a painting then prove to be of value, Elio's effort would be returned with assumed regret to the unsuspecting

owner as worthless while the original could be "discovered"
elsewhere and sold. To summarize Elio Mantoni's potential, he
was a small man by nature, a painter by profession, an Italian
by birthright, a singer by bath rite and currently a courier for
the distribution of spurious banknotes by force of crooked
circumstances. It was this current occupation to which he took
exception. In his youth Mantoni, in common with many
aspiring novices in crime, had overlooked the disadvantages of
his chosen career. Crime may pay, but the large rewards are
reaped by the barons of the industry. For the rank and file work
is irregular and depends upon demand. It is a sad comment on
the progress in industrial relations that little thought and no
effective action has been taken to improve the lot of the
evildoer. A man employed in a protection racket himself has no
protection. There is no trade union to act on his behalf and
should he strike he will be struck down, for society has yet to
evolve a law to safeguard the career of the lawbreaker. Elio
Mantoni therefore had to do what he was told and, although it
was not his trade, he had been acting for the last months as an
unwilling commercial traveler. Travel he disliked: in this case
it also involved danger, which he detested, and all the
mummery of signs and passwords, which he despised.

Apart from the song—an insult to the intelligence—there
was the tie—an insult to art. To have to wear a bow tie was
sufficiently bad, but that it should be in black and scarlet
horizontal stripes was anathema. In such a tie as that he would
not be found dead: but in such a tie as that he had been found
by the police. It was the tie—the tie, he was sure of it—which
had led the police pigs into searching him. It must be evident
even to their dull minds that such a man as he would not wear
such a tie—except from some base motive.

Those pigs of the police, to stop him at Passports and: Would
he mind stepping this way? Nothing personal; simply that some
passengers, picked at random, were asked to cooperate in a
check for drugs. No, it was not necessary to strip; just the coat,
the trousers and the shoes would do. Then quick hands patting
him to ensure. Apologies. Nothing personal. They were certain
that he would understand.

Yes, he had understood; with his suitcase already there in the
room waiting for him to produce the keys; everything unpacked, repacked, his briefcase emptied, refilled and returned,

and their pretended lack of interest in himself. Oh, no, nothing personal. How much of a fool did they consider him?

Elio Mantoni took a deep breath through his nose and expelled it slowly through his mouth to control nerves and clarify the brain.

Innombrables—that was the word he had forgotten. How ridiculous to disturb himself; to forget that the words of the song were written in his notebook. Impossible to think straight after the shock of being searched. And ridiculous to disturb himself for that: the pigs had been fooled. Had not the search proved him to be innocent? His volatile spirit soared, then sank. Unless they were playing with him—always suspecting. They might still be watching him—waiting. His mind took another plunge and panic swept over him. If they were to see the transfer of the money he would be searched again; arrested. But how could he give warning when he did not know who would do the transfer—or how—or when? It could be any type of man. It could be a woman. Also somehow he must report that he had come under suspicion. They would have to keep him out of England for a time, even though the pigs had proved, could prove, nothing against him.

Out of England; he began to feel better. No more of this perilous traveling with briefcases full of false money. They would have to put him back to his own, to his proper work, to painting. He drew himself up to his full five foot three and a half inches. He knew—because they had told him—that there were two stolen paintings on which he would soon be required to work. And now, undoubtedly, once he was free of England, that was what they would set him to do. Painting new masterpieces on old. And he would be back in his element. Encouraged, his ego once more self-inflated and his thirty-four-inch chest expanded, Mantoni strutted to the doors of the Heathrow Airport departure lounge and looked around for an empty table. There was none. He chose one at which a middle-aged woman was concentrating on a plate of variegated cream cakes. An hour's delay. Always delay, and always the excuse: due to the something of the incoming aircraft. And every extra minute would increase his danger. He bought a double whiskey at the bar, took it to the table and sat down, putting his briefcase on the floor beside his chair. He noted the tag on the woman's cabin-flight bag: GENOVA. A compatriot? He realized that she had stopped eating to stare at him. The cream-flecked mouth curved.

"*Buon giorno.*"

"*Giorno,*" he replied curtly and turned his head.

She flounced her shoulders and retreated into her preoccupatio with the cakes. Mantoni considered. A country-woman? It could be woman . . . No, he decided, she was not the type to . . . *Ma allora* you could not know. They were clever, using people who would never be suspected. But then—his thoughts flicked again to fright—he had been suspected. Even now he had the sensation of being watched, was on the point of looking round, when he was distracted by the arrival of a thin, elderly little woman escorted by a young man. The woman settled herself on the chair next to his and the young man announced that he would fetch her tea and biscuits. She protested. He insisted and, placing his briefcase on the remaining chair, went to the counter. Elio Mantoni tensed. The briefcase was not unlike his own; this might be the man. . . . As the young man was returning with the tea and biscuits an older man of whom Elio failed to get a clear view tried to push his way to the table. The young man was overbearing and the other retreated. Elio had started to hum the verse from Rimsky-Korsakov's "Song of India." The young man ignored him.

"If you'll wait here, Miss Seeton, I'll come back for you before your flight's called and hand you over to a stewardess, so you've nothing to worry about."

The elderly woman thanked him: he responded with a bored smile, picked up his briefcase and left.

Elio stopped humming. Covertly he took stock of the newcomer. No, no, no, small and old and gray; even more innocent than the cake woman. But . . . No, ridiculous. His imagination was running away; inventing danger where there was none. He was allowing the pigs, the pigs, the pigs to rattle him. *Ma ancora*—still, still he felt eyes upon him. In a quick survey of the lounge his glance locked with that of a man at a table against the wall. The man looked away, but Elio knew; knew that the other had been watching. Police? Or . . . ? His agitation increased with the sense of being trapped. Once more he would start the signal. He began to hum.

Three men with diverse interests had watched Mantoni enter the departure lounge.

One, a Frenchman, sat on a low upholstered banquette

beyond the cafeteria. He could have modeled for, had been modeled on, the typical British business executive: bowler hat, dark suit, black shoes and by his side the inevitable rolled umbrella and heavy briefcase. The only incongruous note in the City, though here it was almost obligatory, would have been the carrier bag which held a bottle of duty-free whiskey and a carton containing two hundred cigarettes. He paid no attention to the flight announcements since, as he had explained with a slight accent when checking in his luggage, he preferred to be nearly three hours early to waiting about in town with nothing to do. He held a newspaper at which he glanced occasionally, but for the most part he watched the throng in the cafeteria with an air of indifference. On Mantoni's appearance it was not so much the manikin he noted as the bow tie with its black and scarlet stripes. He also observed the black briefcase under the Italian's arm. Waiting until Mantoni was seated, he slowly gathered his possessions and sauntered toward the table. Halfway there he saw that an elderly woman accompanied by a young man might reach the table first and he began to hurry, but his progress was impeded by a family party: a mother, for safety, holding the hand of the eldest child, who, in her turn and for the same reason, held the hand of the next in years, who held the next, who held the next, who held the terminal, a tot who clutched the string of a nodding monkey in a cart. It was this last that proved to be his undoing. Thinking that the cavalcade had passed, he advanced, knocking the cart under a chair, and was set upon by the tot, who wailed, clung to his trousers and kicked his ankles. The family turned on him as one in assorted octaves of expostulation and by the time that he had extricated himself it was too late. He lunged toward Mantoni's table only to be met by a stiff shoulder and a disdainful stare.

"I say, old man, no need to shove, y'know. Plenty've room for all; 's matter o' fact I'm not staying." The young man collected his briefcase from the fourth chair. "There you are." He turned to his companion. "If you'll wait here, Miss Seeton . . ." The rest of the sentence was lost to the Frenchman as he moved away. Flute, that chair was useless. It had to be next to the striped bow tie or to make the exchange would be difficult—too evident. He left his newspaper, carrier and umbrella on a seat at a nearby table while he went to the counter and ordered coffee. He would have to find other means.

The second man who watched, Detective Constable Haley of Fraud, had hurried to the cafeteria after hearing the report on the abortive search of Mantoni and his possessions. Knowing that the Italian's flight to Genoa was delayed, he thought it likely the little tick would fill in his time there—would probably be needing something strong for his nerves. If, however, he decided to sit outside by the plate glass windows, the detective constable could move to a spot where he could keep an eye on him. Haley chose a seat at a table in the center against the wall opposite the end of the bar, from which he could watch both sides of the lounge without having to turn his head. He noted Mantoni's swaggering arrival. Cocky little ass—but under the bluster, he decided, Elio was edgy; his forehead was shining with sweat. What awful gear these Italians went for: purply suit with a blue stripe—more like pajamas; and as for the tie, and a bow to boot, black and red stripes—godawful. Anyway the little jerk'd got himself a whiskey and plumped himself down near a fat woman stuffing herself with cakes. She looked clean enough—hardly the type to pass him the doings—though at that you never knew. Well, if she tried it on he'd have 'em both to rights. When he'd really need to keep his eyes skinned was if anybody joined 'em. The detective constable was distracted for a moment by the sound of shrill vituperation: a mother and her brood had ganged up on some city type and were screaming abuse at him. Seemed the cit'd pinched the baby's bottom or kicked it or whatever. Didn't look the type but . . . A movement at Mantoni's table caught his attention. A youngish character was putting a briefcase down on a spare chair. This could be the chummie—codfish type with a forehead and chin both running off the face like they were ashamed of being there; small blame to 'em. He was with a woman who'd sat herself down next to Elio. Elderly type from the clothes. Come on, Elio, lean back and let's have a dekko at her; probably the cod's ma or auntie. Haley watched Miss Seeton's escort fetch tea and biscuits, have a brief word with a man who tried to push his way to the table, then pick up his case and leave. The cod'd had what looked like a bit of a barge-in with the city type. Anyway the cit'd sheared off and the cod'd scarpered, so he couldn't be the chummie unless it was the old girl herself. Which would be clever. Mantoni took a gulp of whiskey and leaned back in his chair. Good, now he could see her. . . . Be damned. The detective constable was startled into half rising from his seat. Be double damned. It was Miss Seeton—the Yard's MissEss. Mantoni swiveled in his chair and for a second the eyes of the two men met. Haley blinked as if coming out of a daydream and deliberately checked the time on the wall clock against his watch. He was nonplussed. Miss Seeton—here? The one the Oracle was always using? Who'd let her in on this, what gave and why hadn't someone warned him? Had something new cropped up? At a guess he'd guess the Oracle must've cooked this up with Fraud. Fair enough, but why? What was the Oracle up to?

"They,'" said Chief Superintendent Delphick, "are mad."

Sergeant Ranger surfaced slowly from the papers spread out upon his desk. If the P.M. report said that it was uncertain whether rape had preceded murder or t'other way about, did you file it under M or R? Better cross-index and put it under both, or even perhaps . . .

"Yes, sir." When the Oracle was in that tone of voice, better to agree and find out what you'd agreed to afterward.

The internal telephone on the chief superintendent's desk buzzed: he lifted the receiver. "Delphick. . . . Yes, sir, actually I am—or as free as one ever is. . . . Yes, I've read it and I . . . Oh—I see. Certainly, sir. I'll come up straight-away." He dropped the receiver back into place. "Mad," he repeated. "Stark, raving mad."

"Yes, sir." Somebody'd got under the Oracle's wool all right, which meant somebody'd be sorry for something sometime.

Delphick pushed back his chair and got to his feet. "You agree with me then?"

"Yes, sir."

"Even though you don't know what I'm talking about."

"No, sir."

"Try that for size." Some stapled sheets of paper fluttered onto the sergeant's desk and the chief superintendent left the office.

Sergeant Ranger glanced at the last sheet. It was signed by Sir Hubert Everleigh, the Assistant Commissioner (Crime). Crippen. What had old Sir Heavily dreamt up now that had put the Oracle right offside? Better find out before he came back. The sergeant settled down to read the confidential memo. *MissEss*—the word seemed to leap at him from the page and he frowned. But the Oracle hadn't needed Miss Seeton to do any sketches lately, and so far as he knew everything down at her half-pint village was quiet. What went on? Surely she hadn't started getting up to mischief on her own again. He concentrated on the memorandum: . . . *to be seconded for special duties abroad* . . . But you couldn't go seconding somebody who wasn't on the Force. And however off you might think it was to have Miss Seeton mixed up with the police, after all she was only on retainer as an artist. You didn't go bouncing elderly drawing teachers round the world pretending they were policewomen; it simply wasn't done . . . *the Bank of England* . . . *the Banque du Lac, Geneva* . . . *forgery* . . . *highly confidential* . . . *The Home Office has agreed upon representations from the Foreign Office* . . . The F.O.? The sergeant put down the papers in complete bewilderment.

Sergeant Ranger's mystification was understandable. Only recently he had spent the day at Plummergen, Kent, the village where Miss Seeton lived, on a visit to his fiancée. He had become engaged to Anne, the daughter of a doctor Knight who ran a small nursing home outside of Plummergen, soon after Miss Seeton's arrival there consequent upon her having been left a cottage on the death of an elderly relative. Her advent had been coincident with her having been witness to a murder in London which had brought her and her facility for sketching a recognizable likeness to the notice of Scotland Yard. The repercussions of the affair had spread from the village through half of Kent and had entailed a protracted visit by Superintendent Delphick, as he then was, and his sergeant to the local inn before the case was brought to a conclusion.

But, the sergeant reflected, when he and Anne had dropped in on her the previous Sunday, Miss Seeton had been gardening, with no cloud on a serene horizon. So that gave her exactly four days less the odd hour to become an expert on forgery, to intercept a pass from International Finance and dribble it down the field ahead of half the British government. How in hell did she do it? Why did everything she touched go poopsie? But surely even she couldn't poopsie half the ministries. Or was the whole thing some pretty off-joke? And "highly confidential"? Miss Seeton? She'd hit the headlines

every time she'd waved her umbrella. And as for banking and
forgery, she couldn't add two and two. The Oracle was right,
they must be crackers—the Bank of England, this Swiss bank,
the F.O. and the Home Office, the lot of 'em—stark, raving
crackers. He stared at the memo in disbelief: . . . *the Bank
of England . . . the Banque du Lac, Geneva . . .*

"Your call to Geneva, sir."

"Thank you."

"M. Telmark of the Banque du Lac is on the line."

"Thank you." Jonathan Feldman, second in command to
Lord Gatwood, the governor of the Bank of England, lifted the
receiver. "Karl? Jonathan here. We finally got it organized and
she's on her way, and she'll call on you at ten tomorrow
morning as arranged. . . . No, not a soul knows a thing,
except the police and the Home Office—and of course the
Foreign Office . . . Yes, Lord G. had to get on to the F.O.
eventually in order to bring it off. The police were being
sticky . . . What? Sticky? Oh—difficult, difficult. The assistant commissioner was difficult, the commissioner was difficult, the Home Office was difficult—I suppose they don't like
loaning out their star operatives—and it wasn't till his lordship
got the F.O. to lean on them a bit that they gave in. All this fuss
and palaver over that funny little old thing . . . Yes, nobody'd suspect *her* of being a sleuth, and she keeps it up all the
time. The whole way through my interview with her she stuck
to being . . . What? No, stuck . . . Oh, I see. No, it's a
verb this time and means something quite different. Anyway
she played the innocent—you should've heard her: Forgery?
Oh, dear dear dear and tut. And she was afraid she knew
nothing of banking—or not in that sense, if I knew what she
meant. . . ."

". . . *and I'm afraid that I know nothing of banking, Mr.
Feldman. Though, naturally,*" Miss Seeton corrected herself,
"*one has one's own. Account, that is. But very small. And then
the statements . . .*" She sighed. "*So difficult nowadays,
when they have asterisks instead of red.*" She was dubious.
"*Or is it black? Sometimes it's a little hard to find just how one
stands. One always thinks of asterisks in connection with
footnotes. But in a bank, apparently, it means that everything is
all right.*" She had another moment's qualm. "*Or else it means
that everything is not.*"

Jonathan Feldman laughed dutifully. Obviously she got a kick out of playing it wide-eyed. "I'm sure, Miss Seeton, you're far too prudent to overdraw, and besides"—his eyes twinkled—"in a policewoman it wouldn't be the thing."

"Oh, but I'm not," she protested.

"Not overdrawn?"

"Not . . . ?" For a moment Miss Seeton had lost the thread. "Oh, good gracious, no. That would be truly dreadful, and quite beyond my means. But I'm not," she reiterated, "in the police. Or not in that sense. But merely attached, as it were, when suitable, to draw—Identi-Kits, they call them— whenever, for some reason, photographs are not. Suitable, I mean."

Jonathan Feldman was enjoying himself. Here was a worthy opponent in a verbal fencing match. Nothing could shake the pedestal of naïveté on which she had elected to take her stand. He was unable to resist, however, letting her know on occasion that he saw through her. Even the assistant commissioner had tried to make out she was not a detective and certainly no banking expert. Did they all imagine that no one read or remembered the newspapers, with their headlines: BATTLING BROLLY BARES BANK FRAUD—CATCHES CROOKED CASHIER? *He composed his expression and spoke gravely.*

"Quite, Miss Seeton, I fully understand. With regard to your assignment, you are officially on holiday and, as you so rightly maintain"—his lips twitched—"you know nothing of police work or banking, and your call tomorrow morning on Karl Telmark at the Banque du Lac is purely a private visit to give him greetings from me as a mutual friend. He'll make all further arrangements with you personally."

"He does," ventured Miss Seeton, "speak English?"

"Perfectly. Here"—he handed her a fat envelope—"is your passport and money for the journey in English and Swiss currency. I understand you haven't been abroad before."

"No," she acknowledged, "and I'm afraid that I . . ."

"Nothing to worry about. One of our clerks, young Penrod, is taking you to the airport and will stay with you till your flight's called, and there'll be a car to meet you in Geneva." He stood up. Miss Seeton rose. "Now I don't think there's anything else except to remind you of the delicacy of the situation and the need for complete secrecy. It only remains to wish you luck and to say"—he suppressed a chuckle and spoke

*with added solemnity—"that in spite of your lack of both
knowledge and experience I'm sure you'll do your duty and
that we here at the Bank, indeed the country, will be in your
very capable hands."*

*Speechless, Miss Seeton gazed at him in distress until she
saw the ill-concealed mirth. She smiled. Of course, how silly of
her. Mr. Feldman was teasing. Secrecy. That would be the
reason, one supposed, why they did not wish to use a foreign
artist for whatever it was they wanted drawn. But all those
embarrassing suggestions about financial matters and forgery,
in relation to herself, had been just his banker's way of being
waggish. Miss Seeton was comforted.*

Jonathan Feldman laughed in reminiscence. "Well, there it
is, Karl, and it's over to you. She's perfect for what you want.
Stemkos'll never guess she's having a look-see over his affairs.
But don't let her fool you with all that innocence stuff. When I
was pulling her leg about it at the end she relaxed for a second
and gave me a knowing smile. No flies on that one; she knows
just what she's about. . . . Right, you might give me a ring
after you've seen her and got it all organized your end, and tell
me how things go. . . . Right. Bye."

"Corymbe of the Foreign Office here. I want to speak to the
home secretary, please. . . . Harry? I've just had Jonathan
Feldman—you know, Lord Gatwood's dogsbody—on the
line. . . . No, nothing's gone wrong. Just to thank me and
would I pass on thanks to you, so this is the pass. Though I
never understood why you made such a fuss about letting her
go in the first place. After all, you can see the Banque du Lac's
point of view. I don't know how many millions Stemkos is
worth—he's probably lost count himself—but if I were a bank
and my richest client started throwing forged notes about, I'd
want to play it pretty close to the chest myself, and since all the
forgeries so far have been English notes I should've thought
you'd have been only too glad to have one of your people on
the spot. . . . But how many times have I got to tell you they
don't want anybody else, and we can't afford to offend the
biggest private bank in Switzerland. Good Lord, even I've read
about her, and the way the press crack up this MissEss of
yours—who dreamt up that idiotic code name anyway?—
you'd think the Yard depended entirely on her. . . . Yes, I

know you said so, but you're not going to persuade Geneva, or Jonathan Feldman, or Lord Gatwood himself—or me, for that matter—that anybody solves three or four cases, or whatever it was, by accident. . . . Well, have it your own way. I don't care whether she does it by mistake or magic. They wanted her, they've got her, so now it's their lookout. Better just pray she waves that wretched brolly of hers the papers are always on about and turns up trumps."

"I want to speak to the assistant commissioner. . . . Which?" The home secretary became testy. "Sir Hubert Everleigh, of course, A.C. (Crime). . . . Hubert? The F.O.'s just been on to me with a vote of thanks from the Bank of England and the Banque du Lac, so everyone's satisfied at last. All this upheaval about that schoolmarm of yours—it's incredible. She's given me more headaches than—At all events it's settled and that's the end of it. If I hear the word Seeton again I'll resign. . . . No, no one knows except ourselves, the Bank and the F.O. . . . She's where? . . . Oh, at the airport. Good, then we can all relax."

Should he, D.C. Haley wondered, phone the Yard and ask for instructions? No, better hang on a bit and see how things shaped. Mustn't queer the old girl's pitch. Obviously she knew what she was doing. Comes straight in with a young man in tow—good bit of cover, that—and plumps herself down at Elio's table cool as you please. No wonder the Oracle thought the world of her. Looking at her you couldn't believe she was anything but what she seemed; a little old ex-schoolmarm off on a spree and rather wishing she wasn't and had she packed everything and would the neighbors see to the cat? He'd give a lot to know what she was really thinking behind that innocent deadpan.

How plaguing it was, thought Miss Seeton, to have a thing on the tip of one's tongue, so to speak, to remember a tune perfectly well, yet not to be able to remember what it was. She concentrated as the gentleman sitting next to her hummed the refrain once more.

"Dee dee—da da—da da—de de—dum—dum."

Foreign, she felt sure. Something to do with India? No, Russian . . . Of course. That was it. And by Tchaikovsky,

she expected; he generally wrote the music for the Russians.
She stared about her. Quite fascinating: the clatter and the
clack; the busy men and women serving food and drinks; the
busy men and women cleaning tables and the floor; the officers
and girls in uniform, striding forward, strolling back. And,
above all, everywhere, people; such varied people; mostly
waiting; yet all these dissimilar people had one common bond;
they carried, or they guarded, baggage. Instinctively Miss
Seeton looked down at her own overnight case. Her larger case
had already gone on ahead. The very efficient, no doubt kind,
but also, perhaps, rather insistent Mr. Penrood from the Bank
who had brought her here had arranged for it to be weighed
when they had first arrived. He had insisted upon paying for
something called overweight, of which he appeared to dis-
approve and about which she felt a trifle guilty. She should not,
perhaps, have, after all, included so many drawing materials.
No doubt they would have some reasonable substitute in
Switzerland. And then the case—relabeled by the young lady
in charge of the weighing process, who had also given her a
receipt and returned the folder containing her ticket, with
various printed labels concerning her luggage stapled to it, and
a piece of pasteboard which Mr. Penrood had insisted she
should keep in her handbag in readiness, though, when she had
asked him in readiness for what? he had merely smiled and said
that he would explain when the time came and the young lady
had laughed—had been dumped upside down and moved
slowly away on a conveyor belt. The case, of course. Looking
now at the label on her overnight bag, Miss Seeton could not
restrain a smile at the quaint printing done with a matchstick
dipped in ink by Martha, who helped two mornings a week to
keep the cottage clean. Martha had impressed upon Miss
Seeton the necessity for boldness and clarity with regard to
labeling, especially when foreign travel was in question. The
MISS E. D. SEETON had almost succeeded in drying before
Martha had smacked it with a piece of blotting paper, but the
GENEVA had fared somewhat worse. The result, though
undeniably bold, and clear as to who was traveling, was not
quite so clear as to where.

Where? Miss Seeton collected her thoughts. She really must
not, she admonished herself, allow the allurement of a new
environment to distract her mind. Where was Mr. Penrood? He
had promised that he would return for her in plenty of time,

and would deliver her to wherever it was she had to go and hand her over to a hostess, which, although, naturally, well-intentioned, had made one feel, just for a moment, like some awkward parcel which couldn't be trusted through the post. And it was very important that she should catch the plane. Or, she deliberated, would that be the wrong expression? Was it, perhaps, only trains and buses that one caught? Well, at all events, that she should be on the plane. And, there again—she frowned—did one say "on" or "in"? It was, she knew, correct to say "on" a boat—though, in actual fact, one was generally "in" it. Except, of course in very small boats, like punts and things. Though, if memory served, in the case of a day's boating, it was the river that took the "on," the punt the "in." But having never traveled by airplane—having, in fact, never traveled abroad at all—one was afraid that one knew little of the technical terms. However, since she had been told that there would be a car to meet her at the other end and to take her to her hotel, it would be so very rude not to be there on time. And, unless there was another airplane later going in the same direction, she would miss her appointment at the bank tomorrow morning. And in so vast a place and amongst such a crowd it would, surely, be so very easy for Mr. Penrood to lose his way. Again she looked around her: a myriad faces, in all colors, in all styles of headgear; anticipatory, strained, sad, carefree, glum, laughing, chewing, indifferent, anxious faces and, at a table opposite the end of the refreshment counter, the face of a gentleman who gave her a broad wink as their glances met. Miss Seeton ignored the impertinence.

Give her best, thought Haley. Never batted an eyelid. At that he'd been a b.f. to wink. Although he'd caught sight of her once at the Yard over that child murder business, she wouldn't know him from a dotted line. You'd got to admire her guts—busting in on a setup like this. She'd find herself in right trouble if she didn't watch her step, or somebody didn't watch it for her; these chummies weren't playing for pence. Well, since she'd got Elio well under control for a bit, he'd take time off to report. Asking the man next to him to hold his place, Detective Constable Haley went to one of a row of telephone kiosks from which he could command a view of the Italian's table.

Haley put down the receiver. This beat cockfighting. The inspector hadn't had a clue she was here—nothing'd been said to Fraud. He stood watching Miss Seeton. She wouldn't've muscled in on their biggest, hush-hushiest case in years off her own bat. How in hell had she heard of it anyway? Even the Treasury hadn't been let in on it, which meant there was something pretty screwy somewhere. The Oracle must've sent her here on some ploy of his own. Did that mean Elio'd been up to something they hadn't heard about? Couldn't've; Fraud'd been watching the little squirt like a hen with one chick for weeks. And now the inspector was off to some high-powered confab in the A.C.'s office; perhaps that'd explain things. Lucky he'd rung when he did, only just caught him, and he was to report anything he considered of importance direct to the inspector in the A.C.'s office. That should go with a swing—a mere D.C. busting in on the phone when Sir Hubert was in the middle of chatting up some of the top brass. And seeing all of 'em in Fraud had been told to keep their traps shut, what was all this high-powered powwow in aid of anyway?

"Deputy Assistant Commissioner of the Special Branch, Commander Conway and Inspector Borden from Fraud—sorry, sir, from C6—and Chief Superintendent Delphick from C1, sir."

Sir Hubert Everleigh sighed. You took time and trouble learning the name, rank and occupation of every officer under you, and then a firm of business consultants was called in and headquarters was reorganized and, though their occupations and names remained the same, all your senior men were regraded and retitled. He glanced at the box that had made the announcement, thanked it and asked it to send his visitors in. He waved them to chairs as they entered.

"Good afternoon, gentlemen." He addressed the head of the Special Branch. "I asked you to sit in on this, Mr. Fenn, because I think it's possible, even in my opinion likely, that your department will become involved and it struck me that such an involvement would be perhaps somewhat less involved if you knew how the case stands at the moment, the latest developments and its and their implications. I have here"—he indicated two typescripts on his desk—"an informal report, perhaps I should say a series of notes, prepared by the commander and Inspector Borden which the inspector has kindly typed himself and which I suggest that you and the chief superintendent may find helpful as a reference during our discussion. I regret that you were not given this in advance, but these two copies"—he handed one to Fenn, Delphick moved forward and picked up the other—"are the only ones in existence. For reasons which should become clear by inference, I prefer that no one else has an opportunity to read the contents. Nor do I wish a copy of the report to leave this room."

Deputy Assistant Commissioner Fenn bowed formally and took a seat. "Thank you, Assistant Commissioner." He smoothed the papers upon his knee.

Delphick's eyes skimmed down a list of numbered paragraphs and dates on the first page: *Mme Stemkos . . .* Stemkos? That'd be the shipping millionaire. *Mme Stemkos with Librecksin (secretary) . . .* Then Stemkos himself; Librecksin again; Madame again, and a lot of guff about deposits at the Banque du Lac, Geneva. And the upshot seemed to be that when some of the big clearing banks such as the Swiss Bank Corporation and the Credit Suisse sent their English notes back to the Bank of England one hell of a lot of them were forged fivers. Well, well, you'd've thought Stemkos would've had enough of them ready without printing a little snide on the side.

A paragraph had caught the attention of the Special Branch.

7. *Owing to the excellence of the forgeries, particularly with regard to the quality of the paper, Interpol has not yet been informed, since the Bank of England would prefer for the time being to pursue discreet inquiries on their own account.*

In Fenn's estimation any inquiries that were not conducted under his aegis were a waste of time and to call them discreet would be laughable. He came as near to a sneer as the time, the place and the company would allow.

"These discreet inquiries? The Treasury investigators?"

Sir Hubert ignored the tone. "No, Mr. Fenn, not at this stage. I am aware," he went on as the other began to protest, "that the normal procedure in such circumstances is to inform the Treasury and hand the matter over to their investigators, but in this case we are not yet convinced that the circumstances are normal. You see, the excellence, to be more accurate, the perfection of the paper employed can only mean in practical terms access."

"Are you implying," demanded Fenn, "that someone at the Bank . . . ?"

"Not necessarily. In the classic phrase, we have reason to
believe that someone who is at the Treasury could conceivably
be involved. Consequently both the Bank of England and we
would prefer, if it is possible, to keep the matter—er—under
wraps for the time being." He turned to the two men from
Fraud. "Now before we go over the ground for the benefit of
Mr. Fenn and Chief Superintendent Delphick, has anything
fresh come to light?"

Commander Conway shook his head. "No, sir. Nothing that
has got us any further. But I should like to ask, since the
Murder Squad Oracle is sitting in on it, and particularly
because of something we learned in a report from Heathrow
only a few minutes ago, whether there hasn't been some
development we don't know of."

The assistant commissioner put his fingertips together and
studied them. "A fair question, even pertinent, and the answer
is, yes there has, but," he went on as the commander and his
inspector leaned forward, "I must hasten to add, or to qualify,
that the development in question has nothing to do, at all
events not as yet, with murder. I fear"—he hesitated and gave
a brief smile—"that an element of farce has recently entered, I
should say has been forcibly injected into the case. A Miss
Seeton, a retired drawing mistress who is on a yearly retainer
to us as an artist— and, I should like to emphasize straight-
away, in spite of somewhat extravagant accounts of her
activities in the press and a tendency which she undoubtedly
has for becoming more deeply involved than either she realizes
or we intend, that that is the full extent of her commitment to
us—has been engaged, seconded would be perhaps more apt,
to Geneva to investigate the Swiss end of the affair."

The deputy assistant commissioner, the commander and the
inspector gazed, incredulous, at Sir Hubert. Delphick, who
already knew of the step from the confidential memorandum he
had received, tightened his lips, awaiting an effective opportunity for protest. Finally, Inspector Borden:

"You—you must be joking, sir."

"No, that would be most improper, very ill-timed. Her visit
is to be unofficial, though officially sanctioned, and we have
naturally informed the Swiss police as a matter of courtesy.
Actually she has been engaged by the Banque du Lac as a
private—no, in view of the fact that the whole thing had to be
arranged through official channels, perhaps one should say an
undercover—investigator. It was partly on account of this that I

asked Chief Superintendent Delphick to attend. Although I
have met Miss Seeton on one occasion, he knows her
comparatively well—was indeed originally responsible for her
becoming entangled in police work. I thought it might help if
we all had some idea of our MissEss, of her character and of
her reactions to given circumstances. I won't say of any move
she is likely to make since her gyrations have always appeared
to be completely unpredictable." Sir Hubert settled back in his
seat. "To bring you up to date, MissEss—we may as well
accustom ourselves to using that title since the Banque du Lac
insists upon doing so; they apparently think it's our code name
for her and not, as it was, a mistake on the part of our
computer—anyway, MissEss has left, or"—he looked at his
watch—"to be strictly correct, must be due to leave at any
moment for Geneva. Now it is a fact that whenever Miss
Seeton has been in contact with or"——he glanced at Delphick—"put in touch with any form of crime, she has
unconsciously, maybe one should say she has unwittingly, had
the effect of one of those lawn weed killers which startle the
plants into excessive growth until the plants, in this case the
crimes, have blown themselves up, distorted themselves and
finally solved themselves or killed themselves through their
own overstimulated energy."

"You," Commander Conway marveled, "you really think
she may get on to something out there?"

Sir Hubert was brisk. "Certainly not. She's far too guileless,
too innocent, to get on to anything, at all events in the context
you're suggesting. But she has a genius for poking her
umbrella into hornets' nests unbeknownst to herself. If that
happens here our fraudulent friends may very well think she
has got on to something and the consequent ructions might end
by bringing them into the open."

A strange expression had developed on Inspector Borden's
face. He cleared his throat. "I—it's—" He stopped. Then,
answering the assistant commissioner's unspoken query: "It's a
bit funny, sir, you should've said all that about her bringing
them into the open because she's having a cup of tea with one
of them now."

Miss Seeton put down her cup. Not, she feared, very
palatable. So very strong. Really, she reflected, that strange
little gentleman next to her, in the rather colorful suit, must
have that tune quite dreadfully on the brain. Though, again, of

course, it might be nerves. As Elio Mantoni pushed his
unfinished whiskey glass aside she noticed that his hand was
shaking. Yes, nerves, she opined. Some people were, she
knew, frightened of flying, though quite why it was difficult to
understand, because, surely, there must be less risk of an
accident in an airplane, since there was more room than, say, in
a car. Room in the air, that was.

Mantoni bent, opened his briefcase, took out a notebook,
closed the case, turned a page and studied it with a frown. His
frayed nerve ends were raw. Why had nothing happened?
Anyone could see his terrible bow tie to identify him—and
then the song to make all certain. But nothing, nothing. And
there might not be much time. If they called his flight . . . If
he left without the forged money he might be blamed. Or had
the pigs arrested someone and he did not know, and there
would be no transfer, and the pigs were playing cat with mouse
with him? In desperation he decided to sing the words in the
hope that the password would reach the right ears and whoever
it was would see the urgency. If he allowed the words to come
while he was reading, searching for something in his diary, that
would be natural, yes? His humming changed to words.

> "Les diamants chez nous sont innombrables,
> Les perles dans nos mers incalculables;
> C'est l'Inde, terre des merveilles."

There, Miss Seeton congratulated herself, she'd been right.
It was foreign. No doubt the gentleman himself was Russian.
So very difficult, she believed. Even the Russians themselves,
one understood, admitted that it was more difficult to learn than
English; in which case one did wonder a little why they didn't
adopt, say, English instead. And, then again, surely, if more
countries spoke the same language, there would be, perhaps,
less misunderstandings. For instance, Chinese speech, from
what one had read, depended not so much upon what they said,
as upon how they said it. Which must, one would have
thought, lead to certain difficulties. And even, sometimes, one
would have supposed, for them. For the Chinese.

"You permit?"

Miss Seeton's attention was jerked from problems in the
abstract to the particular. A gentleman from a neighboring
table wished to borrow the sugar bowl. She smiled and
nodded. The man put a briefcase on the floor, took the sugar to

his own table, replenished the bowl there, returned, put back the sugar, picked up a briefcase, smiled, bowed and departed. Oh. Miss Seeton found herself in a predicament. She half turned in her chair to watch the gentleman's retreat. Oh. Now that was very awkward.

On the point of leaving the phone booth, D.C. Haley paused. The old girl looked worried. What had bitten her? She'd turned round to watch that chap who'd borrowed the sugar. Actually it was that city type who'd kicked the baby. Nothing in pinching a bit of sugar to throw her that he could see. Dared he plonk himself down on the vacant chair at her table? Better not. Could queer her pitch. Might as well stay where he was for the moment, long as nobody started queueing for the phone. Gave him a chance to see without being seen. Uhuh—that man at the bar, the colored man, was watching Elio's table. Watching Elio, or MissEss? Mean anything? Come to think of it, that black man'd been at the bar for quite a time. Stringing his drinks out—didn't remember seeing him buy another in the last quarter of an hour or so. Automatically Haley made a mental note of the man. Better include him in his report just in case.

The man at the bar, Xerxes Tolla, was the third man who had watched with interest when Mantoni had entered the departure lounge. He knew through a contact in the airport that the Italian had been stopped by the police and searched. If Elio'd been tagged he'd best keep him abroad for a while—switch things round. He'd written a note and arranged for it to be handed to the Italian when he boarded the plane, telling him to carry straight on to Geneva, catching the early-morning flight out of Genoa, changing at Milan. There was the picture deal coming up in Geneva and the little clot was needed for that, and after that there'd be the Stemkos jewel theft insurance do in Paris— he could help out with that too. It would mean somebody new for London. Still it was time for a change—never push your luck. In any case Elio was no good for this present job—too excitable, and beginning to run scared. The only thing he could do was paint. But you had to keep switching the men on this money-carrying or the customs became wary. Which meant using whatever men were on tap. He weighed the problem. The French fellow'd be no use if he couldn't make a better job of getting to Elio's table than falling over his own feet and half a dozen children and then calling attention to himself by having a blaze-up with the entire family. Made quite a neat job of swapping briefcases at the end though. Point was, had anybody twigged? Were the fuzz still watching Elio? If so, he'd need to be ready to make a move himself if they picked up Elio again. His eyelids hooded. Rather looked as though that old woman at the table might've noticed more than was good for her: she'd leaned round to stare after the Frenchman and seemed a bit fussed. Yes, she was turning back to Elio. He'd stake a dollar she was going to say she was afraid there'd been a slight mix-up.

"I'm afraid," said Miss Seeton; she hesitated. Really, it was very awkward. She was sure, but, then again, one did so dislike to interfere, or appear to make a fuss. But it could, one could foresee, prove to be so embarrassing to find oneself wearing the wrong pajamas, toothbrushes and things like that. Well, possibly not pajamas in a briefcase. But papers and things. It was so hard to decide whether one should say something. Or not? "I am rather afraid," she informed the humming gentleman, "that there's been a slight mistake."

Mantoni closed his notebook and stared at her. Finally he spoke. "No meestake."

"Oh, but really there was," Miss Seeton insisted. "The gentleman who came to borrow the sugar was carrying a briefcase very like yours, and, if you remember, he put it down in order to take it back. The sugar, I mean. And when he returned it and picked it up, the briefcase, that is, I'm sure . . ." She faltered under the other's inimical regard. "That is to say, I think, or, perhaps, I should say that I got the impression, that he took yours by—"

He cut her short. "No," he repeated, "meestake." To prove his words he picked up the briefcase beside him, opened it, dropped his notebook into it and zipped it shut, tucked it under his arm, gulped the remains of his whiskey and left the table.

The woman opposite Miss Seeton stopped in midcake to regard Mantoni's retreating figure. *"Non simpatico,"* she summarized. She transferred herself to the chair that he had vacated, pulled her plate toward her, then bent to examine with interest the label on Miss Seeton's case. *"Genova?"* she inquired.

"Yes," agreed Miss Seeton.

The woman flashed a smile of sympathy, rumaged in her handbag and produced a small book entitled *Conversazione in Inglese*, ran a plump finger down a page, found what she sought and announced, "You too are delay."

"Yes," admitted Miss Seeton.

Her new acquaintance beamed with satisfaction. It was evident that to her a shared delay was a correct basis for amicable relations. Noticing Miss Seeton give an anxious glance at the clock on the wall, her companion waved a piece of cake in airy dismissal.

"Non si preoccupi." She put the cake in her mouth and indicated a spot near the ceiling. "You see," she explained through crumbs and cream, "say *quando*." Again she had resource to her book on conversation in English. "Say when and where go."

Miss Seeton's eyes followed the directional finger. A small screen like that of a television was set upon a crossbeam. She had time to read the heading AMSTERDAM before the screen blacked out. She smiled her thanks. Now, should Mr. Penrood be, for any reason, delayed, and after all, time was getting on and there was no sign of him, and also she didn't find the lady's voice on the loudspeaker quite easy to follow, she would be able to manage for herself by keeping a watch for the word GENEVA on the little screen, which would also, apparently, tell her where to go.

Where to go? D.C. Haley found himself in something of a dilemma. Elio had sat down on one of the banquettes outside the cafeteria, and he was in duty bound to keep the little twit under observation. Contrariwise, MissEss seemed to have taken over and it didn't look as if she gave a damn about Elio making off. Probably'd found out all she needed of his plans for the time being and would move in on him when she was good and ready. Anyway at the moment she was busy chatting up the fat lady with the cakes. Haley compromised by going to the bar. From here he could keep an eye on Elio, would be on tap if MissEss needed a spot of help and at the same time could get alongside the black man and try and size up whether he connected in on this or not.

"Going far?"

Xerxes Tolla took his time. He studied the fresh ingenuous face. One of those who got a kick out of dark skins? No, he surmised, an idle example of white trash asking futile questions. "Home," he replied.

Good parry. Haley was interested. Your ordinary citizen answers an ordinary question in the ordinary way. This sounded more like a stall. Maybe he'd been right about this fellow. Instead of asking where home was, he let his jaw drop; his expression became vacuous.

"Oh, good show. Me, I've got to hang about till the little woman shows up. We're off to Gay paree for a bit of a lark."

Not one of those, decided Tolla. He signaled to a barman and pushed his glass forward. "Again."

"Oh, no, old man," Haley volunteered. "On me. After all, bit of a celebration, what?"

Tolla shrugged. Let the scum pay. The day was not far off when white vermin would come crawling to their black masters for the price of a drink.

Xerxes Tolla believed this. Any group that has at one time suffered oppression will always view an alleviation of their lot or improvement in their circumstances, not as attempts by a more enlightened age to introduce parity into an inequitable regime but as a sign of weakness to be exploited.

When the African protectorates had taken on adult responsibility and had celebrated their independence and their state of emergence by creating states of emergency, Tolla had returned to his own country and offered his services. The offer was welcomed by the new government. They had been approached by an intermediary who, although he refused to be specific, gave them to understand that he was representing a combine of powers; at first with an oblique suggestion, then more clearly and, finally, when their receptiveness was beyond doubt, with an open proposition. The ex-protectorate's paper money was still printed in England and though of a different design, on the same paper as English banknotes. For a considerable consideration, would they be willing to demand increased supplies of notes, for which they could blame the deterioration in the quality of the paper over recent years, their own humid atmosphere and careless usage by the natives? An official at the Treasury in London would then authorize an extended run of paper from the mills. The only provable falsity to which they would be committed would be the acknowledgment of undelivered consignments of notes, since the surplus paper would be retained in England for the printing of forgeries on a scale

sufficient to undermine England's economy and bankrupt the
country. The ex-protectorate government's response was enthusiastic: there is nothing like a little matricide for stretching
the wing span of a fledgling nation, and Tolla's arrival in the
midst of these delicate negotiations was opportune. Here was a
man with the trading experience, the expertise and the
underworldwide connections they needed to cut them in on a
percentage of the market.

Xerxes Tolla had learned the elements of his trade in the
kindergarten for contraband dealers, the watches run from
Switzerland. He had operated principally from Geneva, where
he still kept a flat up in the Old Town. Recently he had found
that in England, America and Germany the police were
treading hard upon his profits, though he was satisfied that no
suspicion had been attached to himself. In New York he had
lost a large consignment of heroin to the Federal Bureau of
Investigation, in Munich a parcel of stolen gems had been
seized and four minor members of his organization had been
arrested. In England on the Kent coast a group of illegal
immigrants had been met upon their arrival by customs officers
instead of by the Essex farmer who was due to collect them.

Tolla's price for serving his country had been diplomatic
status with its corollary diplomatic immunity. This was
granted, the more readily since it cost nothing, and he became
attached in a minor role to his country's consulate in London
though his main function was to act as liaison with their
representatives abroad and to attend, in unconscious irony,
trade delegations throughout the world. The arrangement
suited both Tolla and his government: he was free to pursue his
smuggling activities in comparative safety, while they would
take fifty percent of the yield from the circulation of the forged
notes. Their backers, too, were satisfied: the greater part of the
distribution was taken off their hands by a professional with the
right qualifications, which saved them trouble and also secured
them against international embarrassment should the plot to
break England's economy and enforce successive devaluations
chance to be exposed; inevitably it would appear to be a direct
deal between the traitor at the Treasury and the ex-protectorate
concerned.

In spite of the illegal immigrant fiasco, Tolla's opinion of the
English police force was derisory. His only personal contact
with the police had been at a diplomatic party attended by Sir

Hubert Everleigh. The assistant commissioner's trick of quali-
fying every statement that he made had struck Tolla, who in
common with most criminals had little humor and no appreciation of subtlety with words, as irritating and effete. Even when
congratulating the new attaché upon his recently acquired
diplomatic status, Sir Hubert had failed to be straightforward.

"It is notable," he had remarked, "or at all events it is
certainly worthy of note, when a man of your caliber, maybe
experience would be the better word, is recognized—or should
one say acknowledged?—by his government."

"The fact that this man is recognized—or should one say
acknowledged?—by his government gave us a starting point
for the investigation. You do not," observed Sir Hubert, "or
you do not in the normal way, employ a criminal unless you
intend to turn his propensities to account."

The head of the Special Branch's temper was beginning to
fray. "You suggest"—he looked accusingly at the assistant
commissioner—"with all due respect, that Stemkos and/or his
entourage are involved, which is a matter for the Swiss Sûrete,
the Bank of England and the Treasury investigators. And now
you're dragging in someone called Tolla and his government
but without as far as I can see a thing to back it up. And
you"—he addressed Commander Conway—"hint this and
imply that, but where in all this rigmarole can you show me
one scrap of evidence?"

The assistant commissioner cleared his throat. "Here." He
pointed to two apparent five-pound notes which lay upon his
desk beside a magnifying glass. "One of those constitutes the
most suggestive evidence."

Fenn moved to the desk, tilted the Anglepoise lamp, picked
up the glass and began a minute study of the notes, being
careful not to get them mixed. Delphick rose, selected a five-
pound note from his wallet and joined him. The others waited
in silence. Whenever Fenn replaced a note on the desk
Delphick tried comparison with his own. After a minute or two
he grinned at his colleagues from Fraud, shrugged and returned
to his seat. Fenn took more time. Finally he put down both
notes and the glass.

"They are distinguishable?"

"Oh, yes," Sir Hubert assured him. "The numbers, of
course, but that means waiting until the duplicate appears. In

the ordinary way no forged note will pass the routine scrutiny
of a bank clerk. These can and do. To give you exact details, if
you think they'll help . . ." He searched for and found a
letter on his desk. *"Any flaw in the design is reported
immediately by the engraver concerned and then registered to
facilitate comparison should this at any time become necessary. An imitation of the plastic strip woven into the paper,
applied later, will rub off when damped. And the critical
watermark is made by a Dandy Roller and the use and control
of the Dandy Roller in the industry is necessarily extremely
rigid.* Better controlled, I feel," he commented, "than
their sense of humor when naming it. *The currency for last
year was as follows: £10 notes—£278,000,000; £5 notes—
£1,677,000,000; £1 notes—£957,000,000.* Which I suppose,
since only a little over six million pounds' worth of forgeries in
fivers has come to light so far, still gives us a definite edge on
the forgers." He put down the letter and looked up, bland. "I
do trust, Mr. Fenn, that you find that helpful."

"Surely," said Fenn impatiently, "if it's that serious the
Bank of England can call in the issue and bring out a new
design as the Bank of Scotland did some years ago?"

"They may have to," conceded Sir Hubert flatly.

"But it wouldn't do any good," put in Commander Conway.
"Now they've got the paper they'd soon copy the new one or
one of the other notes and we'd be back on the merry-go-
round."

Seeing from Fenn's expression that he was liable to say
something outrageous, Delphick decided to draw the fire in
order to give the deputy assistant commissioner time to simmer
down. What was the matter with him? Didn't look so much that
he'd got out of bed on the wrong side as that he'd fallen off the
end on his head. Surely Fenn must realize that there were limits
beyond which even their lordships of the Special Branch
couldn't go. He interposed quickly:

"What I don't understand is all this Stemkos stuff. One: with
all his millions, what on earth does he want to get mixed up
with snide for? Unless you're figuring that he's part of some
foreign backing behind Tolla and company, in which case I
should've thought he'd've been careful to keep out of the
limelight himself. Two: why he and his wife and secretary are
the only ones listed as actually passing the snide."

Commander Conway grinned. "Good point, Oracle. Re the

foreign backing angle, could be, looks a bit like it, but frankly we don't know. On the face of it and on his reputation to date it's difficult to see him being palsy-walsy with Tolla and his lot. For your other point—that was just a stroke of luck. As far as we know Stemkos and Company are the only people who've passed big amounts at a time. The luck was Jonathan Feldman being Johnny-on-the-spot in Switzerland for a powwow with the clearing banks when the Swiss Bank Corporation in Geneva got a large dollop of English notes from the Banque du Lac. He and the S.B.C. combed through 'em straightaway and found over a couple of thousand pounds' worth of the snide. For once they were in time to pinpoint where they'd come from and after that it was easy. Lord Gatwood popped over to Geneva for a heart-to-heart with Telmark of the Banque du Lac. They got down to comparing deposit dates against clearance dates and the result's pretty damning. Lord G. hit the ceiling and came back to get things organized and Telmark landed on the ceiling just after him and screamed for your Miss Seeton. No normal gang"—his voice became edged and aimed at Fenn—"would've laid on this lark—too much time and too much outlay."

"For too little profit," added his inspector.

"Too little profit?" echoed Fenn.

"Well, think, sir; just to produce the notes alone—without any of the rest of the organization such as getting hold of the paper, bribes, contact men, distributors; plus the fact you're probably selling your notes at less than half their cash value— you'd need a first-class engraving printing press. That's going to run you into a pretty penny. Then with your camera and the equipment you'll want for setting up for the—at a guess I'd say they're using the tri-mask process—" Seeing the other's blank expression, "Roughly, sir, it means developing your photographs in three different colors, on three different steels for each side per note. All that lot's going to tot up the bill a bit. And the scribe who etched those"—he indicated the notes on the desk—"after they'd got the photographs on the steels is a top man: he wouldn't come cheap. And then apart from the three steels a side, there's the overprinting of the numbers." He shook his head. "One way and another, I wouldn't say you'd get much change out of a hundred thousand, probably nearer double. But it all comes back to the paper. Most times your snide merchant will pick the holiday season because of the tourists, then'll set up for a quick turnover and a fast get-out. As long as the paper's near enough with the watermark and the strip to fool the public that's all that worries him. Once the banks are on to it he's had his lot, pockets the profit and calls it a day. But here the paper's right. And that can't be right, if you see what I mean. The etching," he enthused, "is a lovely job. There are flaws but you've damn well got to hunt for 'em. And to me it all adds up that there's more than just money at stake. Somebody for some reason has backed this bit of graft to the hilt."

"Even if you're right," snapped Fenn, "I can't see that you've a shred of proof that politics come into it. There's nothing about an ex-protectorate in this"—he tapped the report, which he still held—"but if this man Tolla's behind the distribution of forgery—and you say he's been involved in smuggling for years—why shouldn't he be doing it in the ordinary way of business purely for his own pocket? Which seems to me far more likely. As far as I can see, from what I've heard to date, none of this concerns my department. Why exactly am I here and what do you expect me to do?"

An awkward silence ensued. "There is," said Sir Hubert at last, "a former M.P. who changed his political affiliations, lost his seat and was fobbed off with a post in the Treasury."

"Estevel, the turncoat?"

Sir Hubert nodded. "From information received we know that he and Tolla have met on several occasions though they appear to have been at some pains to keep these meetings secret. Their meetings could be explained by the fact that Estevel has recently become interested in, and voluble on, the racial question—but then why the secrecy? I fear that it has occurred to our somewhat skeptical minds that in turning his coat the reverse may well prove to be one of many colors."

"But," objected Fenn, "I still don't see how all this connects up with the paper you're so worried about."

Commander Conway took over to explain the arrangement with regard to the printing of notes, adding, "Only twice in history has the paper for snide been perfect: the Great Bank Note Conspiracy of 1862, when paper was stolen from the Portal mill, and—now. We've run a quiet but thorough check and all the paper is accounted for. Only one odd thing has cropped up." He spread his hands. "You can't call it proof, but even you will admit it could be a pointer. Some months ago

Tolla's government asked for a large extra consignment of notes, giving various reasons, amongst them the poor quality of the modern paper, which of course we can't deny since we ourselves found the ten-shilling note uneconomic to produce and had to substitute a coin.''

"And did they get their extra cash?" asked Fenn.

"Sure—okayed by Estevel, signed for, sealed and delivered. Everything very much on the up-and-up, and it's going to be the devil to prove any different. Estevel covered his tracks well, but there it is, our one lead, with enough coincidence round it to stink of fish. And me, I'd take a bet on it.''

"Which," remarked Sir Hubert, "if you accept the premise, Mr. Fenn, and since it embraces both national security and a foreign government, does put the ball in your court. I should perhaps add that Chief Superintendent Delphick's mention of the possibility of some foreign backing behind Tolla's government is, or could be, very near the mark. At least such is our opinion from what little has come to light. Though I fear"—his tone was acid—"at this stage we can offer you no proof. To my mind it is virtually certain that a power, more probably a syndicate of powers—since in international politics your only and temporary friends are those who want something from you—are using the ex-protectorate as a front, and the destruction of our currency with foreknowledge would be very profitable business indeed.''

"Right, we'll get cracking." On his way back to his chair Fenn halted and turned. "But with all due respect, Assistant Commissioner"—he rapped out the compulsory overture to disagreement with a superior—"there's one thing I must stress. You're stating the country's economy's at stake; you're postulating a plot by a foreign government, backed by another foreign power; you're accusing a man who's in confidential government employment—and yet you're allowing the buffoonery of this woman's visit to Switzerland. It's no moment for what you yourself rightly call farce, and I insist that it's stopped at once. With, of course," he added witheringly, "all due respect.''

Sir Hubert's smile was wintry. "With equal—um—respect, Mr. fenn, I'm so glad that you do, and I suggest that you take your insistence to the proper quarter. I have protested, the commissioner has protested, the Home Office has protested, but when the Banque du Lac got Lord Gatwood to bring

pressure to bear on the Foreign Office and the Foreign Office
made an issue of the matter, we all had to yield. There is only
in effect the prime minister left to approach. In spite of the
inadvisability of causing unnecessary offense to one of the
major financial influences in Switzerland, I've no doubt that a
few words from you will have more weight than all that we
have said."

Deflated, red in the face, Fenn sat down. "I—I'm sorry,
A.C., I'd no idea. I—I wasn't to know . . ."

The A.C.'s smile warmed. "Naturally not, and you're not
alone. With regard to the Banque du Lac I feel strongly that
they know not what they do. Karl Telmark, their director, has I
fear completely misunderstood exuberant and reader-catching
reports of Miss Seeton's activities in foreign editions of our
newspapers. And that she was once concerned with a defrauding bank cashier, allied to the fact that she is in his opinion
ideally suited to their requirements in other respects, has
immovably made up his mind. We explained that she had no
idea that the cashier in question was defrauding and that, had
she known, she would not have known what to do. But they
thought we were being modest on her behalf, or obstructive on
our own, and preferred to believe what they had read in print,
and I'm afraid, like the rest of us, you'll have to accept the
situation, idiotic as it is. In my case the strong representations I
made against her going were more, I must admit, for her sake
than for ours, since the poor woman can have no notion as to
why she has been seconded there and will I imagine wander
about or sit in her hotel waiting for someone to tell her what or
who it is they want her to draw, while M. Telmark will
presumably sit in his bank waiting for her to solve their
problems in forgery and high finance, of which she knows
nothing. However, so far as we're concerned we may as well
reap the benefits—to be exact, what, to my mind, are likely to
be the benefits—of the situation. Should the impact of our
MissEss create confusion on the Continent and draw attention
to the Swiss end of the affair, it will provide an admirable
smoke screen for our own investigations at home."

Fenn roused himself from thought. "Sorry to interrupt you,
A.C., but I'm beginning to understand a little of what I read
about your MissEss—the Battling Brolly I think they call her in
the papers. And why in the devil's name Battling? From what
you say of her, she doesn't sound a militant."

"She isn't," Delphick put in. "It was just that . . ." How to explain it? "Well, I suppose it did seem a bit like that the first time we came across her. A young hoodlum was knifing his girl friend and Miss Seeton, who happened to be passing, thought she saw a gentleman punching a lady and poked him in the back with her umbrella, all ready to read him a lecture on good manners. The papers latched on to it and for them she's been the Battling Brolly ever since."

Fenn's smile broadened. "If she really has this effect—is chaos–prone—isn't she liable to be in some danger herself? With millions at stake they'll stick at nothing, and since"—he grinned at Delphick—"she won't have the benefit in Switzerland of the Oracle's protection, oughtn't somebody to be assigned to the job?"

Sir Hubert laughed. "Thank you, Mr. Fenn. It was a point that I hoped you might take."

"I'll put a man on to her."

Give the A.C. credit, thought Delphick. By keeping his temper, except for the one icy blast, he'd got Fenn rowing in with the team and positively keen. He chuckled.

"You'll have to brief your man—Miss Seeton doesn't take kindly to protection in the ordinary way. She's very conscientious, and now that she's retired from teaching children to draw and is retained by us she'll try her level best to do anything she's asked to because she thinks it's part of the job. But don't expect her to understand. You'd never make her see people were trying to kill her—she'd think it wasn't quite nice. What you really want to watch for is when she starts doing quick sketches. Not her usual detailed drawing, but what she calls notes and's a bit ashamed of. They're always worth a second and third look to see what it is she's got on to now without realizing it."

"Well, may her luck hold," hoped Inspector Borden. "Wish I'd known she was going to fetch up with Mantoni though; I'd've sicced her onto him."

"Is that the chap she's having tea with?" asked Delphick.

"Yes, Elio Mantoni, a little Italian cock sparrow about knee-high to a grasshopper. Thinks he's God's gift to art. He's not. Merely the devil's answer to a painting-forger's prayer. Lately he's been hopping in and out of England like a flea with the jitters, so we took an interest. They're using him in this snide racket as a runner. Not," he added quickly with a glance at

Fenn, "that we've got proof of that, but we're pretty sure. We had him stopped today and his luggage searched—made out it was a routine spot check for drugs—but he was clean, not so much a bent penny. I've got a man keeping an eye on him, D.C. Haley—it was he who recognized Miss Seeton—but we're not very hopeful. We've run a quiet watch on our Elio before, but never got a thing on him. How and where they switch the cash we haven't a clue."

The assistant commissioner's mouth quirked. "If he and Miss Seeton are going to be on the same flight I would put it within the bounds of possibility, even probability, that you shortly will have."

"Oh, no, sir, they're both on delayed flights but they're going in different directions. Mantoni's off home to Italy, traveling via Genoa, so there's no chance of their meeting up again."

"You think not? I cannot agree, or cannot agree entirely. I find the coincidence a little too astonishing to think that it will end there. Moreover, the conceit to setting an artist to catch an artist has a peculiar fitness. As I've told you, our MissEss has proved before that she has this strange faculty, one might say misfortune, for attracting crime and criminals. It's small wonder really that though she may never suspect them, they inevitably end by suspecting her. And after being put on this assignment, that she should go straight to the airport and proceed to hold a crooks' tea party seems to me entirely typical of the kind of thing that happens to her. But that nothing further should come of it I should find untypical, unlikely and unbelievable."

Miss Seeton glanced at her watch. There were less than two minutes left of the hour which Mr. Penrood had stipulated. Of course, one realized that the delay might, for some reason, have been prolonged. But still . . . Anxious, she stared around the cafeteria.

"You are unquiet?" asked her companion.

"Yes, perhaps, in a way," agreed Miss Seeton. "I must admit to being a little worried. You see—" She found she had to raise her voice against competition from the loudspeaker. "The gentleman who brought me very kindly gave me some tea and told me to wait for him here, as my airplane wouldn't be ready for another hour. But now it's gone. The hour, I mean.

And I'm not quite sure what I—" She stopped, perceiving that she had lost the other's attention.

"*Ecco*," exclaimed the lady and jumped to her feet.

Miss Seeton realized that she had allowed briefcases and cream cakes to divert her and, with a feeling of guilt, she looked up at the screen. The heading was GENOVA followed by some foreign words, French, she presumed, and some figures which she failed to understand. She collected her handbag and umbrella and stood, uncertain. There was no sign of Mr. Penrood—and, of course, the spelling was wrong. But then, of course, it would be, in such a huge place, and such a crowd— they all spelled their names differently—he might have easily lost his way—in different countries, that was. So very foolish to have missed the announcement in English. And now she didn't even know where to go. Or whom to . . .

"*Non si preoccupi. Presto, fa presto*," cried the cake lady. She grabbed the overnight case and thrust it into Miss Seeton's unresisting hand. "You come wiz me. I see to. *Avanti, avanti*, quick." She clutched Miss Seeton's arm and urged her forward. "Quick for the good seat. I see to."

Abruptly, without a word to Haley, Xerxes Tolla put down his unfinished drink and left the bar. He headed toward the banquettes outside the cafeteria, his gaze fixed on the wide corridor beyond, which leads to the numbered gates for the different flights and the plate glass sides of which look out over the tarmac, where planes line up, and to the runways in the distance. In the corridor he collided with Miss Seeton and the Italian woman, knocking Miss Seeton's case from her hand. With profuse apologies he stooped and recovered the case, brushing it down with a handkerchief from his breast pocket before he returned it to its owner. He bowed and stood back for the ladies to pass. He watched as further down the passage her companion hustled Miss Seeton into the group descending the slope of gate 9 for the Alitalia flight to Genoa.

Miss E. D. Seeton? Something familiar . . . Miss Seeton? It came back to him: paragraphs in the newspapers under preposterous headlines with something about an umbrella. But in the stories Miss Seeton had been linked to, working with, the police—for Scotland Yard. The writing on the label— smudged, yes—but GENEVA, not GENOA or GENOVA. And anyway English people rarely used the foreign spelling even if they knew it. So—it was true she had noticed something about the briefcases. She had been going to Geneva. She was going to Genoa. She worked with the police. He remained for a moment in thought, swung about and hastened back through the cafeteria. Outside the departure lounge he crossed to the counter of one of the stands lining the opposite wall.

"I wish to send a telegram to a passenger on the Alitalia flight AZ 293 and it's important it should catch him before he leaves the airport at Genoa."

The girl handed him a form. "It will have to be telexed, sir, to be there on time."

"But it will reach him?"

"Oh, yes, sir. He'll be called over the loudspeaker while still in customs and asked to collect the message."

"Right." He began to print ELIO MANTONI . . .

The cream cake fancier pushed her way unceremoniously through those who were queueing to board the plane, engaging in spirited repartee with anyone bold enough to protest. Per hand-grip force Miss Seeton followed her. Nearing the air hostess, the Italian released Miss Seeton, fumbled in a pocket and produced with a flourish her boarding pass, marked GOA. Miss Seeton remembered the piece of pasteboard that Mr. Penrood had told her to keep in readiness. Grasping her overnight case in one hand, she shifted her umbrella preparatory to opening her handbag. The umbrella's ferrule jabbed the hand of the man in front of her. Elio Mantoni dropped his briefcase and boarding pass and turned with an oath. He glared at the two women with whom he had recently shared a table.

"Oh, dear. Oh, please, I am so sorry." Miss Seeton was contrite. "I do hope I didn't hurt you. It's so very difficult. And so little room."

While the air hostess stooped to help retrieve Mantoni's possessions, Miss Seeton's guide towed her in triumph aboard the plane.

When Tolla suddenly quit the bar D. C. Haley studied the retreating figure with interest. Whatever else the black man had going for him it wasn't manners. Leaving his drink on the counter he moved back a step to keep the other in view; became alert when the man bumped into Miss Seeton. The old girl'd been looking a bit het and the fat woman'd practically dragged her away. Probably she'd come all over goose pimples after letting Elio out of her sight, that he mightn't be on the flight after all. No need to worry; he'd seen the little squirt go down the corridor toward the gate just after the Genoa flight was called. And now that Elio was under way, with MissEss sitting squarely on his tail, he could relax. This job was wound up. No . . . on second thoughts where was the black man off to now all grim and hot-foot? Forgetful of his drink, Haley went to the door and came face to face with a young man, looked him over, then stood back for him to pass. MissEss' cod-faced boyfriend. Should he tip him the wink? Better hadn't, not his business. The detective constable followed Tolla.

Mr. Penrood sauntering into the cafeteria, approached the table at which he had left Miss Seeton and finding it empty stared at it with disapproval. He glanced round at the other tables, inspected the throng by the refreshment counter, went quickly outside to look over the banquettes, returned with a disturbed expression and stationed himself between Miss Seeton's late table and the ladies' lavatory. He looked at his watch, checked it against the wall clock, glanced again at his watch, but found no comfort. Where the devil had the old dame got to?

"All passengers," announced the loudspeaker, "for flight 813 to Geneva are requested to board their flight at gate number 12."

Oh, hell—could she have gone ahead? But he'd told her to wait for him here. Why the devil couldn't she do what she was told? So he'd been told to stay with her, but for God's sake they couldn't expect him to sit chatting up some old auntie for an hour when there were chattable birds all over the airport. His eyes strayed back to the ladies' lavatory. Could she be ill? He took a step toward it. Should he . . . ? Well, no, he couldn't. But ought he to get someone to go in and have an eyeshot? He scanned the place for a cleaner. There was none in sight. Distracted, he stopped a passing air hostess and explained his predicament. She smiled reassurance and said that she'd get a message put out over the loudspeaker. A cleaning woman came from behind him pushing a mop. Again he sought help. She disappeared in the ladies', but returned with a broad smile and an upheaval of shoulders and mop.

"Ain't nobody there, dear, sick or not."

The loudspeaker broke a silence to ask, "May I have your attention. Will passenger Seeton, on flight 813 to Geneva, please go to gate number 12 for boarding. I will repeat that. Will passenger Seeton . . ."

One of the barmen was eyeing two almost untouched glasses.

"Hey. Sid." He handed one to his assistant.

"What's up?" asked Sid.

"Dunno. Seems it's our birthday, looks like."

"Have you," demanded Penrood, "seen an old woman?"

The barman looked at him pityingly. "Seen a coupla hundred or more."

"Yes, yes, of course, but I'm looking for one . . ." How in hell did you describe her? All old women looked the same.

The barman waved a hand. "Take your pick. Me. I prefer 'em young." He gulped his drink. "Good hunting—sir," he added belatedly.

"This," advised the loudspeaker, "is a final call for flight 813 to Geneva, now boarding at gate number 12."

Desperate, Penrood ran from the departure lounge.

Haley had bought a magazine at one of the stalls. He flipped through it idly, standing well back to allow the noisy, jostling crowd to mill between him and his quarry. Overhead a speaker blared at intervals, too close to distinguish words. He waited for the black man to finish at the telecommunications desk. Having given in his message and paid, Tolla strode to the top of the escalator and hurried down the stairs to ground level. As soon as he was out of sight, Haley tucked his magazine under his arm and threaded his way over to take the other's place at the counter.

"Excuse me, miss." He held out his police credentials. "I know you can't show me the message that dark gentleman wrote without authority, but I'll get on to the Yard and get authority and it'd save a lot of time and fret if you'd be good enough to keep a copy by you so we don't have to comb through a whole heap of 'em later."

A man writing at a table behind her looked up. "What is it, Dot?"

The girl explained. The man rose and came forward. He examined Haley's identification card, ran an experienced eye over the detective constable, then collected and read the telex. Expressionless, he placed the paper on the counter.

"You're quite right, officer. All communications"—he flicked the paper to emphasize his point and the flick spun the paper so that the writing faced Haley—"are confidential and I'm afraid, much as we should like to help the police and"— drawing out the words—"save time where possible, naturally we cannot let you have a copy without the proper authority. However, we'll keep a record of this so that it will be available at once when the authority is produced, which I hope"— once more he slowed his words—"will make it easier for you."

"Thanks"—Haley was copying the telex as quickly as he could into his notebook—"a lot. I'll ring my inspector at once"—he turned the page and continued writing—"and get things moving. I expect he'll be in touch with you." He pocketed his pen and straightened, beaming. "And—er— thanks." He sketched a salute to the man and the girl and moved swiftly to a telephone kiosk. He pulled the door closed behind him as a loudspeaker appealed:

"Your attention, please. Will Miss Seeton—repeat: Miss Seeton—passenger on flight 813 to Geneva, please go at once—repeat: at once—to reception desk, Swissair number 16." The voice began to sound harassed. "Will Miss Emily Seeton—Miss Emily D. Seeton—*please* . . ."

A telephone on the assistant commissioner's desk purred. Since he had given instructions that he was not to be disturbed, Sir Hubert regarded it with curiosity, lifted the receiver, listened, then held it out to Inspector Borden.

"For you."

The inspector approached the desk. "Borden here." He said nothing more for a full two minutes, then: "She wasn't, she's on her way to Geneva . . . She couldn't've." The earpiece began to cluck with excitement. The inspector listened with a gathering frown, but apart from an occasional and incredulous grunt he did not speak. At length he broke in. "Wait, I'll take that down." Sir Hubert pushed a pencil and memo pad toward him. When Borden had finished writing he commended, "Good. Get back here at once and let me have a full report pronto." He cradled the receiver. "Miss Seeton," he said in even tones, "has flown to Genoa with Mantoni."

Sir Hubert appeared amused, Delphick resigned and the commander and Fenn frankly gaped.

"Haley," continued Borden, "is a good boy, and noticing. When I explained she was supposed to be off to Switzerland he was very impressed. Said it was an education to watch her at work. I understand she put on a clever act of looking a bit lost toward the end and fooled some other female into practically forcing her to go. There was a black man hanging about apparently taking a bit too much interest in MissEss. Haley kept tabs on him after the passengers'd boarded. The black man sent a telex. Haley wangled a copy." He tore the sheet off the memo pad. *"Elio Mantoni,"* he read, *"Aeroporto di Genova . . .* The rest's in code, we'll have to get it . . ."

"May I?" Fenn held out his hand. He studied the cryptogram.

IMSS ESEOTN LODOWMNA TA ATBEL OPLCIEASWATRSNFRE
WSICTHDE LFIHGTOT OFLOLWLEIIMNTAE

His upper lip curled. "It's quite a simple transposition"—he took a pen from his pocket and started to write—"like one of the ordinary commercial codes. But then he'd need to keep it simple and anyway sending it in English abroad should be safe enough in the ordinary way. All he's done is to take the letters of each word in threes and put the second letter first. One over is left and two are reversed. Where words have three letters or multiples of three they join the next." He reviewed what he had written. "I think"—he was adding some vertical strokes—"in view of this we'd best get Interpol to ask the Italian police to collect her when she lands, readdress her and send her on to Switzerland tomorrow. It'll give me time to arrange things in Geneva." He handed the paper to Sir Hubert. "There's your plain text, A.C."

The others gathered round to read:

MISS SEETON OLD/WOMAN AT TABLE POLICE/SAW/TRANSFER
SWITCHED FLIGHT/TO FOLLOW/ELIMINATE

Genoa

THE PLANE BANKED, flew back over the sea in full circle, then dropped for the run in.

The air hostess expelled a silent breath of relief. From the moment that the captain had received the telex from Interpol—MISS SEETON ALIAS MISSESS KNOWN TO ENGLISH POLICE STOP ON UNAUTHORIZED FLIGHT TO GENÓA STOP SURVEYANCE IMPORTANT STOP ITALIAN POLICE WILL MEET PLANE AND COLLECT—she had stood guard offering extra cups of coffee and bright conversation, finding it almost impossible to believe that this frail elderly woman was a known criminal. But now in a minute they would be down and all would be handed over to the police.

They came in low over ships at berth. The wheels touched, the plane bounced gently, ran by the water's edge with only a grass verge between it and the sea, as it slowed to the howl of reversing jets, then bore to the right and taxied toward a long low building.

So much smaller, thought Miss Seeton, so—so much less important looking, somehow, than she had expected. Just as the water, from the glimpses she had caught of it from her aisle seat, had looked so much bigger. Bigger, that was, than the Lake of Geneva had appeared from her study of it on the map.

More like the sea. In fact the place had looked really like a
port, giving her a moment's qualm. The legend in huge letters
on a frame over the building in front of her—AEROPORTO
INTERNAZIONALE DI GENOVA—reassured her. The word GENO-
VA dispelled her slight disquiet. She had arrived.

Elio Mantoni, through experience and aggression, won the
battle to be first at the exit door. At the top of the flight steps he
halted, petrified, and nearly lost his balance. Two uniformed
poliemen were stationed at the foot; beyond them others were
standing by two police cars. All were watching the plane; were
waiting. Were waiting, he knew it, for him. Allora, those
English pigs had been playing with him—had traduced him. To
let him go, to build up his confidence, only to arrange for him
to be arrested now when he reached the ground, his ground, his
own country. Should he drop the briefcase, leave it and pretend
it was not his? Impossible. Too late. Pressured by the
passengers gathered behind him, he was forced to descend.
Outwardly calm, but with his stomach churning, he passed
between the two officers, ignored and was ignored by those
near the cars, and led the way to the customs shed. His
passport was given no more than a perfunctory glance and he
moved on to await his luggage.

"Ha niente da dichiarare?"

So this was the trap. To force him into a false declaration,
then to arrest him for perjury, besides entering contraband and
being in possession of false money. Mantoni gazed up at the
customs officer; a rabbit hypnotized by a snake.

Deaf? Dumb? Both? The officer leaned down and ar-
ticulated: *"Ha qualche cosa da dichiarare?"*

Still unable to speak, Mantoni mastered his paralysis
sufficiently to shake his head. Shook it and continued shaking
it until he felt that he would jolt it from its stand. The
loudspeaker rescued him. When the message was repeated the
sound of his own name brought him out of his stupor. Would he
go to reception, where there was a message for him? He
conquered his head-wagging and recovered his speech.

"Son' io," he told the customs officer.

At once the man melted in sympathy. *Povero pochino*—
doubtless flying home to a sick child. It became his turn for
head-shaking: imagining, seeing so clearly, the ambulance, the
race through the streets, the distracted mother, and now the

urgent message from the hospital: Come immediately. The
darkened room . . . the small figure in the bed . . . the
labored breathing . . . And Mantoni's fictional progeny ex-
pired upon the thought. Quickly he marked the luggage.

"*Vada presto! Corra!*" he advised and turned to the next in
line.

Mantoni crumpled the telex in a fury. Who and what did they
consider him? The palette, not the carving knife, was his
weapon. How dared they attempt to oblige him to become a
common assassin? If only he could discuss . . . As always,
Mantoni regretted the system under which members of the
organization seldom met, more rarely spoke to one another and
neither knew nor had direct contact with their employer, or
employers. The most that they could do, should some query
arise, was to write to an accommodation address, or, in case of
emergency, telephone a given number and await new instructions. They were not, however, encouraged to avail themselves
of these facilities. They were expected to obey orders with
efficiency, with dispatch and without argument. Without
argument; without—Mantoni sighed—discussion. And failure
could be rewarded with a swimming lesson in concrete boots.

The old woman had not yet come through into reception. He
moved to a spot from which he could watch the passengers still
waiting for customs clearance. She was not among them.
Then, where . . . ? He hurried to the glass doors which
opened onto the airport in time to see Miss Seeton being
handed into a police car. An officer got in on each side of her.
The doors slammed and the car, followed by its companion,
circled and drove off the arrival area.

Mantoni bit his lip. *Allora,* what did they now expect of
him? That he should invade *la Polizia Centrale,* stab the old
woman, shoot the captain of the police and vanish in the
disorder?

Miss Seeton was the last passenger to leave the plane. The
hostess had asked her if she would mind remaining seated.
There was—er—a gentleman who wished to speak to her.
Having said good-bye with gratitude to her traveling companion, who, in spite of cream cakes, had done full justice to the
meal provided on the journey without ill effect, Miss Seeton
had resumed her seat, mystified but compliant.

With the rest of the travelers on their way to customs, the hostess had beckoned from the top of the steps. One of the police officers, chosen for his command of English, had bounded up into the aircraft. He had set a tone of correctness: had bowed to Miss Seeton, demanding in Italianate English whether she was Miseetone—alias MissEss? Miss Seeton, equally correct, had replied in Anglican French: Wee. The officer was relieved. Here was the true delinquent. The amateur would negate, would bluster, but the professional admitted what was beyond negation without disturbance. He had, he informed her, with others, been requested, on a demand made by Interpol, to meet her, to greet her, and to accompany her to police headquarters. Was she disposed?

Miss Seeton hesitated. It had been made so very clear that she was to insist, should question arise, that she was merely on holiday. But, then again, on the other hand, one could appreciate that Scotland Yard would, through necessity and good manners, have informed the Swiss police that they were exporting an Identi-Kit artist. And foreigners, one had read, set great store by politeness. No doubt the Swiss police had felt obliged to make a gesture. Miss Seeton felt equally obliged. She replied: Wee.

Upon her arrival at headquarters Miss Seeton was taken before a superior officer and supplied with an interpreter. The compulsory police information form which she had filled in during the flight was produced. She was an art teacher (retired)? Wee. Her destination was such and her address so? Wee. And her reason for traveling was holiday—true or false? False, admitted Miss Seeton. The interpreter smiled in triumph, his superior officer smiled in satisfaction and Miss Seeton smiled in sympathy. Brazen, decided the two Italians. She had not entered the length of her stay. Why not? Because, explained Miss Seeton, she did not, as yet, know how long the bank business would take. The two men exchanged glances: a bank robber and brazen—with this semblance of innocence. Then her declaration was, in essential, false? Wee.

Miss Seeton was escorted along several corridors, was shown into a room with a barred window, a bed, a basin with hot and cold running water, an armchair, a table and an upright chair. Her main luggage was brought in, she was asked to wait, the door was shut. And locked.

• • •

Elio Mantoni was tired and his feet hurt him. He had checked in at the hotel where a room had been reserved for him and had then gone to room 117 in accordance with his instructions in order to hand over the briefcase. He had knocked, but there had been no answer. He could not ask for information at the reception desk since he did not wish to establish any connection between himself and the room's occupant. So, later, after two more failures, he had shelved the matter and had concentrated upon discovering the whereabouts of Miss Seeton. None of the hotels that he had telephoned would acknowledge a booking under that name. He had therefore trudged the streets examining upon various pretexts the latest entries in the registers of all the hotels in the directory. He was, in consequence, tired and his feet hurt him.

A small libation at most of his ports of call had led him from questioning his orders to eliminate Miss Seeton, to questioning the sanity of his employers, and by the time that he had reached his thirty-second hotel on a descending scale, his visitations and potations had induced a feeling of defiance. It was too much—it was not to be expected that you could arrange the death of a woman you did not know when you did not know where she was. Without doubt—without any doubt—from the manner in which they had received her at the airport the police were holding a banquet in her honor and would arrange her accommodation when and where they wished.

"Ecco, ecco! Tieni! Aspetta!" bawled the captain of the Genoese police.

Human nature is apt to reflect its geographical conditions. Mexico is subject to earthquakes and the inhabitants mirror the pattern with political quakes which they call revolutions. In Italy, when deeply disturbed the mounts of Etna and Vesuvius erupt: so, under stress, do the Italians. There are few countries in the world where an argument as to which town of a province should be the principal, a matter usually settled by acrimonious discussion between the local councils involved, could break out into a minor civil war. In Italy it can. The Italian is inherently exuberant; scratch the dormant surface and genera-tions of vendetta and extravaganza will ensue. A single agent of police or at the most one car would have been ample for the reception of Miss Seeton. It was typical, after the first advice that they had received from Interpol, that the captain of police should respond to what had appeared to him to be a matter of international import with two police cars fully manned and, considering the woman might have associates on the plane, it was only to be marveled at that he had not called upon the army.

It was many years since the captain had run, but the second message, from Scotland Yard via Interpol, had galvanized him. They had made—he had made—the most enormous error. Extravaganza now reversed, with a clash of gears that could be heard around the town, for fear that his force should become a laughingstock through Europe. He lumbered from his office like a charging elephant in time to catch the young _poliziotto_ who was carrying a tray down the corridor. He glared from the tray to the young man and back again. What, he barked, in the name of all the saints was the idea? How dared they offer a cheap dish of pasta—at that (he peered closer) with a mere smatter of sauce, a grating of cheese and a glass of water—to an honored guest? Did he imagine that this was how amicable relations were stabilized between the police forces of the world? Go, go, immediately—he thrust a handful of fifty-thousand-lira notes at the bewildered young man—to the best, to the most expensive _ristorante_ in town and have them prepare a banquet fit for a king—no, he amended hastily, a queen, naturally, for a queen—and return with it at once.

The captain waddled back to his office, sat and mopped his brow. More ideas came to him. He punched buttons, summoning subordinates. Carpets! Had they carpets? After a consultation someone remembered the strip of red felt they had used for the festa for the mayor. To be nailed, at once, from the door of her room, down the passage, to the toilet. The bath! How could they make the bath, the one, the only functional bath, beautiful? Soap, bath salts, colored towels. The shops were shut. Then demand of their wives, go to their homes and by favor of finesse produce beautiful towels, perfumed soaps, fragrant lotions. And for the toilet—paper. Soft, soft paper in color. Flowers! The market was closed. But flowers were blooming, weren't they? In the public gardens, the squares, the Piazza della Vittoria? Cut flowers and bring them here _subito, subito_.

With his minions running in all directions, the captain relaxed and remopped. He picked up and compared the two communications from Interpol, the second of which had followed a bare half hour upon the first.

The wires had hummed between Genoa and Paris, between Paris and Geneva, between Geneva and Genoa, between Geneva and London, between London and Paris, between London and Genoa. While Deputy Assistant Commissioner Fenn was arranging protection for Miss Seeton in Switzerland and Sir Hubert Everleigh was organizing a telex request to Alitalia for surveyance during her flight and a message to Interpol asking them to settle with Genoa for her reception, for her safety and for her retransmission to Geneva the following day, Jonathan Feldman had reported to Karl Telmark at the Banque du Lac the disappearance of Miss Seeton from Heathrow and, upon subsequent investigation, her inexplicable flight to Italy. Suspecting abduction at best and death at worst, the Swiss banker had contacted the headquarters of Interpol in Paris, which had relayed his report to Genoa along with his demand that the police should ensure her security on arrival. Unfortunately, in translation, instead of being asked to give her *sicurezza*, use was made of the verb *assicurare*, and "make her secure" the Genoese accordingly did.

But how could he have supposed, how imagined? the captain appealed to Fate. He had acted immediately, had done what they had asked, had secured this woman "known to the police," only to find within the hour that she was a member, an honored member, one of the chiefs no doubt, of England's Scotland Yard. But how—he thrust the papers from him—could he have imagined, how supposed?

None of this activity, after an initial and triumphant statement from the police P.R.O. in Genoa anent their capture of the English criminal Miss Seeton, alias MissEss, had escaped the agency representatives of the world press. Reporters, photographers and television crews jostled for position in front of the police station. Pictures of embarrassed officers in uniform clutching bunched flowers, self-consciously carrying towels and scent bottles and, even more self-consciously, rolls of lavatory paper and, finally, three policemen in line supporting loaded trays covered with white damask, were flashed from capital to capital. It lacked only roast peacock in fine feather and a well-tusked boar's head to complete the flavor of a Roman festival.

• • •

Miss Seeton was a little confused: so odd to be met by the
police instead of by the car she had expected; to be taken to a
police station in lieu of her hotel; and even more odd, when
later occasion had led her to try the door of the room into which
they had shown her, to find that it was locked. It must have,
she had decided, to do with that form which she had filled in
incorrectly on the airplane. One had read that foreign police
forces were meticulous in such matters. In Spain, and also in
Russia, she remembered, English tourists were frequently
detained for what appeared, from what was printed in the
newspapers, quite trivial reasons. She had knocked two or
three times upon the door and had called "Excusez-moi" but
had received no answer. They had not yet returned her passport
and, since there was nothing further that she could do until
morning, when doubtless Mr. Telmark from the bank would be
able to put the whole thing straight, Miss Seeton had unpacked
what she needed for the night, had cleaned her teeth and had
gone to bed. So very fortunate that the nice hostess on the
airplane had provided one with that more than adequate tea.

She was awakened by the sound of hammering. For a few
muddled moments she was unable to orientate herself. Was it
morning? She got out of bed, fumbled into her dressing gown
and groped her way to the light switch by the door. She looked
at her watch. Nearly half-past ten. Then, surely, it must still be
night. She tapped upon the door and called, but by now the
hammering had moved farther away and she met with no
response. She tied the sash of her dressing gown and
determined to wait by the door in order to catch the attention of
anyone who passed. The hammering was now distant, but
there were sounds of activity and men's voices. Oh, dear, how
very awkward. Should one dress again?

All was prepared. Everyone was lined up. The captain,
accompanied by the interpreter, advanced, grasped the door
handle, twisted it and thrust. Nothing happened.

"Je suis so sorry," a muffled Miss Seeton cried, "but je suis
afraid la porte est locked."

As the captain turned an empurpled face toward his staff, a
sheepish young *poliziotto* thrust a posy of geraniums and a
cake of soap into his superior officer's hand—this was no

moment for recording that he had only been obeying orders—
fished in his pocket and produced the key.

Miss Seeton was at first discomposed, then resigned and,
finally, indifferent to what seemed to be an endless invasion of
her privacy by gentlemen in uniform. She was, after all,
decently and soberly, if incorrectly, clad, and since their
attentions and intentions, though astonishing, were obviously
well-meant, and considering that they completely ignored the
fact that she was in night attire, she, too, would disregard it.

The captain, having shaken her hand with difficulty, hampered as he was by the geraniums and the soap, stood to
one side of the door looking both imposing and idiotic. The
interpreter, unencumbered, shook hands freely, aligned himself
beside his chief and the two of them remained in this position
of command to observe, to criticize, while the troops de-
ployed. Flowers! But no vases. Jam jars and two pails were
found in a cleaner's cupboard, emptied of their contents, filled
with water and crammed with blooms. The surplus served to
decorate the bathroom and the lavatory. The hand basins in the
room and in the bathroom were both half full of soap, wrapped
and unwrapped. Bottles of bath essence and lotions were
lodged and dislodged everywhere. The moment for the grand
entry had come. The three tired men supporting their loaded
trays advanced. The table was too small. They backed and
waited while two more tables and a pair of chairs were
produced from nearby offices. The scene was set, the legions
withdrew and the captain with the interpreter stepped forward
to address his honored colleague and to make formal explanations and apologies. The locking of the door—how could she
forgive? Incompetent misunderstanding of orders to hand the
key to her. Her accommodation—so nude, so poor. But they
had had so little time, not having been advised until too late of
her arrival. But now, with regard to the advanced hour, they
had done their humble best to make amends. He did not expect
this flummery to be believed but hoped that she would have the
grace to accept it and not raise the awkward question as to why
they had not engaged a room at a hotel. Meanwhile might they
offer her a light repast? They whipped the damask from the
trays to disclose rows of hot plates; they lifted the covers with
pride. There was: risotto di scampi; three different kinds of
pasta; fritto misto alla Fiorentina with its exotic mixed grill
including forcemeat balls, sweetbreads, brains, boned cutlets

and chicken livers; asparagus browned in butter with grated
cheese and fried eggs; a bombe in a Thermos bowl; a
Neapolitan spiral of short crust with honey, nuts and candied
peel; a pottery bowl containing a cheese and egg dip over a
spirit lamp waiting to be lit; bottles of red wine, white wine and
brandy; coffee, cream; cutlery, glasses; butter and a basket of
assorted breads. Miss Seeton gasped.

"But je ne peux pas, possibly, manger tout cela!" Sensible
of the disappointment that she would cause, she realized that
she would have to do her best. It was, after all, so very, very
kind and they had taken so much trouble. To say nothing of the
expense. She appealed to the interpreter. "Won't you—voulez-
vous non manger too?"

The interpreter translated the painstaking Anglo-French into
rapid Italian. The idea was received with enthusiasm and the
three of them drew forward chairs and settled down to what
was beginning to take on the aspect of a maximal feast in the
dormitory. In view of the number of dishes through which she
would have to wade, Miss Seeton pecked, the interpreter ate
and the captain of police, whose girth gave him the advantage,
stuffed.

During the meal Miss Seeton was told that arrangements had
been made for her flight to Milan in the morning and the
interpreter would accompany her. Milan? She couldn't go to
Milan in the morning. She had an appointment with the bank.

When this information was relayed the captain's eyes
narrowed. *Allora*, they were about to learn the reason for her
visit.

"What bank?"

The Banque du Lac. The interpreter was nonplussed. There
was no such bank in Genoa, nor had he ever heard of one in the
whole of Italy.

"Non, non," she explained, "in Geneva—in Swiss."

But—the interpreter spilled ravioli on the table—they could
not get her to Svizzera in the morning. Not possible. There was
no direct flight. She would have to go via Milan and the plane
from there to Ginevra was in the afternoon.

No direct flight . . . ? Afternoon? The uncomfortable
feeling that she had experienced when seeing all that water
before they landed came back in force.

"Where," asked Miss Seeton, "am I?"

She was told. She was appalled. Then embarrassed. And she

had been speaking to them in French. How silly they must think her. And all the trouble she had put them to. Oh, dear. Between repeated apologies, she gave them an account of what had taken place at Heathrow and how she had come to make such a truly dreadful mistake. On being apprised, the captain of police roared with laughter and slapped the table with appreciation, making the glasses ring. An able one, this one— a prime agent of her class. Pretending in the first part to believe the story of their error; now, in the second part, she offers them this *buffo divertimento* of the lady with her cream cakes. Naturally not expecting credence, but knowing that they must pretend to give it credit since it could not be disproved. Unless the wine—he drained his glass, refilled Miss Seeton's and his own—loosened her tongue . . . But no, he was beginning to have respect for this one. Able. Very able. They would not learn from her why Scotland Yard had sent her here. Principal officials did not suddenly alter their destination without reason. He gave it thought. They would be in force tomorrow at the airport, keep a close watch and try to establish her intentions. And he would telephone his opposite number in Milano to scrutinize her every word and look, supposing that she might have, or try to make, a contact. Or . . . was she following someone—some international criminal? He must examine the lists of passengers.

Slightly glazed, they finished dipping bread in cheese and put the coffee on to heat. Now for the morning—for breakfast? Miss Seeton repressed a shudder. What could they offer? Anything, anything she wished, she had but to command.

"Just," Miss Seeton ventured, "some weak tea, toast and jam."

The interpreter and the captain exchanged a glance. Tea? Toast? Where could they obtain . . . ? They countered this with coffee and hot rolls. And of course *marmellata*. Well, no, not marmalade, she didn't care for it. But just butter would do if jam was difficult. Reassured that in Italy jam was *marmellata* and that marmalade was something else again, Miss Seeton once more shook hands, bade her guest-hosts good night and trod the wrinkled red felt to the facilities before retiring finally to rest.

Fifty-three hotels were all that could be—all that should be—expected of a man. Only lodgings were left. *Allora*, it was not—it could no longer be—his responsibility. His plane left at eight in the morning for Milano, so they must arrange whatever deaths they wanted for her—and for the doing, they could do themselves.

Mantoni decided to treat himself to an expensive dinner, washed down by two bottles of Vernaccia di Solarussa. It was a little bitter for his taste but he found consolation in the fact that it was the highest-priced wine on the list. He topped the stuffed peaches of his dessert with three shots of the wormwood-flavored Miele del Grappa and succeeded in convincing himself that his claim for expenses would be sympathetically viewed. By now the night, like Mantoni, was well advanced. Fortified, he returned to his hotel in a mood of belligerence. He collected his key, took the lift to his floor, walked down to the first floor and knocked on the door of room 117. He waited. Waited, then thumped. There were creaks, a thud, heavy footsteps and the door was thrown open to reveal a huge man, pajama buttons straining to contain the doormat-fronted barrel which served him for a chest. Bleary-eyed from sleep, he looked ahead, looked left, looked right, looked down. The thick lips under the heavy mustache parted and he gave a raucous laugh.

No. This—this was too much. It was beyond. He had been plagued by English pigs, put in peril by Italian *polizia*, he had survived danger, he had been ordered to commit death and through it all, undaunted, he was now completing his main mission. He was no one to be mocked by a witless gorilla.

Mantoni swung the briefcase forward and up. The giant let out a howl and fell back clutching it to his tender pain. The little man closed the door. David and a stone—Elio and a briefcase—it was all one; either way Goliath fell. Swollen with rich food, heady wines and vindicated self-esteem, Mantoni swaggered to his room and swerved to bed.

Jonathan Feldman was stuttering with rage. "How d-dare you send her to Italy . . . ?"

"We didn't." The assistant commissioner's voice was mild.

"All right, if we must qu-quibble over words, allow her to

go to Italy first without warning me? What are you going to say to Lord Gatwood? What am I supposed to say to Karl Telmark? D-do you realize he sent a car to meet her—and don't forget he's paying her—and not only does she make a fool of him by not turning up, but there's headlines and photographs in all the papers that she's p-playing the fool all over Italy. Good God," he exploded. "The whole idea was to keep things quiet and now this—this misguided missile of yours is splashed in every headline. I can't understand—"

Sir Hubert raised a hand in restraint. "Nor, Mr. Feldman, as yet, can we." How was it that a modest retired drawing mistress, of a retiring nature, had the trick of setting everybody by the ears including, apparently, hardheaded banks and hard-boiled government departments? "Misguided missile." A happy smile; he must remember it. Perhaps a word to the War Office: the next time a cold war hotted up it might be an idea to launch her into the trouble spot, which should give the troublemakers enough troubles of their own to prevent them from troubling other people. England's secret weapon? Sir Hubert composed his face. "I feel bound to emphasize that we at the Yard were against Miss Seeton being let loose on the Continent, particularly in regard to matters so far outside her scope as counterfeiting and finance, and that it was M. Telmark who, through you and the Foreign Office, overruled us. You, if you remember, gave us to understand that you would be responsible for seeing her onto the plane to Geneva. I hardly feel, therefore, that we should be held accountable, or not directly, for the fact that she finished up on a different plane to somewhere else. However, I have done my best. After your telephone call I arranged for Commander Conway and Inspector Borden of Fraud, who are in charge of our side of the investigation; for Deputy Assistant Commissioner Fenn of the Special Branch, who has kindly agreed to hold a metaphorical umbrella over her during her sortie abroad; and for Chief Superintendent Delphick and Sergeant Ranger, who know her better than any of us, to be present at this conference in the hope that between them they'll be able to answer any queries that you—or Lord Gatwood, or M. Telmark, through you—wish to raise."

The commander cleared his throat. "All we know—and don't forget we've never met the lady—is that she's gone chasing down to Genoa after Mantoni, whom we know to be a

small-time artist turned crook and suspect of being a carrier for
the snide. How she got on to him we don't know, but why she
decided to follow him is fairly obvious."

Fenn roused himself. " 'Fraid I can't help. I set things up to
keep a watch on her in Switzerland, but her sideskipping to
Italy's caught me on the hop."

Sir Hubert looked a question at Delphick.

The chief superintendent cogitated. "Granted my sergeant
and I know her and that she has worked with us or for us on
three cases, but I think all it's taught us of her is to expect the
unexpected. The chief thing seems to be ready, when she
explodes a bomb by accident, to pick up the pieces quickly,
reassemble them and learn what's going on."

"All right, all right." Feldman ran a hand through his hair.
"According to you I asked for trouble. All right. But none of
you"—he glared at them all accusingly—"ever warned me
that the lady was a bomb."

Milan

WHAT, MISS SEETON wondered, were those?

They were flying low and she was intrigued by scores of neat rectangles of water in different colors—shades of green, brown and yellow—while some were almost clear.

The interpreter leaned across. "Rice fields," he informed her.

Rice fields? She felt a misgiving. Rice fields? China? Rice? How very unexpected. "I hadn't realized that rice . . . in Italy, I mean."

"Oh, yes," he explained. "We grow it a lot, particularly around Milan." With a small sigh of relief Miss Seeton settled back in her seat to enjoy the shifting panorama as they dropped to land.

One hostess stood guard by the curtain which divided the tourist from the first class, where Miss Seeton was ensconced, while another led her to the exit the moment that the plane came to a halt. The interpreter, carrying her case, blocked the other first-class passengers for sufficient time to ensure that his charge disembarked alone. After shaking her warmly by the hand, the hostess watched Miss Seeton descend and sustained a benign smile for the benefit of the battery of cameras lined up below. *Ecco*, she apostrophized in silent criticism. To be such a very important personage and yet to wear such clothes—and such a hat. Never, never would she understand the English.

The captain of the Milanese police advanced. The pictures in tomorrow's papers should be impressive since the tarnish on the gold braid, the uniform's indifferent fit and the scruff of an unsuccessful shave would not be patent. He took Miss Seeton's hand and bowed over it while his retinue inclined in unison like a well-trained chorus. Cameras clicked and whirred, interviewers pushed forward, microphones at the ready, only to be waved aside. Miss Seeton was led to a car, shook hands with the driver, was ushered into it, the captain and his second in command—another handshake—spread a rug across her knees, put a cushion to her back, took their places on either side of her, the doors were slammed, the rest of the *polizia* jumped into the two escorting cars and the three vehicles moved sedately forward some six yards to the main doors of the airport, where they all unloaded, Miss Seeton was unwrapped and wafted past passports and customs to the refreshment end of the lounge. Milan, determined to be not a whit behind Genoa in canceling an error, was showing that Italy understood the deference due to an esteemed colleague and was refuting the morning headlines in the world press: BATTLING BROLLY JAILED—LA SEETON DÉTENUE—LA SIGNORINA SEETON IN CUSTODIA—ARREST OF YARD'S MISSESS.

Although Miss Seeton, traveling first class—so kind, but so extravagant of them, and the champagne, too, so palatable, but inclined to make one sneeze—had not seen the passengers in the tourist class, they had seen her. Among them, Elio Mantoni had watched her quasi-royal send-off and touch-down with mixed feelings. At least he knew once more where she was even if the knowledge, for the moment, was of little use to him and did nothing to alleviate his hangover. He would have several cups of strong black coffee and then, with nearly three hours before the flight to Geneva, he would have time to go to an alleyway off the eastern approach to the Castello Sforzesco where he would acquire a pistol—a pistol with a silencer—and he would take the first opportunity.

Miss Seeton, at a table for four, was flanked by the high command, while the rest of the police party, grouping themselves at satellite tables, brought her sandwiches, cold sausages, cheesecake and coffee. Toying with her food, she was distressed to note that the coffee cup was not clean, though naturally it would be impolite to draw attention to it. She waited patiently for it to be filled and it was not until she saw her companions sipping that it dawned upon her that the black stain at the bottom of the cup was in fact the coffee and that she would get no more unless she swallowed the bitter brew. Putting down her cup and taking in her surroundings she saw— good gracious, what a strange coincidence—the gentleman who had hummed at London airport. She smiled and nodded. Unknowing and out of key she began to hum the "Song of India."

The police captain, watching her carefully and having noticed her signal to a distant table, wondered if this tuneless excursion was part of some prearranged directive. Deliberately, in baritone, he joined in the aria and others of his force, taking their cue from their chief, supported him. Miss Seeton blushed. How rude of her to hum. But what a popular tune it seemed.

Mantoni glowered. *Allora*, so she derided him, derided him in public with all her friends of the *polizia*. She wished him to understand that she knew what he was doing—what he had done—and that she found him ridiculous and was only awaiting her opportuniyy. *Allora*—so. He got up. This was now personal. This was vendetta. He would go at once to the dealer he knew of and when he had his pistol—and its silencer—she would find that it would be he, he who would be making the opportunities. And soon.

Geneva

"LADIES AND GENTLEMEN, in a few moments we shall be passing Mont Blanc, which you will be able to see on your right if the clouds allow."

Mont Blanc. That should be very impressive. Miss Seeton took her traveling sketching block and pencils from her handbag on the empty first-class seat beside her and continued to stare out of the window, ready to be impressed. Really, it was quite difficult to appreciate that all these balls of cotton wool, just below one—so like those that were conveniently sold in plastic bags by chemists nowadays—were, in fact, clouds. And that the very solid-looking snowfields, that stretched almost as far as one could see, were not. Snow, as well. And, right over there, in the distance, that blue lake, with its sandy shore, was merely a break in the clouds and the effect of the sun gilding the edge around it.

Oh. Suddenly, or so it seemed, a grayish-brown crag of rock jutted above the cotton wool quite close. Very close indeed. One side of it was almost bare, with dark streaks, while on the other it looked as if someone had carelessly spilled a can of whitewash. So that little bit of rock must be—she leaned forward to peer behind her—must have been Mont Blanc. How

very odd that up here clouds should look like snow and snow
like whitewash. So very topsy-turvy.

The name Mont Blanc brought realization that they must
now be over Switzerland and the memory of her two previous
and abortive flights caused her to flush with embarrassment. So
extremely careless of her.

It might have comforted Miss Seeton to know that her case
was not without precedent. The history of confusion between
Geneva and Genoa dates back many centuries and even so
recently as 500 A.D. both cities occasionally spelled their
names Genua. There is a tradition which holds that Saint
Nazarius was the first bishop of Geneva although this is
incorrect since that saint belongs properly to Genoa. It is of
course possible that the august gentleman, making Miss
Seeton's journey in reverse, had originally arrived in Geneva
only to be redirected. In modern times such errors are less
common. According to the airline authorities, bewildered
travelers making the incorrect landfall are rare and such cases
do not occur "more than a dozen or so times a year," but if
pressed these same authorities will admit that misplacement of
travelers' luggage is "rather more frequent."

They dropped below the clouds and Miss Seeton's interest
revived. Those samples of colored veneers such as one saw
displayed in the windows of high-class timber merchants must,
she supposed, be really plowed and planted fields. Then little
pools. In gardens. Of most peculiar shapes in highly improbable blues and greens. The plane flew down the length of Lac
Léman and Miss Seeton watched through the window with
satisfaction. How exactly it resembled the map that she had
memorized, with the city spread across the end of the lake.
And here it would, perhaps, be more tactful to remember to
call it by its other name, Lake of Geneva.

Geneva: city of intrigue; where Machiavelli would have felt
at home; where delegations come from every other land and
every other delegate is other than they seem; where informers
sell to spies and spies are counterspies and only unite to
undermine the United Nations; where dubious financiers put
doubtful gains into unnamed accounts and use the city as a
springboard to new lives in brighter sunshine at their shareholders' expense; where deviation from accepted standards is

accepted as the norm; where infiltration is the order of the day and honesty is more suspect than the lie.

Genève: city of humane wealth; where the native, the resident, the Law, regard the foreign antic with passivity; where all is uncovered, all discovered, yet comment on discovery is rare; where the miscreant who oversteps will soon be asked to leave—why pay for his support?—but should a prison term prove politic the term will be short before his removal under guard to the frontier of no return.

Elio Mantoni joined the passengers clustered on either side of the luggage chute where it levels off for the last few yards of its length. Some had porters in attendance, some had managed to secure one of the small supply of trolleys, while others had neither and waited ready to grab and cope with their impedimenta as best they could. In Geneva travelers await their baggage at ground level. On the other side of the airport building their transport lands and discharges their belongings upon the ground. That their cases should then appear through a hole in the high ceiling and glide down a long, steep causeway toward their owners is one of the unquestioned, mysterious quirks of foreign travel.

Mantoni was keeping a lookout. Nowhere was there a sign of that horrible woman. She had vanished. She had boarded the plane and had been waved upon her way by half the *polizia* of Milano as though she were someone of the grandest importance—but now, no. She was hiding—watching, waiting, to see what he would do. *Allora,* he would do nothing. He too would watch, would wait—would see what she would do.

The luggage began its descent. As it trundled by him, Mantoni pulled his case from the conveyor belt but remained where he was as though anticipating more manna from the heavens. Suitcase after suitcase was snatched from its slow progress and borne away in triumph until but three remained, huddled against the end barrier, unclaimed, unloved, disconsolate. Casually he inspected them. One of them bore a label printed in smudged ink: MISS E. D. SEETON—GENEVA. Then where . . . ? She could not have—not even she—altered her destination in midair. He would delay himself, would follow the case, or her, or both and so discover her hotel. And, once discovered, he would make his plan and he would be avenged.

Avenged. He gripped his new briefcase with a sense of anticipation.

At Milan, intercepting the nodded sign and glance from the captain of police at Miss Seeton's table to one of his subordinates, Mantoni had been prepared. He had eluded the agent who had tried to tail him, but when he had reached the shop in the alleyway near the castle he had found that the pistol he was purchasing, with its silencer attached, was too long for any pocket. After a consultation with the dealer he had decided to buy a briefcase as well, a case with handles and a zip fastener, and in this the pistol now reposed ready for the moment when, the zip unzipped, the hand inthrust, the pistol fired, the zip refastened, the marksman walked away showing no sign except the fallen body of the victim. The fact that Mantoni had never yet fired a pistol did not bother him. He was confident. The armature was pointed at the enemy, the trigger pulled and—*phut,* the enemy dropped dead. He'd seen it done in films. A simple exercise performed by common hired assassins and well within his scope, demanding little of the expertise of hand and eye such as he had and which it took to wield a painter's brush. And—understood—he'd practice.

He considered the newspapers tucked beneath his arm: such vulgarity; that woman and her photographs spread over the front page. And the headlines: LA SEETON E POLIZIA FANNO FESTA DI MEZZANOTTE! He would—it would be wise—keep out of sight. He stepped on the mat which opened the glass doors, hailed a taxi, told the driver he wished to follow a friend to her hotel when she came out, threw in his luggage, climbed in and, with his briefcase held across his knees, he settled down to wait.

A policeman was studying the *Journal de Genève* with disapproval: a photograph of a line of uniformed men carrying trays covered with white cloths and a black arrow pointing to an embarrassed officer clutching a fistful of bottles in either hand; above it the caption: A GÊNES C'EST LA POLICE QUI RÉGALE! MLLE SEETON S'EN RÉGALE! Further down the page was a picture of a woman descending from an aircraft, subtitled *Mlle Seeton à Milan.* He grimaced; those Italians— too emotional. She'd find things different here in Switzerland: no fuss; no midnight feasts in police stations; no photographers and reporters to greet her; no one to meet her save his driver and himself, who'd escort her to her hotel, see her safely in and, after that, whatever she did, it would not be their onions. Where was she? He stared around. The other passengers had gone and now a new lot were coming through. She'd been on the plane—he'd checked. And though the face in the photo wasn't so clear, he could not have missed those clothes. Buying herself something duty-free? A drink? A call of nature? But with all this fresh crowd now arriving it might not be so simple to place her. Better get back to the car where he could watch the line of doors more easily. He went out, got in beside his driver and settled down to wait.

The chauffeur of the car ordered by Karl Telmark of the Banque du Lac stood, solid, patient, by the center exit. No sign of her—except her case there; he'd read the label but didn't care to touch it till she came. Luckily he'd seen pictures of her—plenty in the papers. But now the place was filling up again. Best to attend outside. Safer. He got in behind the wheel and settled down to wait.

Two plainclothesmen from the Swiss Sûreté, their clothes—dark suits, dark ties, dark shoes, white shirts, fawn raincoats, felt hats with feathers in the bands—so plain, so uniform that they were that in effect, glanced at each other, shrugged in unison. Some ladies didn't travel well. No doubt that was why . . . But, even so, she could not now be long delayed. Not for them to ask for information at the desk. For them to shadow, to watch, to be discreet, unnoticeable. But with a new flight—no, two flights—coming in, it would be more discreet, less noticeable to get back to their car. They turned as one, strode out as one, encarred as two and settled down to wait.

A young man was expostulating at an information desk. "But after all, I say, you know, she must be here. There'll be fair old ructions if she's got lost again. You've got to find her. After all, that's her case"—he pointed to where Miss Seeton's suitcase rested lonely and abandoned against the barrier—"and if that's there, where's she? After all, I'm from the embassy—in Bern, you know—and the consulate here asked me to whiffle along and pick her up—meet her, you know—and do a spot of looking after, so you'd better stir your stumps and find her." The girl at information could not help him. She telephoned here, asked questions there, but no one seemed to know. The young man, now popeyed with frustration, turned away, surveyed the ever-increasing throng of travelers. Stay by the case? Or sit outside? Outside'd be best with all this mob. He went to his car reluctantly and settled down to wait.

A smartly dressed woman stood close to the wall. She had been standing there now for quite some time, toying with *Vogue*. In her thirties? Early? Late? It was difficult to tell. Fair hair brushed back tight to the head, twist-rolled, brilliant blue eyes alight with laughter and intelligence; no beauty, but she would outshine all women in whatever company she chose to grace. Fashionable? She gave the impression that, whether or not she followed fashion, fashion followed her.

She had watched, expressionless but with amusement, Elio Mantoni's shifting from foot to foot, his distracted glances around, his oh-so-casual examination of the label on Miss Seeton's case, and then his departure. That bulge in his briefcase—could it be a gun? He was, she guessed, seated in a taxi outside, waiting.

The uniformed policeman's dilemma, before his final retirement, had made her smile. He, she imagined, was still waiting, still outside.

That chauffeur, so correct, had also glanced at Miss Seeton's case and then had gone outside. To wait?

The young man—diplomatic?—in a fever of fiasco, of bafflement and failure, after getting no satisfaction from information—he too had gone outside and was, she was sure, still waiting.

For herself, she had finally guessed Miss Seeton's whereabouts. Better, for the moment, not to intrude; not to interfere. It would appear that this Miss Seeton had the trick—conscious or not—of attracting publicity. And publicity, vis-à-vis Miss Seeton, was something that she preferred to avoid. She glanced at her watch, lifted her shoulders a fraction as though deploring the nonarrival of some friend, passed between the glass doors near her, went to her scarlet Lancia sports coupé, slid into the driver's seat and settled down to wait.

Four cars and two television vans crept down the lane formed by the vehicles parked on the left and those drawn up with their drivers by the right-hand curb waiting for passengers. The leading car stopped; in consequence its followers braked, while in the rear other cars were forced to halt and, not understanding the delay, began to play a cacophony upon frustrated horns. From the first car the driver jumped, opened his back door with a flourish, bowed, and from it stepped Miss Seeton. He accompanied her into the airport building. They returned, he carrying her suitcase. They were interrupted. Miss Seeton's appearance had acted as a signal. Doors opened down the line of waiting cars, except for the taxi in which Mantoni kept his vigil, and the scarlet Lancia of which the occupant remained in place to observe and to admire.

The uniformed policeman intercepted Miss Seeton and her cavalier, demanding explanations. The young man seconded to the consulate from the embassy in Bern interposed, expostulating. The chaffeaur ordered by the Banque du Lac intervened with mild insistence and the two men from the Sûreté, indisposed to interfere, stood back to listen.

The policeman required the man's identity. Thrudd Banner, World-Wide-Press. Humph. And where had he been—he and all these others? He waved at the cars and television vans. And where, where then, had been Miss Seeton, instead of with her luggage as was to be expected? In the V.I.P. lounge, giving a press conference. Humph again. A press conference? The young man from the embassy grew shrill with horror. But that was exactly what he'd come there to prevent.

"Too late, friend. Too bad," said the reporter.

"But look here, after all, I say, she can't, she's much too tired, she's not responsible."

Thrudd Banner winked at Miss Seeton. "He says you're gaga, ma'am."

The young man spluttered. "I—I—you don't realize who I am."

"Too wrong; I do." He did. They all knew Thomas ffoley, Tomfool, attaché at the embassy. Bern got rid of him on any and every pretext and sent him to Geneva. The consulate here had become adept at inventing errands, harmless ploys, to keep him from their hair, and both cities prayed for the day when he'd fall flat on his foolish face and be recalled.

"If you print one word without permission, I—I'll speak to the ambassador."

"Do that, and write me what he says. I'll frame it."

Thrudd could afford to grin. MissEss had proved good copy,

earning his high regard. In verbal thrust and parry she had, in
his judgment, matched or outmatched the lot of them, wielding
her words with wit and all the skill with which reputedly she
wielded an umbrella.

"And what is your opinion, ma'am, of life in jail in Italy?"

Miss Seeton looked reproving. What a way to put it. Like a
naughty little boy asking silly questions during class. Still—her
opinion? "Oh, very high," she assured him earnestly.

"And would you tell us," asked a female cub, "your reason
for coming here?"

Her reason? Why, of course. "A holiday."

And was this her first experience of foreign travel? Oh, yes,
indeed. And did she, when on holiday, normally go a long way
round to get where she was going? Oh, no. But then, of
course, this was not. Normal, she meant. Not normal? Then
she admitted that there was, in this case, some extraordinary
reason behind her jaunt to Genoa? Oh, yes. Quite extraordinary—pens poised, they leaned expectant; microphones were
lowered on their booms; cameras came to close-up—the
extraordinary likeness of the names, that was. And what was,
Thrudd insisted, her opinion of the police in Italy? So very
kind. And such good food. So thoughtful. So understanding.
Though, perhaps, almost too much of it—the food, she meant.
Would it be true to say she'd come to an understanding with the
police in Genoa? Well, one hoped . . . And had she, they
chorused, come to a further understanding during the three-
hour conclave at Milan? Well, yes, she thought so. Or did hope
so. They had certainly seemed most understanding. And very
kind. And so hospitable. Except, of course, the coffee.

"Tell me, MissEss," Thrudd finally had asked with an
appreciative twinkle, "so that I don't misquote: in all this
misadventure—as you claim—if the Italian police had misbe-
lieved you, what charge would they have preferred on your
arrest, a mischief, a misconduct, or a misdemeanor?"

She looked perplexed. She didn't quite . . . Was worried,
then she smiled. "You see, it was," Miss Seeton told him, "a
mistake."

And that, Thrudd decided, had given him his heading:
MISSESS' MISTAKE?

And where, the policeman wished to know, did M. Banner
think that he was taking the English miss? To her hotel, where
else. He would not. The officer drew himself up to the full

height of his importance. His orders were, his duty was—and both would be accomplished—to escort the English miss to her hotel.

Mild but stubborn, the chauffeur pointed out his orders were, his duty was—and for both he would be held answerable—to escort the English miss to her hotel.

In stridulous tones the attaché overrode them. He felt his reputation was at stake. He had been entrusted with, at last, a significant assignment. He must not fail.

"I represent the British embassy—the consulate—and I'm afraid I must insist that Miss Seeton is handed over to my charge."

Finally the matter was arranged; without reference to Miss Seeton's wishes: ffoley would drive her, the chauffeur would follow with her luggage, the policeman would act as escort, thus fulfilling both his orders and his duty, and Thrudd, if all this was okay by MissEss, would follow; the rest of the news hounds having already gained the most of what they wanted.

Once clear of the airport, the other press cars and the television vans cut on ahead, leaving Thomas ffoley to grind his gear changes sedately and in triumph. Firmness, that was what was wanted with foreigners. Britain could still look after her citizens when they got themselves into a spot of trouble when abroad. Just put your foot down and be firm.

He put his foot down firmly at a traffic light and his and Miss Seeton's heads both jerked in unison. The chauffeur, with her cases, swore and braked; why couldn't the English sot learn to drive. The police driver had more time and, back of him, Thrudd Banner, the two men from the Sûreté and Mantoni's taxi eased to a halt. The lights changed. Thomas ffoley stalled his engine, clashed his gears and jolted forward and the cavalcade set off again to wend its slow way down into the city, toward the lake. In the rear the owner of the scarlet Lancia kept an eye upon them all.

Miss Seeton found it strange. Foreign travel. So very unexpected. Or, should one say, so very different from what one had expected. Admittedly she had traveled rather more, and slightly farther, than had originally been intended—though, privately, she felt that, mortifying though her mistake had been, it was one that many might have made in the same circumstances. But it was surprising what a lot of people took

an interest. The police she could understand, up to a point.
They were extending politeness to a colleague. Not realizing
that, in actual fact, she wasn't. Or, at all events, not in the
sense they seemed to think.

They had reached the lake and the car came to another
abrupt halt. To hooted indignation from behind, ffoley crossed
from the right-turn lane to turn left over the Pont du Mont
Blanc. Miss Seeton recovered her balance.

"Could you tell me, Mr. ffoley," she ventured, "to what
hotel we're going?" The car swerved. Oh. One should not,
perhaps, talk to a gentleman when driving. ffoley recovered.

"But after all—look here—I say, you said you were on
holiday."

"I am."

"Well, that's what I mean. After all, good Lord, you must
know where you booked." He was beginning to regret his
chivalry: thought he was rescuing an elderly lady in distress;
now it appeared the old dame was slightly dotty.

Miss Seeton sensed something of his feelings. "I did not"—
her voice was a little tart—"make the booking myself, Mr.
ffoley. They told me that there would be a car to meet me and
take me to my hotel, but they did not say its name. So,
naturally, I . . ." She stopped, realizing that the car in
question had been ordered to meet a plane from England
yesterday, and not one from Italy today.

"You're at the Richesse; with all the confabs that've been
going on everybody knows that. What firm—who are these
'they' who booked you in without telling you?"

"Er—some friends made all the arrangements for my
holiday."

Did they just? Then in spite of how she looked she must be
rolling. The Richesse mightn't be him—old hat, unscenic—but
they could charge. Cost you a quid to cough. Hang on a bit—
she was from Scotland Yard. Couldn't be all that dotty. Maybe
she was here on some hush-hush do. Yes, that'd be it—then
something cropped and she'd switched to Italy. Geneva was
always up to its chin in hush with everybody having confabs on
the strict q.t. Well, this was one where he'd got himself onto
the inside track. Somebody's sent for her, someone with
money. Better stick around a bit; might do the old career a bit
of good.

At the far side of the bridge he turned to the right along the

Quai du Mont Blanc, past the Brunswick Monument, swung
the car left without waiting across the oncoming traffic to the
latter's mechanical and vocal fury, down the Rue Adhémar
Fabri, which borders one side of the triangle forming the Place
des Alpes, slid by a line of parked cars in front of an awninged
terrace, to pull up near the pavement before the wide, shallow
steps which lead to the entrance of the Hôtel de la Richesse.

In the fleeting glimpse she had had of it in passing, the
monument, with its likeness to a scale model for the Albert
Memorial, had given Miss Seeton a restorative sense of
familiarity. She felt pleased that her hotel should be so close to,
and look out upon, such a reminder of Kensington Gardens.
Her hotel? All sense of familiarity left her as a smiling porter in
plum-colored uniform, peaked cap in hand, held her door and
helped her to alight; as three smiling boys in like-colored
uniforms hurried through the revolving doors and down the
steps; as an aproned luggage porter with a welcoming smile
appeared from a basement at the side. She stood aghast. Oh,
dear, how very unsuitable. What could Mr. Telmark have been
thinking of? Even if, as she supposed, it was to be for only one
night, or, possibly, two, it was still so very—well, really, there
was no other word—unsuitable. One had expected, naturally,
some superior sort of boardinghouse; so many of them called
themselves hotels. But this—the Hotel of Riches; and it so
evidently was—oh, dear, it was—it really was—unsuitable.

While Miss Seeton stood debating the suitability of the hotel
and of herself, the chauffeur handed her cases to the luggage
porter, saluted and drove off; the police car drew up and halted;
Thrudd Banner decided that if the police could double-park so
could he too—for a moment. He jumped out and took up his
position to get a picture of Miss Seeton as she entered; the men
from the Sûreté stopped behind him. With cars parked against
the curb outside the hotel and others opposite angled between
white lines backing onto the garden of the Place des Alpes, this
double-parking had left only a single lane. Mantoni's taxi
driver waited for a break, pulled out, but as he came abreast of
Miss Seeton Mantoni ordered him to halt. The Italian wound
down his window. He was within a foot of her. Such an
opportunity might never come again. It was irresistible. He
thought quickly, looked back. A red car was coming up in their
rear. That would stop the police—delay pursuit. If the taxi
driver realized what had happened he would hold the pistol on

him, force him to drive on, at speed, and, when they were clear, hit his head, shoot if necessary, abandon him and disappear. *Allora*. Mantoni raised his briefcase.

The owner of the scarlet Lancia, blocked by the taxi, sprang from her car and stepped forward with determination, stood in front of Mantoni's window, waved at her car in explanation and said:

"Mais, je vous en prie, monsieur."

Mantoni glared at her. His driver turned to stare and mentally wolf-whistled, engaged his gear and drew the taxi forward. Mantoni's opportunity had gone. Already Miss Seeton had moved to the pavement with the hall porter—it was too far—always, always, this interfering woman was between his aim and them. Frustrated, he said to the driver to drive on. So, so, this then was not the time. But—and he noted it—this was the place. Tomorrow, tomorrow he would be prepared.

One of the hotel bellboys grinned a question. The fair-haired woman smiled and nodded. He took the Lancia and drove it away while she went lightly up the steps and into the hotel.

Flanked by the policeman and by Thomas ffoley, Miss Seeton followed through the revolving door, pushed by another smiling boy. She was led to the far end of the reception desk, her passport number was recorded, a young man, very correct in a black suit, collected her key and preceded her to one of the two lifts, opened by yet one more smiling attendant. She turned to thank her convoy, shook hands with the policeman, who assured her that he was at her service; shook hands with Thomas ffoley, who declared that he would call on her tomorrow to see how she was shaking down. The lift ascended and she emerged at the third floor.

Her room was large; her suitcase and her overnight bag awaited her. Really, for a hotel, the room was very large; a comfortable-looking bed, an armchair by a table with a standard lamp, a writing desk, another chair, another lamp. The correct young man opened doors: showed her the bathroom, the hanging cupboards and the shelves; was there anything she wished for—a drink, some coffee, or some tea? Well, a cup of tea she would be very grateful for. Indian or China, lemon or milk? Thankfully Miss Seeton opted for China, weak, with plenty of hot water. It would arrive immediately. And as to dinner? In the restaurant—a set menu? In the grill—à la carte—he would reserve a table? Or, should she be feeling tired, would she prefer the meal served in her room? Catching her expression at his last suggestion, the young man smiled and informed her that the floor waiter would attend on her at seven and present a menu for her choice. Should she require anything else before, she had only to ring or use the telephone. He bowed, he smiled again, withdrew.

The tea arrived and, on the tray, an envelope. A letter from Karl Telmark suggesting that, in view of all that had taken place, it would be better if she did not come to the bank, for fear of publicity, and that he would do himself the honor, with her permission, to call upon her at her hotel the next morning and discuss her plans. Discuss? Her plans? But she had none. She was here to work—to draw—for him. Poor Mr. Telmark and that missed appointment for this morning. It was very worrying. One felt so guilty at the trouble one must have caused. And then the police in Italy—they had seemed quite sure that she had had some other reason for arriving there and, when she had explained, they had laughed and made such a fuss over her—and all that food. It had, of course, been very kind, but just a little worrying. And, even here, in Switzerland. So many people to meet her at the airport—she'd understood that no one was to know—and newspaper people, too. The whole of the last twenty-four hours had been so strange and really rather worrying.

Dutifully Miss Seeton settled down to worry—and she failed. She looked at the bed, then went and sat upon it. It was, as she had thought, most comfortable. Most . . . comfortable. She caught herself yawning. The whole hotel—most comfortable. No. Comforting would be more correct. One had feared that it would be intimidating. For someone like oneself, that was. But, no. Everyone had smiled, was welcoming. She yawned again. She'd been up very late last night—and it had been an early start this morning—with two journeys. There were still a couple of hours before they would come about her dinner. Really, she . . . She slipped off her shoes, lay down and pulled the coverlet over her. Worrying, of course, but comforting . . . and comfortable . . .

And so, instead of worrying, Miss Seeton fell asleep.

Elio Mantoni had done a hard night's work. He had reconnoitered the Place des Alpes until he knew every foot of the ground: the ornamental pond behind the Brunswick

Monument; the small café restaurant, between the outside
tables of which runs the main shortcut crossing the Place, to
diverge into little paths ending on the pavement of the Rue des
Alpes; the slope down to flat ground at the far end where the
Rue Bonivard separates the Place des Alpes from the huge
expanse of the Place Dorcière with its bus terminals and heavy
traffic, from which vantage point he could see—but could also
be seen by—the entrance to the Richesse; last, and best, the
footway, screened by evergreen shrubs, leading from the café
tables to the back of the parked cars in the Rue Adhémar Fabri.
Here, sheltered from sight by the shrubs and cars, there was a
clear view of the hotel terrace and, across the road, at an angle,
of the door to the hotel itself.

His reconnaissance over, he had crossed the lake, returned to
the Old Town and climbed the steep steps of the Passage des
Degrés-de-Poules to the first of the two plateaus formed by the
bastions below the cathedral. The passage steps are as
precipitous as their name implies, though whether "de-
Poules" refers to chickens or to prostitutes appears uncertain;
presumably the latter, since no self-respecting chicken would
attempt the sharp ascent, sinister even by daylight. It is kinder
to picture that in times gone by a bedizened lady sat at a
window or draped a doorway near the top to act as a reward
and consummation for any breathless mountaineer.

Ill-boding though the place might be, it was deserted. Few
people go there even by day and it was, in Mantoni's
estimation, an ideal rifle range. For his first endeavor he aimed
quite simply at the wall of the Rue Farel. The Rue Farel is not a
street in the generally accepted meaning of the term. It is more
in the nature of a brick support for the bastion above and
disappears in a slow bend where the lower platform narrows. It
is ill-lit by a dim lamp set in an iron bracket. At this Mantoni
leveled his briefcase, fired—and missed the wall. After twenty
minutes' practice he had improved and twice had come within
two feet of the wall bracket. The silencer was satisfactory; he
was pleased with it. It made no more noise than someone
suffering from indigestion. Mantoni, the amateur assassin on
payroll, was not to know that silencers are unprofessional, save
in exceptional circumstances, since, apart from the unwieldly
length, they make for indifferent aim.

A shadow moved. Two sparks of green fire menaced him.
He sighted and pulled the trigger. A flurry of movement and

the green sparks disappeared. Putting down his briefcase, the elated Italian danced a short *pas seul*. He'd mastered it, his aim was true, he'd killed a cat.

Round the diminishing curve of the Rue Farel, tail high with indignation, stalked a cat. Never before had this place been used for target practice, with things that went *phut* and whistled through your fur.

He'd killed a cat! Tomorrow, down by the lakeside there, he'd kill just such another. In mistaken triumph Mantoni snatched his briefcase and ran down the passage steps to return to his boardinghouse, the Hotel Magnifique, there to enjoy the refreshing, dreamless sleep of the unjust.

Miss Seeton woke late and felt a little guilty. True, she had no actual appointment for this morning and would have to wait until Mr. Telmark told her what to do. Or, rather, what to draw. Nevertheless a slight feeling of guilt persisted and she hurried through her breathing exercises and her knees—she would do her full regimen of yoga exercises this evening before dinner. Nearly nine o'clock. It would be quite dreadful to feel that one had kept the waiters waiting to serve breakfast. The gentleman behind the desk in the hall good-morninged her. She handed him her key. He told her it was a lovely day. Miss Seeton apologized that she was late for breakfast. He laughed and assured her she was not—that guests had breakfast anytime, but anytime at all, it made no difference, until the hour for lunch. But since it was such a lovely day, sunny and warm, would she not prefer to have it on the terrace? She agreed. He smiled and bowed. A smiling boy revolved revolving doors and Miss Seeton emerged to blink in the strong light.

She moved to her left under the awning—and blinked again, this time in surprise. Goodness. A little extreme, surely, even in these days. Really, more what one would expect upon the stage. And in the morning, too. The makeup, she meant. So— so excessive. In the angle formed by the end of the low balustrade which runs the length of the terrace to the steps stood a blonde, an over-blonde, blond in excelsis. High heels, sheer black tights on superb legs; the clothing extreme, extremely extreme; heavy pancake makeup of a sunburned color, vermilion mouth, the eyes blue-shadowed, the ends of the false lashes tipped with large mascara blobs, the brows drawn in black; the whole surmounted by an effusion, a profusion of blond hair caught by an Alice band and flowing backward in a cloud to reach, had it hung straight, below her shoulders. Surely, thought Miss Seeton, it must be false. Or, some of it at least. There was so much of it. And so improbable.

The blonde gave a tortured smile. Miss Seeton responded primly, "Bongjour," which she trusted was correct.

A waiter hurried forward and led her to a table. Miss Seeton, the crook of her umbrella on the back of her chair, placed her handbag on the seat beside her and sat down, while the waiter suggested fruit juice, bacon-egg, or a *café complet?* Miss Seeton looked blank. Coffee, with rolls, croissants, butter and brioches with jam. Just the—er—that last, it sounded quite delicious. The waiter departed and the blonde moved to settle herself at the table behind Miss Seeton, pressed the bell and the waiter returned to take her order: fruit juice and coffee.

How pretty it all was. The troughs of zinnias all along the balustrade. Geneva seemed full of flowers. In window boxes, in the gardens, everywhere. Miss Seeton was enchanted. Protected from the direct sunlight by the awning, she could look about in comfort. On her right across the road, behind all those parked cars, was such an attractive garden with a little notice on a stand saying CAFÉ RESTAURANT. While, straight ahead, beyond all that heavy traffic, she could see a portion of the lake, where boats were sailing. Close to, and all around her, hopped and twittered sparrows hoping for crumbs. Her breakfast arrived. The croissants were warm and melted in the mouth, the coffee excellent. It was all so very, very charming. And so peaceful.

Karl Telmark had dealt with his correspondence at the bank. Before leaving home he had glanced at the morning papers. Now he studied them carefully: Swiss, Italian, French—all featured Miss Seeton, her activities and her arrival; with photographs. Later, when the English and American editions were on sale, added to the interest roused by last night's television feature, the situation would be worse. He instructed his secretary to cancel two appointments and left shortly before nine. He would call at the Richesse, have a word with the proprietor and arrange to see this woman, this MissEss, privately in her room. She should, evidently, be up and dressed by nine o'clock.

The proprietor made inquiries and informed him that his guest had had early-morning tea and was now upon the terrace having breakfast. The two men sauntered casually out onto the steps so that M. Telmark could gain the advantage of an unnoticed preview and assessment of his temporary employee. The ruse was unsuccessful since all he could see were Miss Seeton's shoulders and the back of a most ill-chosen hat.

Nineish. Thrudd Banner had decided to catch her before she was likely to go out. Last night he'd rung a friend in London to try and learn a bit more about her and the general idea seemed to be that once things started happening to her they didn't stop till half the criminal population was either in jail or dead. Copywise, he'd been advised, she was a good investment timewise. So he thought if he could winkle out of her, chattily, something of her movements or her plans, he'd get a rough idea of where to keep tabs on her.

He crossed the Place Dorsière, had to await his chance to dive over a pedestrian crossing in the Rue Bonivard and reached the garden of the Place des Alpes. He looked toward the hotel and grinned. That hat—there couldn't be two like it in the world; there it was, sitting on the terrace drinking coffee.

Thomas ffoley did not care for early rising and deplored the Swiss habit of starting work at eight. However, this morning, with his career in mind, he had made an effort. He'd skipped breakfast—he'd give himself an innings when he got to the hotel. But with these old girls you never knew. They might go jaunting off at any old time instead of staying decently put until about eleven. He'd better, he supposed, get there around nine.

The traffic in the Rue Bonivard was heavy so he paid off his taxi at the bottom of the Place des Alpes—he hadn't been able to wangle a car out of the consulate again. No good bringing his own bus—nowhere to park. In front of him he saw that awful reporter fellow who'd been with her at the airport yesterday. Well, just as well he'd turned up really. After all, with fellows like that about she'd need a bit of help, and at the same time he'd be able to get a bit of an idea of what was what and what was on.

The sky was a cloudless blue, the sun was shining and Mantoni felt on top of his world, in full mastery of himself, his weapon and events. He had bought a cheap Japanese camera

and had affixed it to his briefcase so that when unzipped and
ready for the fray, in raising it, he would appear to be a tourist
taking photographs. Also the viewfinder of the camera would
improve his marksmanship. His intent was to follow his quarry
when walking in the street, come up behind her at a crowded
moment, fire at close range, rezip, and saunter on, one of a
throng who had not noticed the elderly lady who had slipped,
had stumbled, fallen. He had forgone breakfast at the Hotel
Magnifique, where, although included in the charge, the meal
was not magnificent—the croissants stale, the jam a watered
jelly.

Now, at a table outside the café in the Place des Alpes, he
was enjoying a second pot of coffee, a second plate of
croissants with butter and black cherry preserve. At intervals
he would leave the table like any tourist to give the impression
of taking photographs. It appeared that he was particularly
interested in recording the frontage of the Hotel de la Richesse
and, finally, at a few minutes past nine o'clock, his perseverance was rewarded. Lurking behind a shrub, he raised the
briefcase with its camera and peered across the road. There on
the terrace in plain view, almost opposite him, sat Miss Seeton.
And the distance was no more than last night when he'd killed
the cat. It was—irresistible. It was Fate. He pulled the trigger
and in the camera's eye he watched Miss Seeton's head—and
hat—fall forward, sideways, then vanish from his sight
beneath the table. He'd done it. His orders—and his vendetta—were accomplished. He'd done it—as he knew he could.
The Italian restrained, contained himself. This was no place to
indulge in triumphal dances. Aglow with pride, he sauntered
through the garden to the Rue des Alpes, turned left, then
waited dutifully until the lights signaled permission to cross the
quai, and lost himself in the pedestrian crowd that flowed
toward the bridge.

The blonde at the table behind Miss Seeton, lifting the heavy
mascaraed lids, surveyed the garden of the Place des Alpes. A
small man, half concealed by shrubs, was preparing to take
photographs. She shook a cigarette from a packet, rose and put
her hand on the back of Miss Seeton's chair.

"Say, excuse me." Her voice was low and pleasantly
modulated. "Could you favor me with a light?"

"I'm so sorry," apologized Miss Seeton. "I'm afraid that I
have no matches. I don't smoke."

In removing her hand the blonde dislodged the umbrella, which fell and caught between her ankles, making her lurch. To save herself she clutched Miss Seeton's shoulder, pulling her over, and she, Miss Seeton, Miss Seeton's chair, the tablecloth and most of Miss Seeton's breakfast, all landed in a tangle on the tiles. There was a whining buzz: a small hole appeared in the window just above them; the glass starred and fragments tinkled; and in the hotel writing room, to the accompaniment of cries and exclamations, part of a large mirror on the farther wall disintegrated and cascaded to the floor.

Among the onlookers the crash caused various degrees of consternation.

The proprietor sighed: another careless waiter; another tray; more cups; more glasses; more stains upon the carpet. He retired into the hotel to learn the damage.

Thrudd Banner's ever-ready camera had caught the moment of the befalling; now he raced forward and from below the balustrade snapped a quick shot of the starred window, showing, unless he was off the beam, a bullet hole.

ffoley dashed after him. "Look here—stop that—after all you can't do that—look here, after all—look here—" How like these awful fellows who take awful pictures just at the wrong moment. Anyway, he'd jolly well see these never got into print. He'd throw a scare into the fellow—quote the embassy—pull rank—and put his foot down. Thank God he'd beetled over early—just in time. This would show the consulate—show them in Bern as well—that he was Johnny-on-the-spot and on the ball.

Down the street a man in a fawn raincoat and a felt hat with a feather in the band had run back to his car to contact the Sûreté headquarters. His counterpart ran ahead and up the steps, onto the terrace, where, joined by Thrudd Banner and Thomas ffoley, he helped to raise Miss Seeton to her feet, replace her chair and restore her blond companion. Two waiters collected and swept up the debris, produced napkins to dab at spotted clothes and laughed away the accident. The ladies were not to distress themselves, they would be re-served at once.

Karl Telmark had watched the fracas on the terrace with misgiving. Who or what was this MissEss who traveled in wrong directions, who surrounded herself with publicity when she should not, who missed appointments and who now could not eat even a simple breakfast in a respectable hotel without overturning herself, her breakfast and her chair—without counting an exaggerated blonde? The proprietor's news arrested his thoughts and redirected them. So—that was why she had thrown herself to the ground: to dodge a bullet. So—already this MissEss must have discovered something of the Stemkos affair. So—the affair must be more dangerous than he had supposed. Evidently this was no moment to approach her. It would be best . . . yes—he would write her a note inviting her to dinner and arrange with the proprietor to send her there by taxi. At least in his own home no person could learn of their meeting nor would she be likely to precipitate an escapade. Distantly he heard the wail of a police siren. He must go. The police already knew, through Scotland Yard and Interpol, of his engagement of her and could, should they wish it, question him privately. As for the rest, it would be better for MissEss, and for himself, that none of the staff nor the spectators should learn of the connection.

A police car tore around the Place Dorsière, through the halted traffic on the Rue Bonivard and stopped at the hotel. Four men in uniform: one stayed with the car, two sprang to the terrace and the other entered the hotel. The moment they took charge the man in the fawn raincoat had a brief word with them and left. Questions were asked, statements were taken, trajectory and line of fire were estimated, measured and the spot where the would-be killer must have stood was pinpointed. More questions were asked, more statements taken, but nothing of any help became apparent. Miss Seeton failed to get the drift: she'd heard nothing—seen nothing. Except the destruction of her breakfast. Which was her fault. So stupid of her to leave her umbrella hanging there. When she was shown the bullet hole, it could be, she was quite convinced, nothing to do with her. It must be, she imagined, some form of demonstration. The blonde was unhelpful. No, there'd been no bang, except—she rubbed her hip—where she'd fallen. But at that she guessed in a way it had been lucky. Seemed like falling over her own feet and knocking everything to hell had got this poor lady out of the line of fire. The hotel staff was equally unaidful. No, they'd heard nothing—only the crash of glass. So that the few facts that the officers could establish were: where the criminal had stood; that there'd been no sound of a shot; and the bullet they dug from the wall behind the mirror.

A message came through on the car radio and was relayed.

Would Miss Seeton do them the honor to call at the Hôtel de la Police and make a formal statement that afternoon? Miss Seeton, slightly surprised, agreed and the officers departed.

While the ill-assorted quartet of Miss Seeton, the blonde, Thrudd Banner and Thomas ffoley settled down to a newly served breakfast, Elio Mantoni continued rejoicing on his way. He heard the far-off siren and he laughed. What they would need would be a hearse. He marched up the hill in the Old Town to his boardinghouse and behind him crept, as though looking for a place to park, a scarlet Lancia.

Miss Seeton's interrogation during the afternoon at the Hôtel de la Police was another failure: they failed to elicit the information they were seeking; she failed to understand what it was they sought. The formality of her formal statement was soon disposed of and the inspector to whom had been assigned the task of questioning her, primarily on account of his excellent command of English, got down to business. Would she care to reveal what it was she had discovered of such importance that someone should risk shooting at her in a public place in full daylight? No? Would she care to reveal the exact nature of the investigation she was to make on behalf of the Banque du Lac and whom it concerned? No? Would she care to reveal why—when they had been given to understand by both their English colleagues and M. Telmark that her visit was to be in strict secrecy, on a private matter which concerned the bank—she had, instead, decided to arrive with the utmost publicity? No? It had not been a ruse to flush—that was the correct word, was it not?—the criminals into the open? No? Would she care to reveal the reason for her journey to Italy and whom—the inspector leaned across his desk, eyebrows raised in challenge, lips twisted sardonically—whom had she been following? No? Elio Mantoni? He flashed the name at her. His shock tactics failed as dismally as had the rest of his questionnaire. The only response he got was a look of complete bewilderment.

The inspector sat back in thought, idly tapping the desk with a pencil to the destruction of its point. Before him lay various reports concerning Miss Seeton and her activities.

A copy of a report from the agents of the Sûreté who had been on the scene at the time of the affray:

In their opinion and from their observation it was certainly

Miss Seeton who had been the target and not the blond young
woman who had just arrived behind her. As a rider—again in
their opinion, and from their observation—the speed with
which MissEss had flung herself to the ground dragging the
blonde with her for safety had not been the reaction of a
woman of the age that she purported to be. In their opinion—
and from their observation both that morning and, to an extent,
on her arrival at the airport the previous afternoon—none of
her movements quite tallied with her looks or with the way she
dressed. The consensus of their opinion—and of their observation—was that she was likely to be a woman in her late thirties
to early forties cleverly impersonating a woman of more than a
certain age, her only error being—refer above—an undue
youthfulness of carriage and of movement.

A report from his own men:

In their estimation and with regard to their measurements,
the line of trajectory proved conclusively that the bullet—
unless one could allow for a very indifferent marksman—was
definitely aimed at someone sitting at the table and not at the
person standing behind, an outrée blonde named Mlle Vanda
Galam. The lady in question, Miss Emily D. Seeton, had
refuted any suggestion that she could be the target, but again—
in their estimation—she must have been. For the rest, neither
from the hotel guests, from the staff, nor from the passersby
had anything of assistance been established.

A notification, rather than a report, from Italy:

The Genoese and Milanese police wished to advise their
comrades in Geneva that it would appear (so far as they could
apprehend) that MissEss had probably been following (or
possibly in touch with) a certain Elio Mantoni (Italian citizen)
who had arrived (and left) on the same flights as MissEss.
Questions through Interpol had established that Mantoni
(though never condemned) was known to associate with
criminals, was an artist employed (suspected only) in a
criminal scope. MissEss had not spoken of him or (so far as
was known) to him, but at the Milano airport (circled as she
was at the time by their men, she could have done no other
without showing her intent) signaled to him by smiling and
then humming a song (possibly some prearranged code?) and
the said Mantoni had immediately quit, eluding the officer who
attempted to follow him, and Mantoni had only reappeared in
time to catch the plane to Geneva.

"This song." He glanced up quickly. "What was it?"

"Song?" Miss Seeton gazed at him. "I'm afraid I don't quite follow."

"The song you"—he checked the Italian communication—"that you hummed at the airport in Milan."

"Oh." So difficult to explain. "That tune, you mean. It was, I fear, a little rude of me, but, you see, I had it on the brain. There was a gentleman—a Russian, I thought, though, of course, he may not have been; but he certainly wasn't English—at the same table while I was waiting for my plane. In London, I mean. He kept humming it. Then sang it. Before he lost his pajamas. No," she corrected herself quickly, "how silly of me. That was, of course, only my immediate impression at the time. I realized, afterward, that it would be far more likely to be papers, in a briefcase. Don't you agree?"

It was the inspector's turn to gaze; his turn not to follow. Ask a simple question—the name of a song—and she riposted with some fantastic history of a Russian in pajamas—or out of them—at Heathrow. So this was her trick: to say too little or too much; and either way to infuriate. Perhaps then this song had some importance, since to avoid a direct reply she was taking refuge in some man's pajamas. Well, he would listen and it could be that she would give herself away. Grimly he nodded.

"Continue."

"Well, really, that was all. Except that, naturally, knowing the tune, it stayed in one's mind. And when I saw him again at the airport—the other one, I mean—"

"At Genoa?"

"Oh, no. I didn't see him there. Though I do remember him being on the plane. He was sitting further up on the other side. But when we were having coffee I noticed him at another table, and it reminded me. And I suppose I must have, without realizing it, starting humming it."

"The name of this song?"

"I don't know."

The inspector strove for patience. "You said you did."

"No, indeed I didn't." Miss Seeton appreciated that perhaps she had not made things quite clear. "Or, rather, yes. I did. Say that I did, I mean. Because I do. And I have an idea, though I'm not sure, that it may be by Tchaikovsky. But when I said 'I know it,' I meant 'know it' only in that sense. Because I don't. Know its name, I mean."

He shrugged and made a note. If she was determined to evade he would ask Milan. It was a pity that their advice on the Italian, Mantoni, had arrived too late to be of service. They would have to go through the motions of trying to trace him but by now he would, without doubt, have disappeared with a new name and a false passport—if he was still in Switzerland. But as a lever to prize information out of this woman he was useless—for the moment. But wait . . . Mantoni was an artist. This woman taught—or had taught—art. M. Telmark was a director of the art museum. Could that be the connection? He would put the point to his superiors. There had been an alert only this morning through Interpol to all countries concerning the theft of some paintings from a private collection in England. He debated whether to question Miss Seeton on this but decided that it would be a waste of time and temper. Evidently she was one of those who piqued herself on working alone—the anathema of all normal police routine. In any case the Sûreté were keeping her under observation for reasons which they had not chosen to divulge—or not to him. Let them deal with her—and might they enjoy it. For himself, as far as he could, in spite of her pigheadedness, he would continue to investigate the shooting, would make his report, would suggest a surveillance of the Musée des Arts and would agreeably disembarrass himself of the affair—and of her.

He stood up, thanked her with heavy irony for her help and conducted her out to a police car, collecting Miss Galam on the way. The blonde had insisted upon accompanying Miss Seeton in case her evidence should be wanted. But, since she had no evidence to give beyond the statement she had already made at the hotel, the inspector had seen no object in wasting his time on her. He studied her now as she followed Miss Seeton into the car: good legs—yes; but, for the rest—no, not to his taste, too overdone.

For Miss Seeton the afternoon had been full of surprises. First that Miss Galam should have persisted in going with her to the police station in spite of the police driver's objection. Then to discover what a very charming, quiet young person she had proved to be, with that low and restful voice and not in the least brash as, frankly, from her appearance, one would have expected. She had been struck upon their arrival at the wide modernity of the Boulevard Carl Vogt to find that the main police station was such a very up-to-date building. Like a block of offices. Which, if one considered, was, one supposed, only natural, over what appeared to be a row of uncompleted garages.

The inspector's attitude, too, had surprised her. The taking of her statement on the shooting had been perfunctory, which, of course, was not surprising, since she knew nothing about it; but what had surprised her was his insistence upon matters which, surely, hardly came within his sphere. It had seemed so curious that he should question her engagement by Mr. Telmark, when, since he himself had employed the word "secrecy," he must have been perfectly well aware that she could not answer. Or rather, should not. Though in actual fact, as she had not yet met Mr. Telmark and did not know what it was he wanted her to draw, she could not. It was true that she had been told in London that it concerned, in some way, the forgery of English banknotes, and that a Mr. Stemkos, a millionaire whose name one had frequently seen referred to in the newspapers, was concerned in, or disturbed about, it. But beyond that she knew nothing and it was certainly not within her province to mention this to the inspector if Mr. Telmark, for some reason, had not seen fit to do so.

Slightly odd also had been the friendliness of Miss Galam. Maybe she was lonely. They had had tea upon their return to the hotel and Miss Galam—no, one must try to remember to call her Vee, since although her name was Vanda she was Vee to all her friends—had suggested they should dine together. Miss Seeton had refused in view of a note which she had received from Mr. Telmark inviting her to dinner. This note had proved to be the most unexpected phenomenon of the afternoon—and her greatest worry. She had been unprepared for such a contingency and the Promenade Saint Antoine sounded such an imposing address. Did one dress for dinner? Or did one not? There was no one that she could ask. Fortunately she had packed her black lace, the only dress approaching evening wear that she possessed, and so, she supposed, the black lace would have to do.

The black lace did. Mme Telmark was wearing an afternoon or cocktail dress so that Miss Seeton's ensemble with its jacket, though out of date, was not out of place.

The Promenade Saint Antoine had proved to be even more

imposing than one had feared. What she had not expected were
the curious and sharp contrasts of its locality. Except for the
drive down from the airport through a comparatively new part
of the city, all that Miss Seeton had seen of Geneva on either
side of the lake shore had been broad, flat streets, many lined
with trees, all thronged with people; wide spaces interspersed
with grass plots dotted with flower beds; yet more trees; more
people.

Now, climbing high into the dimmer lighting of the Old
Town, there were no people; only the occasional passing car
whose occupants were invisible. Houses dropped below them
and Miss Seeton watched with fascination through the windows as the taxi ground in second gear round the hairpin bend
of the Rue Théodore de Bèze. The rough stone walls between
which they were traveling began to shorten, to become on her
right a railing above which showed the tops of trees and an
old—surely a very old—building at the back of which she
noticed, when they drew level, the railings turned at a right
angle to form, between them and a high wall, the dark mouth
of a narrow passage.

Brighter lighting made her turn her head. The wall on her
left had ended at a more modern road. No. Rather, a short
bridge over another road beneath them. The wall leading to the
bridge bounded a rising slope of grass on which was, she had
just time to glimpse, some statuary. Then, passing the end of
the bridge:

"En voilà," remarked the driver. "Promenade Saint Antoine."

Wide, very wide, with mansions to her right and on her left
rows of trees with cars parked in double ranks beneath them.
And then an ornamental iron railing to save one from falling to
the parallel road below.

The Promenade Saint Antoine: highest and greatest bastion
of the old fortified city. It is difficult for the tourist, for the
foreign resident, indeed for many of the Genevese themselves,
to appreciate the incongruous intricacies of the Old Town
without some knowledge of its history. The original settlement
on stilts on the marshland between the rivers Rhone and Arve
had proved to be indefensible against attack. The inhabitants
therefore had climbed the hill behind them to build themselves
a fortress. Years later the Romans drained the marsh and
erected sumptuous villas, extending their occupation to the

lake shore. This colonization in its turn had fallen before barbarians. Once again the natives retreated up the hill to strengthen and expand the town.

By 1814 Geneva was beginning to feel isolated, requested permission to join the Confédération Helvétique and, early the following year, the Congress of Vienna found time between dances to ratify the merger. With this security the city grew and in the Old Town moats became roads and bridges crossed them, resulting in a maze of anachronistic inconsistencies. On one side of a road a broad flight of terraced steps may lead with dignity to a modern thoroughfare while opposite, a precipitous cobbled slope serves as a reminder that this same thoroughfare in olden days was water.

Miss Seeton's taxi drew up before a small house set back in an angle between the imposing dwellings which bounded it. How, she wondered, did one pay the taxi—so unlike a taxi; more in the nature of a private car, with a chauffeur, except for the lighted word TAXI on its roof—and how did one tip? She solved her problem by offering her purse.

"Voulez-vous prendre ce qui est usual. Je ne comprend pas le money." The driver laughed and assured her in English that all was arranged and paid for.

Miss Seeton passed under an iron trellis arch with a hanging lantern and mounted the steps to ring the bell. She found it strange in such surroundings that her hostess should answer the door and stranger still that it was Mme Telmark who cooked and served the delightful meal. Miss Seeton had yet to learn that in Geneva domestic help was almost unobtainable and that in consequence, unless the hostess was particularly adroit, in general dinner parties were planned through an agency or given at a hotel or a restaurant, which relied for the most part on Italians for its staff.

After dinner her hostess excused herself and M. Telmark tried to get down to business. He tried to elicit the reason for the attack on her that morning. She didn't know. And, in any case, she did not consider that it was. Or, if it was, it hadn't been. An attack. On her, she meant. He tried to discover what it was she had found out that made her dangerous. She hadn't found out anything. And, as for being dangerous, the mere idea was ridiculous. He tried to ascertain why she had gone to Italy. She was full of apologies. Such a silly mistake to make. He asked why she had chosen full publicity and given a press conference on her arrival here. Oh, it hadn't been a conference, she assured him. They'd just asked her questions and she'd answered them. Wryly he recalled the heading and the final line of Thrudd Banner's article when the foreign papers had arrived that afternoon.

> . . . MissEss insists that everything that happened has been a mistake. One must not doubt a lady's word, but on the other hand to take Miss Seeton at her own face value might well prove a MISSTAKE.

Now, remembering Jonathan Feldman's warning not to be fooled by her, Karl Telmark did not believe one single word she said. He shrugged. If she was determined to be a soloist there was nothing he could do, but he considered it foolish as well as dangerous. Resigned, he gave her the facts with regard to the paying in of the forged five-pound notes into the Stemkos joint account. He also gave her papers: a copy of the account as it currently stood; a list of the deposits, with the dates and names of the depositors; the dates when the notes had been sent from the Banque du Lac to the clearing banks; when the forgeries had been discovered in England; and a summary of his subsequent discussions with Jonathan Feldman and the governor of the Bank of England. All these papers, he emphasized, were extraordinarily private and in the normal fashion should not be allowed to quit the bank. But the circumstances in this case were abnormal, and it was essential that she should be in full possession of the facts if she was to appreciate the position. He was entrusting them to her and he would be grateful if she would return them to him as soon as she had assimilated the contents.

Miss Seeton looked at him blankly. "But, surely, Mr. Telmark, it would, in that case, be very much better if I didn't take them. And I fear that it is very unlikely that I should ever understand them. I am not," she apologized, "very good at figures. And, again, to look at someone's private bank account would be so embarrassing."

"You needn't feel"—the banker produced his new word with pride—"sticky about that. Heracles Stemkos has many accounts all over the world. The only one among those he has with us to which we have traced these forgeries is a joint one with his wife."

"I see." Miss Seeton tried to. "It isn't possible, I suppose, if you don't yet want to mention the matter to him, to ask Mrs. Stemkos privately about it? Oh, no," she realized, "I do see that wouldn't do. Mrs. Stemkos would be bound to mention it to her husband."

"I doubt it," Telmark's mouth twisted. "The Stemkos ménage is also sticky. She's his fifth wife and very much younger—like all of them except the first. And unless appearances and gossip are false, her current affair is her husband's secretary, Anatole Librecksin."

Miss Seeton attempted to visualize such a life. Five wives. It seemed a lot. Perhaps Mr. Stemkos was looking for something he had never found. And then the young wife. Her reason would, presumably, be money. And one could understand that she would become bored with an elderly husband who was probably tied to his business. On the other hand, if one made a bargain one should keep it. Or, if one failed to, surely one should be, at the least, discreet. With a feeling of depression Miss Seeton put the papers in her handbag and rose. Mr. Telmark still hadn't told her what, or whom, it was she was to draw. Evidently he was determined that she should grasp the background first. It was natural, she supposed, for bankers to have an absorption in figures. And difficult for them to recognize that ordinary people, like oneself, had not. Indeed found them rather muddling. Still—she would do her best.

With unconscious volition she crossed the room to study a picture on the wall. So many pictures. And most of them so very modern. And not all of them quite easy to understand. She had identified a Braque, which she did not care for—part of a violin, peeping through mostly angular shapes in rather depressing grays and greens and browns, that might mean anything. But this . . . Surely a Marquet. Boats at a quay-side. Quite lovely. In the foreground, water: the delicacy of the coloring blending and shadowing till one could see the movement; feel the ripple.

The banker watched her with amusement; snapped his fingers. "*Mais voyons,*" he began; corrected himself. "You must forgive me, I had almost forgotten that I was entertaining an expert." He showed her his collection of paintings; expatiating on line, form, color, brushwork and the balance of composition, though he lost Miss Seeton when he delved into the overlap of unrelated objects in their relation to the subject as a whole, and the perspective of nonperspective in flattened surfaces and horizontal planes.

Explaining that he was a director of the art museum, he insisted that in two days' time she should attend the *vernissage*—for a moment this word stopped them both and they had recourse to a dictionary. The word *vernissage*, they learned, meant private view, or, alternatively, varnishing day. Miss Seeton also discovered that the art museum was not a museum as she understood the term but more in the nature of a cross between the Tate Gallery and Burlington House. It had a permanent collection of pictures on display but also acted as a gallery for exhibitions and sold the artists' efforts on commission.

"Perhaps," observed M. Telmark, "you will be able to explain to me the popularity of a painter in whose work I can see no merit—but it sells. He is an Italian and, like many small men, full of his own importance and of an exaggerated temperament. I will be interested in your opinion of his work." He went to the telephone and ordered a taxi to take Miss Seeton back to her hotel.

They stood on the doorstep to await the car's arrival. At once, under the trees some way down to their left, an engine started up and a car slid forward. The lights, including the word TAXI on its roof, were switched on and it pulled up in front of them. Its driver, a dark-skinned man, remained at the wheel while M. Telmark opened the door for Miss Seeton, at the same time paying the fare. The taxi drove off down the Promenade Saint Antoine in the direction opposite that from which Miss Seeton had arrived.

No sooner were they under way than another engine, already idling, was revved high, sidelights were switched on and a small blue Peugeot shot from under the trees ahead of them straight across the road, forcing the taxi to a halt with a scream of brakes and a stream of bad language. Both drivers jumped out and Miss Seeton recognized the driver of the small car as Miss Galam—Vee. Vee and her opponent engaged in furious French argument and Miss Seeton decided that it was time to intervene. Hearing the taxi door open, the man broke off, swung round and rapped:

"Get back in, madam. I'll take you on when this fool has moved her idiot car."

Vanda Galam turned, saw Miss Seeton and exclaimed, "My, you of all people. What a break." She opened her passenger door. "Come on, I'll take you back." She leaned into her car, picked up her purse and addressed the taxi driver. "Fair enough, you speak English, so you've guessed we're friends. I'll take the lady back with me." She opened her bag. "Just tell me your fare to the Richesse and you can cut along."

The man protested. He'd been called from the rank and had instructions to take the lady to the hotel. He would prefer to carry out those instructions rather than trust her to a mad-woman who hadn't learned to drive.

"That will be all right," Miss Seeton assured him. "You see, my friend is staying in the same hotel. And," she added to Vee, "you don't have to worry about the fare. He has already been paid." She got into the Peugeot.

The dark-skinned man cast a quick glance up and down the promenade. His hand went to his pocket. Vee's hand shifted in her purse.

"Don't try it, sonny," she muttered. "Just be on your way."

He saw the snub barrel of the pistol protruding from her bag. Suddenly they were spotlit in the headlights of another car parked beneath the trees behind them. Xerxes Tolla slowly withdrew his hand, empty. He jumped into his taxi, banged the door, slammed his gears and stamped on the accelerator.

Vee shut her bag and gave the sad rictus that served her for a smile as she got back into her car. "You know, I somehow got the impression there he didn't like me."

"I expect," opined Miss Seeton, "that it was nerves. Or rather, one should say, reaction to them. After all, he did have to stop very quickly."

"True enough." Vee laughed, remembering the blaze of light. "Took off quickly too."

She took off in her turn and in contrast to her catapulting start now drove with sedate control.

Well, well. Thrudd Banner huddled low in his seat. He couldn't have chosen a better parking place—front row, but nicely shadowed by the trees; front row stall seat for all the action. So MissEss was just a schoolteacher on holiday, never been abroad, knew nobody, but sets out after dark to visit bankers in their homes with, looked like, half Geneva following. Too true when he'd been told that where she was the action was, and she'd repay watching. And she'd almost had him fooled this morning over coffee till he'd been in half a mind to apologize for the MISSTAKE article. Well, it was the last time she'd give the runaround to Mrs. Banner's little boy. And what gave with the Galam blonde? Falling about the terrace with MissEss while somebody did target practice. Which, he wondered, had been saving which? And from whom? And afterward the Seeton, with her hat off center, sitting there mild as milk and twice as natural. *Shooting? Good gracious. She'd thought that somebody'd dropped a tray. But shooting . . . Were they sure? How very odd. It must've been an accident. Or perhaps a demonstration.* Too right it'd been a demonstration, but against which of them? *At her? Oh, dear me no and goodness. What an idea!* And did she know Miss Galam? Were they friends? Wide-eyed at once. *Oh, no, they'd only just met that moment, down there on the floor.* And dealing with that fool Tomfool's questions like a schoolmarm keeping a tiresome child in place. Then the police putting her through it. MissEss as bland as butter. *No, she'd seen nothing; heard nothing.* And by and large had said nothing—all three monkeys in one.

Yet off she goes to spend half the afternoon at police headquarters—with the blonde tagging along. Up here this evening to Telmark's house. Telmark? Thrudd debated. Was something up at the Banque du Lac he hadn't heard about? Soon as she appears a taxi pops out from along here where no taxi should be, and the moment they were under way the Galam jet-propels out and nearly crashes them—nice bit of driving, that. A colored taxi driver? Could be, he supposed, but it was the first time he'd seen one in Geneva. And then the Galam trundles off with MissEss as if she'd never driven over 20 mph. And now . . .

Thrudd watched as the headlights to his left, which had interrupted Vee Galam's discussion with the taxi driver, were switched off and a car with sidelights only, two men on the front seat, drove out and took the same direction as the Peugeot. He turned his ignition key. Better tag along and see everybody safely home. As he pressed the starter, lights to his right caught his eye and a taxi crossed the bridge at the Rue Théodore de Bèze to draw up at Karl Telmark's house. Too late, chum—Thrudd grinned as he departed—you've missed all the fun of your fare.

• • •

Miss Seeton was worried. She was sure that Vee must know where she was going. She seemed so very capable. But . . .

"Are you sure," she ventured, "that this is the right . . ."

She stopped. On their left a short bridge crossed the road below. Perhaps . . . No. She was sure, quite sure, that this was not the other bridge because that, the other one, so very like it, was at the other end. Besides, although there was a grass slope with trees beyond, before some buildings, it was on the wrong side. Of the bridge, that was. And, in any case, there was no statuary.

"Right—in what way?" asked Vee.

"Because—" Miss Seeton watched the promenade narrow to become the Rue Beauregard and curve down a gentle slope with a drinking fountain set into the wall on their left, a wall which gave way to railings as the street forked down to join a wider road. "Because," repeated Miss Seeton—really the topography here was very difficult to follow—"because, although I realize that we're going down, it was the other end. When I came up, I mean. And steeper," she explained.

"Don't let it fret you; we'll get there just as quick this way and the roads are better." And better lit, she reflected.

Miss Seeton relaxed. Vee did not. What was the car behind them? They'd doused their headlights now but she'd had no chance so far to gather who was driving. Friend of the taximan? And who'd that black chap be anyway? Could be this Tolla she'd been briefed on, though why was he doing his own dirty work? Didn't sound the type. What the hell had MissEss stumbled on that made her so damn dangerous? If only the old girl knew, or they could find out, they could spread the load a bit and take the pressure off.

Vee kept glancing in the mirror as the car behind crept down the Rue Beauregard, followed by—good for him—another car she recognized; that beat-up yellow Volvo belonging to Banner, the press man. Well, between them they'd got the other car nicely sandwiched. Vee too relaxed. Admitted, in this game take nothing—take nobody—for granted, but she'd still take a bet that Thrudd Banner was clean. Just doing his job and would help out if things got out of hand. She hesitated. Should she whip the car round to the right here at the Rue Daniel Colladon, narrow, dark and tricky? But it would get her back to the Bourg de Four and from there she could cut through the Old Town down the Rue Verdaine and take the Mont Blanc bridge

instead of one of the earlier ones. It would soon prove if the car
behind was really after them, and with Banner doing a follow-
up, between them they should be able to deal . . .

Vee abruptly right-angled the Peugeot off the brightly lit
width of the rue de la Croix Rouge into the narrow gloom of
the Rue Daniel Colladon. Miss Seeton, thrown against the
door, saw for a moment a precipitous cobbled slope to a lower
road before the car was hedged by a narrow street. The car
behind them turned in turn and the light fell so that Vee could
see the two men on the front seat. For God's sake, she chuckled
to herself, identical felt hats and raincoats—it must be the boys
from the Sûreté, and MissEss was traveling home in motorcade
as per always. Fair enough, but what went with the opposition?
Had the black taxi driver given up? And where was the little
Italian runt?

Elio Mantoni was in his element. With the edge of his brush
he slashed a streak of vermilion between a chocolate brown
square and a lime green ovoid, then stood back to admire the
effect and to obtain a true perspective of his work; though
whether Karl Telmark would have recognized any perspective
in the flattened planes of the daubs or even admitted a relation
in the unrelated colored spludges was doubtful.

No such consideration bothered the artist: all that was
lacking to complete his happiness was a studio with a north
light instead of a small bedroom on the top floor of a third-rate
hotel. He had delivered two canvases to the art museum that
morning.

With a palette knife he smeared more chrome onto the
canvas which, together with the one drying over against the
bed, was due shortly for exhibition in Paris. How, Mantoni
wondered as he superimposed his effusion over the last folds of
the robe which draped Tintoretto's *Madonna of the Seven
Rivers,* could anyone with artistic sensibility prefer such
carefully executed compositions by dead artists to his own
living, immediate, breathing inspirations. He had reported
yesterday the success of his mission to eliminate Miss Seeton
and today he had scanned the newspapers, at first with
trepidation and then with mounting indignation, at finding no
mention of his exploit. And then this afternoon he had received
a terse message asking why he had failed in his assignment.

Mantoni was dumbfounded. Failed in his assignment? How

could he have failed? Had he not, with his own eyes, seen her fall? Or had she, like other cats, many lives? If so they could rest assured that he had taken one of them. Shrugging off the mystery, he had concentrated on, and lost himself in, painting. In this, at least, he found satisfaction. And tomorrow, at the private view, he would find further satisfaction in watching people admire his work, with no danger of interference from old women.

"How d'you do. How d'you do . . . No, to me it's all quite new. I find it charming."

In such a crowd the term "private view" struck Miss Seeton as a misnomer.

"How d'you do. How d'you do . . . No, I hadn't heard. . . . Did you? But how alarming."

Miss Seeton was beginning to feel that she had strayed into some well-practiced social minuet.

She was disappointed. She had looked forward to this occasion thinking that for the first time since she had left England she would be on firm ground, meeting people who understood and appreciated art. Possibly even meeting the artists themselves and, although she might not necessarily understand or even like their work—if it was very advanced, that was—it would still have been interesting to learn something of their aims and their techniques. But no one in this gathering appeared to be interested in, or even to look at the pictures. It was more like some fashionable cocktail party: they were actually serving drinks and little snacks. Fortunately she did know one or two of the company. Vee was there, looking more startling than usual in a dress with a skirt slit right up to the hip. And that newspaperman, Mr. Banner. And that rather tiresome Mr. ffoley. And Mr. Telmark, of course, who kept introducing her to people whose names she failed to catch. And, although everyone was talking, rather shrilly, and for the most part with their backs to the paintings, no one had even mentioned the dreadful news in today's papers.

BIG ART THEFT

RAID ON STATELY HOME

The Duke of Belton, returning with the Duchess from a holiday in Turkey for the reopening of Belton Abbey to

the public, found that thieves had stolen four canvases
from his well-known collection of paintings. Among
them were Gainsborough's portrait of the 4th Duke with
Duchess and the famous Madonna of the Seven Rivers by
Tintoretto, valued at over £30,000.

She'd seen the Tintoretto once, on loan at Burlington House,
and that it should now be in the hands of thieves was really
quite, quite dreadful.

Miss Seeton eased her way out of the chattering throng and,
catalogue in hand, set about a serious study of the exhibits.

Yes, really, she decided, "exhibits" was the only suitable
word. Many of them were not paintings at all, but consisted of
pieces of scrap metal and the sort of things that one threw into
the dustbin, all glued or nailed higgledy-piggledy onto a sheet
of cardboard or a wooden panel. One of these latter had an old-
fashioned lavatory chain with a china handle inscribed with the
word PULL. She trusted that no one would obey this injunction
since the chain was attached to a jam jar, half full of water, in
which one small goldfish circled endlessly round its cramped
quarters. More a matter, she felt for the RSPCA than for an
exhibition. No. 59. She found it in the catalogue, entitled
Puss-and-Pull. No. 60 was a board on which, among assorted
iron-mongery, a broken rusted bedspring jutted out with a large
glass eye impaled upon its prong. She found it faintly distaste-
ful and did not bother further. Beyond were three oil paintings
on canvas and Miss Seeton grew more hopeful, but the first of
them somewhat dashed her hopes—distortion without drafts-
manship. The next was a collection of rough geometrical
shapes in violent colors: surely rather old-fashioned in style;
reminiscent of Delaunay's *Window,* or Léger's *Woman in Blue,*
both, if she remembered rightly, executed before the 1914 war.
Only, of course, nothing like so well done. This present one,
she meant.

She was preparing to pass on when something about the
design recaptured her attention and she stopped. Oh, now she
saw . . . That was very interesting. She moved back, moved
forward, then from side to side, studying the work from
various angles. Yes. Really very interesting indeed.

Beside her M. Telmark spoke. "So you have found one of
Alberti's masterpieces of which I told you. Now, can you
explain to me where the attraction lies and why they sell?"

For the first time Miss Seeton noted that both this and the canvas beyond it had a red spot pasted in one corner.

"Say," Vee's low voice came from Miss Seeton's other side, "don't tell me you go for that godawful daub. You've been circling round it like a tigress scenting meat."

Miss Seeton performed the introductions and Karl Telmark appealed to Vee.

"Perhaps you, Miss Galam, can persuade our expert to diagnose the reason for this man's popularity."

"Come on," Vee encouraged her, "give."

"It's so difficult to describe." Miss Seeton's hands began to flutter as she sought for words to formulate her feelings. "It lies, I suppose," she said finally, "in the technique—no, perhaps one should say method. It's something that I've not seen before. To compare it with Sickert's later work, or with Cézanne, would be wrong. No spots, you see." Faced with Vee's blank expression, she elucidated. "Paintings that at first sight seem just colored spots, but then, as you gaze at them, the form beneath emerges until the form becomes all. And they disappear. The spots, I mean. Except, of course, here," she admitted, "there are no spots."

Vee was about to protest when the banker forestalled her. "Continue. You see some design below this colored mess?"

"Why, yes indeed. Don't you? It's"—Miss Seeton's hands strayed again—"so difficult. It catches one at certain angles and then goes again. In a way it's like a mockery of—more accurately perhaps a satirical comment on—the style so popular in the early nineteen hundreds. I—I . . ." A comparison at last occurred to her. "You know Picasso's portrait of Ambroise Vollard"—Vee did not but Telmark did—"where the face looms at one pinkly through squares and rectangles, mostly grayish? The squares and rectangles, that is." Vainly her fingers tried to delineate the portrait in the air.

Both her hearers by now were interested; Karl Telmark because he understood something of what she was trying to express; Vee because something in her briefing on this woman had clicked in her memory.

While the banker searched the Alberti work in vain for hidden meanings, "Got some paper on you?" asked Vee.

"Why, yes." Obediently Miss Seeton produced a sketch-book from her handbag.

"Good. Now try to put down just what it is you see."

Miss Seeton took a pencil and stood abashed, uncertain. Then suddenly her pencil began to streak across the paper. It was, thought the fascinated Vee, rather like watching somebody engaged in automatic writing. Under Miss Seeton's flying pencil, in sure strokes, a large black hat took form, beribboned and befeathered; beneath it, voluminous hair; a lady in a fichu; a narrow waist, full skirt; one arm hung down encircled by a diaphanous scarf; her other hand reposed in the crook of the arm of the gentleman coming into shape beside her, in powdered wig and eighteenth-century clothes; behind the pair a tracery of foliage; a few more deft touches and by the lady's skirt a dog looked up at her.

Miss Seeton was lightly superimposing oblongs, squares and circles on her sketch as Vee looked across the gallery. A fair-haired woman whose animated face and whose style made her outstanding was talking in a group. Their glances met and with a nervous gesture Vee smoothed the back of her own blond mop of hair before returning to her vigilance on Miss Seeton.

Karl Telmark gave up his futile attempt to find significance in the Alberti composition and looked over Miss Seeton's shoulder. "Good"—he beamed—"now let us see what it is that you remark in this . . . *Merde,*" he exploded, then apologized. "*J'demande pardon,* but this—this cannot be true."

"Well, no," agreed Miss Seeton, "I'm afraid it's not, because, even to give any kind of true impression calls for color. And"—sadly she surveyed her sketch—"of course, it's only very quick and very rough."

"But I tell you this"—manners lost in agitation, he prodded her drawing with his forefinger—"this is not possible."

"Nonsense, Karl." The fair-haired woman had joined them. "All things are possible—it says so in the Bible. Only to us mere mortals some things appear so much more possible than others."

"Mélie—" The banker tried to collect himself. "Miss Seeton, Miss Galam—Mme de Brillot. Mélie," he urged, "look." He indicated the sketch.

Mme de Brillot did: briefly she eyed Miss Seeton's work; the original on the wall; then Miss Seeton's impression of it once again. "So clever," she pronounced, "and the insight—so penetrating. Karl, I have need to telephone. I came to ask if I might use your office."

"But certainly. You know your way. Forgive me but I must think. There are affairs to which I must attend."

"Precisely." She took his arm. "And so you shall escort me. Offices are for thoughts and for attention to affairs." She turned back and the blue eyes gave Miss Seeton the sensation of being bathed in brilliant, laughing light. "Such a short encounter—it must be corrected." She slipped a card from her bag. "My address; we will arrange something when Karl is not so occupied with his affairs." Quickly she impelled the unwilling banker on his way.

Off keel, Karl Telmark paced his office. "Mélie, you don't understand. It was the Belton Gainsborough that that woman drew—one of the four pictures discovered to have been stolen from the Abbey only the other day. Every gallery and dealer in the world has been notified and she—she drew the Gainsborough as being under the Alberti. Oh"—he tried to laugh it off—"a coincidence, of course—she had seen it somewhere sometime, something brought it to her mind, just coincidence, but I—I cannot take the risk. I will have to close the doors and allow no one to leave until it has been investigated, and above all Alberti must be kept here." He made for the door.

Amélie de Brillot was perched on the desk; she had dialed and was awaiting an answer. She looked around. "Too late, Karl. Don't trouble yourself with doors; Alberti is gone."

He stared at her. "How do you know?"

"Because I saw him leave when Miss Seeton began to examine his pain—" She turned to the telephone. "*Allo . . .*" She gave a number, adding the word "Urgent." Again she had to wait. "Sir down, Karl. Nothing will be resolved by marching in circles." She spoke into the receiver. "Good—" and began to summarize: "Two suspect pictures at the art museum, overpainted. Possibly two more at Hôtel Magnifique, pension in the Rue Melun. Registered there under Elio Mantoni, alias Alberti, artist. Short, just over five foot, slight build, age in the forties, full mouth, brown eyes, heavy eyebrows, thick dark hair average length."

"Beard and mustache," hissed Telmark.

She waved him to silence. "If you send a car immediately to the hotel you should be in time to collect the pictures, if there. Possibly Mantoni too. As Alberti, disguises himself with a

beard and mustache but is unlikely to be wearing them now."
She lowered the receiver while orders were being given.

Telmark was gaping at her. "Mélie, how do you know all
this?"

"By the use of my eyes and such wits as the good God gave
me." The receiver quacked; she lifted it. "*Hein?*" After a
moment she addressed the banker. "Who bought the pictures?"

"An agency, Bertauld (fils) et Laurent."

"And their principal?" He shrugged. She gave the telephone
the name of the agency, adding, "Principal unknown." The
telephone asked a question. No, she replied, they could put one
of their own men onto it. She herself did not wish to be
involved in any way. In response to another question she
laughed. But no, there was no haste with regard to the
paintings here. A buyer could not remove a picture from the
gallery until the end of the exhibition without permission,
which would not be given. And, she advised the instrument,
discretion would be wise. If the paintings were innocent no
harm was done and if they were, as she suspected, from the
Belton collection in England, the less the criminals knew as to
how the pictures were recovered and returned, the more
confusing it would be and in consequence the more probable
that they might make mistakes. She thanked the telephone
punctiliously for its speed, for its efficiency and above all for
its discretion, replaced the receiver and sprang off the desk.
"There; all is arranged and we can return to the gallery."

Karl Telmark sat watching her. He had known her for some
years: the fashionable, witty Mélie de Brillot; she came and
went, always at the right place at the right time, in Venice for
the season, then probably Rome, Paris for clothes, New York
for Christmas—or it might be Japan—and always among the
right people; she had a flat here near the Plaine de Planpalais
but was seldom there and took many of her meals at the
Richesse, where the staff adored her; always smart, always gay
and amusing; ever on the move. He remembered once at a
dinner party remarking that if anyone wished to get in touch
with Mélie quickly they should fire the letter into the air by
rocket and whatever jet she was traveling in could collect it in
transit.

Now he saw a different woman, who dealt with a matter
which should be the prerogative of the police; gave orders

which she expected immediately to be obeyed. Who—or
what—was she? He had accepted her as she appeared, without
thought. Impelled to think, it struck him that she was
essentially alone: she had no intimates of whom he knew, but
was mostly to be seen among a galaxy of acquaintances, or by
herself.

"To whom were you speaking?"

"To whom but to a friend," she mocked. "Karl"—before
he could speak again—"I will conclude a bargain with you. I
have saved you an embarrassment, a scandal in the gallery, to
be made to look an idiot." He nodded. "In return you will
remember only that you brought me here to telephone, nothing
more. Evidently you are too much a gentleman to listen at
doors when I am talking in private with a friend. It is agreed?"

He grinned and answered in English, "I suppose I'm stuck
with it."

She laughed delightedly and replied in kind. "Okay. And on
our way back to join all those very rich, very fashionable, very
amusing people—" As though a current had been switched off
her vivacity left her: she looked old, tired and embittered; the
transformation was as shocking as it was sudden. With a
visible effort the current was switched on again and her eyes lit
up. "—you shall tell me who has been instructing you in
English slang. Not, surely not, your nice Miss Seeton?"

Ruefully Miss Seeton studied her drawing before closing her
sketchbook, which years of teaching art had made it second
nature for her to carry, and returning it to her bag. "Impossible," Mr. Telmark had said. Rather an abrupt way of putting it,
perhaps, but, yes, it was a very rough jotting. And obviously
had conveyed nothing to him of what she was trying to
express. But when one's impression depended so much upon
the violent contrast in the abuse and use of color, it was quite
justified, she admitted, to say "impossible." Because, of
course, it was. Without it.

She continued her tour of the gallery accompanied by Vee,
whose pithy comments on and scurrilous interpretations of the
works on display were, she felt, for the most part justified.
Miss Seeton began to enjoy herself.

"Now, that I admire." Miss Seeton and Vee turned: blue
eyes sparkled at them. "To dare anything so original as to
study the masterpieces at a private view."

It was that Mrs. de . . . the lady who had given her a card
and gone to telephone—with the intriguing face bones. Like a
child caught in a misdemeanor, Miss Seeton said hurriedly:

"Miss Galam was explaining them to me." Vee choked.

"You are an authority, Miss Galam?" asked Karl Telmark.

"Sure. With these"—she waved a hand—"all you need is a
filthy mind and no inhibitions and you're home every time."

With the return of Mme de Brillot and the director of the
museum, other people began to converge upon the group,
entailing more introductions.

"How d'you do. . . . Why, yes it's true. . . . I should
have said that one or two were quite disarming. . . ."

"Miss Seeton, Miss Galam—M. and Mme Stemkos."

"How d'you do?"

"How d'you do?" Very beautiful, of course, but perhaps
rather a hard face. That thin mouth. Mrs. Stemkos, Miss
Seeton judged, wouldn't wear well. Mr. Stemkos, she thought,
on the other hand, was rather a jolly person. Somehow he
brought to her mind Old King Cole in the nursery rhyme. She
was relieved that there was no Mr. Librecksin. Knowing what
one did, that would have been embarrassing.

"Oh, Ana," Mme Stemkos called, "you must come and
meet Miss Seeton, of whom"—a saccharine smile—"we have
all read and heard so much. Anatole Librecksin—Miss
Seeton."

Miss Seeton was duly embarrassed when a swarthy man
took her hand and bowed.

"It's embarrassing," complained Jonathan Feldman.

The assistant commissioner sighed. This was the third
conference on the forged notes, which after all had their own
trivial importance—the trifling question as to whether England
crashed financially or not—and all any of them ever wanted to
discuss was "Should Miss Seeton . . . ?" "Shouldn't Miss
Seeton . . . ?" "Did she . . . ?" "Didn't she . . . ?"
"Why . . . ?" and "Why not . . . ?" Frankly, damn Miss
Seeton—or rather damn the people who'd dragged her into
this. She was welcome to spread her own peculiar form of

disruption abroad, but he had hoped that in her absence they would be free to get on with the job at home. He collected his thoughts and his manners.

"Embarrassing, Mr. Feldman? I'm so sorry."

"Well, it is. I suppose I can understand her not doing a deal with the Italian police but now she refuses to cooperate with the Swiss police—and that's got them properly narked." Sir Hubert caught Chief Superintendent Delphick's eye and both quickly looked elsewhere. "Not only that, but she won't even tell Karl Telmark what she's doing. She either hedges or lies."

"Miss Seeton never lies." Delphick was definite. "On the contrary, she takes such pains to be accurate that she's sometimes almost incomprehensible."

"Call it what you like—in my book it's plain lying. Oh, I'll admit she was helpful over the Belton paintings and naturally Karl's grateful—and it explains why she went chasing this artist fellow round Italy. But why couldn't she say so? And why couldn't she've tipped Karl the wink privately instead of making a drama of it in the middle of the gallery? I suppose, as an artist herself, she thinks art's important, but it's not, compared to money, and damn it, that's what she's being paid for. Karl gave her all the papers to do with the Stemkos joint account: she pretended she didn't want 'em, and he has a shrewd suspicion that she hasn't even bothered to read 'em yet. Haven't you," he demanded, "got any control over her?"

"None," said Sir Hubert flatly, "—or very little. Meanwhile, under cover of her flamboyancy, we have in our modest and less spectacular way made some slight progress. Inspector Borden has been delving into Estevel's background and apart from his political pirouettes, I see from this"—he tapped a report—"that when he has the time to spare from his obligations to the Treasury, he is chairman of Estevel and Conder, Metalcraft, who make"—he referred to the paper again—"carpets. The shares have dropped and the company's reputed to be in financial difficulties, which doesn't surprise me, or not unduly, for I'm bound to admit that I find the word 'carpets' in such a context somewhat confusing. No, Inspector," he continued as Borden prepared to elucidate, "allow me to keep my innocence—and the City its peculiar mysteries. Where else could you expect to encounter metal filings transformed by some sleight of machinery into hessian and wool?"

Commander Conway smiled. "Estevel's firm's difficulties have had their uses; they gave us a lever." He glanced at his subordinate, who took over.

"Well, sir, we've interviewed Estevel twice so far—once at his office and the other time at his flat. We played it on 'People were saying . . .' 'From information received . . .' and 'With a gentleman in his position we thought for his own sake . . .' The first time he was a bit windy and the second, when he was at home, the wind was blustery. He's rattled, and given time he'll break. But time's what we haven't got, so the more MissEss can stir things up, the better."

Fenn stopped doodling on a scratch pad to observe, "She's doing just that. They tried to shoot her the morning after she arrived in Geneva." All turned to him. "It was played down—accident, demonstration, what have you—but it was aimed at her. Tolla's back in Geneva too, and we're pretty certain it was he who tried to kidnap her that same night. So don't worry about her end of it—she's stirring them all right."

Sir Hubert considered, then summarized: "I don't think," he told Jonathan Feldman, "that you need worry about the Stemkos bank papers. Miss Seeton's very conscientious and I'm sure she'll get around to reading them." He thought it better not to comment on what she would make of them. "For the rest: we know she bumped into Tolla at Heathrow, and you tell me she's recently been introduced to Anatole Librecksin; I would suggest that we can leave it to her personality and their consciences to—er—take it from there."

Anatole Librecksin was in a temper. All that he had schemed and worked for during the last few years looked now to be in jeopardy. England had so far shown no sign of panic over the forged banknotes. England—where Heracles Stemkos was a popular visitor, treated with deference, honored and sought after, whereas he, the social secretary who had become recognized in other countries as almost the equal of his master if not indeed the better business brain—a legend which Librecksin had been at some pains to foster—was neglected in this same England as of no account, a mere secretary and, as he had more than once overheard, dark-skinned at that. The new masters to whom he had sold his allegiance were becoming impatient at the lack of reaction on the London Stock Exchange and in the government. He too was impatient, longing to write finis to his calculated affair with Natalie Stemkos before her husband inevitably got wind of it. He and Natalie had salted away plenty, which was by now safely banked in his name—he had played his part well in regard to her and the silly trollop trusted him—but he would need more than just plenty from the moment when things were unmasked. Setting yourself up in another country in the manner in which he intended took vast quantities of cash. This was why, once he had agreed to act as representative for a consortium of international financiers acting in their own interests but with the connivance and for the profits of their respective governments and they had put him in touch with Xerxes Tolla and his smuggling organization for the main distribution of the notes, he had, on learning more of the man, arranged to go in with him privately on two minor swindles. First, a double swindle over Natalie's jewelry: she was to have her baubles stolen while in Paris, claim the insurance and turn the money over to him for safekeeping. Even she did not know that although the colored stones still remained, he had removed all the diamonds, replacing them with zircons, and that those same diamonds were now safely packaged and bestowed under her name in the vault at the Banque du Lac until such time as he felt it safe to ask her to remove them. Shortly, through an intermediary in Paris, arranged by Tolla, the jewelry would be discovered and as extra pocket money to cover their expenses they could claim such reward as the insurance company was prepared to pay. Second, the picture thefts: he had offered to find a buyer, thus saving Tolla trouble. In fact he himself had bought the pictures through an agency in Stemkos' name, intending to resell them later at a profit in America. If things went wrong Stemkos would bear the brunt since all had been done ostensibly by his orders while Anatole, as social secretary, could plead ignorance. But if matters went as planned he would have disappeared before they broke wide open and in the breaking Stemkos would be broken—gratuity which would satisfy his jealousy of his employer and redress imagined slights. For Stemkos, Librecksin knew, would feel some moral responsibility and would attempt repayment of the banks, leaving himself discredited and without money but with Natalie—and a worse fate no man could wish him.

Then, with everything going smoothly, Scotland Yard had acted; sending of all improbabilities this old woman to follow Tolla's man, Mantoni. And now, solely because of her, the forgery deal possibly and one picture transaction certainly were both in danger. Even this present meeting in Tolla's flat was dangerous. He turned on his parttime partner savagely.

"And you admit you don't even know where this wretched little artist is?"

Tolla shook his head, poured himself another whiskey and took a cigarette from a gold box on the occasional table beside the armchair in which he sprawled. "No, not yet. Mantoni was in a panic when he phoned, after seeing a police car outside his hotel. I told him to forget his luggage and the rest of his stuff— we'll get them back later if it turns out to be safe—and to find lodgings the other side of town. He'll be phoning."

"But you let the fool keep the other pictures in his room there?"

"Yup."

"Have the police got them?"

"Too soon to say. Anyway we don't know yet for certain the police were after Mantoni—or, if they were, it could still be for something else. And you can't even be sure the Seeton woman was on to the picture game."

Librecksin was definite. "I'm sure. And if you'd been in the gallery and seen her sniffing around that picture and taking notes on it you'd be sure too. She did everything except take out a tape and measure the canvas. She follows Mantoni half round Italy, then Geneva, then the gallery—don't try telling me she's not on to it, and the forgeries too, or why have late-night meetings with bankers? She's hardly the age or type for a cuddle in the dark."

Tolla sipped his whiskey reflectively. "As to age, I'm not so sure, and the looks could be phony as well. I've seen her on the move, you haven't. No woman the age she pretends to be skitters about as she does." Tolla flicked a lighter to his cigarette and inhaled deliberately. Not sharing the extent of Librecksin's anxiety, he was opting for calm, gaining satisfaction from the other's nervous temper which gave him a brief if spurious authority. "I can find out later what the police know, through a contact."

Librecksin paced. "Does it occur to you you're not doing too well? Looks as though we've lost the Belton pictures; and apropos the notes, England hasn't devalued yet and the Bank seems to be paying up indefinitely; they shouldn't be with the amount in circulation, or"—he stopped and stood over Tolla accusingly—"isn't your distribution quite as good as you make out?"

"My side of it's okay. At a guess"—the black man tapped ash, then cocked his eye and sneered—"I'd say it's you and your doxy who've been milking too much too quickly in lumps from the Banque du Lac." He laughed at the other's consternation. "You and the Stemkos frail got greedy: she—sometimes you with her—kept running round to the Banque du Lac making deposits of snide, and then in the end she takes out a whacking sum in French currency saying she's off to Paris to pick up some trinkets. Does it occur to you"—he mimicked Librecksin's words—"that you're not doing too well? If I can find out all this, likely the Banque du Lac and the clearing banks are way ahead. In which case I'd say the Bank of England's keeping quiet in the hopes of getting who's behind it instead of arsing about picking up small fry."

So. Librecksin swung away and resumed his pacing. It would not be politic at the moment to quarrel with Tolla. And at that the black fool could be right. Maybe the satisfaction of using Natalie's trust in him and Stemkos' trust of him had led him into snatching too much too quickly. He must get Natalie to retrieve from the bank tomorrow morning the package of diamonds, which she believed to be jewelry of his own, and find some safe hiding place which couldn't be connected with him but would leave them available should things go sour. And yet—he stopped at the window, looking down on the roofs of the Old Town—and yet they should not. Even though he had taken risks to grab money while there was time, it should've been all right, would've been all right, could be all right if it wasn't for this woman. He turned back into the room.

"Why the devil didn't you get rid of her at the start?" Tolla shrugged. "I tried."

"Tried?" he scoffed. "All your gunman did was to knock out a window and you, when you actually had her in your taxi, you go and hand her over to another woman."

"I told you"—Tolla was exasperated at the reminder—

"wherever she goes half a dozen people spring out of nowhere. You can't go blasting off in front of witnesses."

"The next thing"—Librecksin continued to needle him— "will be we'll have her taking a trip to Paris and telling the insurance to hold payment on the jewelry."

"Don't worry," Tolla said. "They can't watch her round the clock. We will. I'll set it up, with extra men for safe measure, and the first time she's alone she's had it."

"Better," Librecksin advised, "bring her in and question her first. Once we know what she's told the police we'll know what we have to face."

1. *May 13.*   *Mme Stemkos paid £2,000 into her & husband's joint a/c . . . said she and husband had been helping people who had taken money from sterling areas during currency restrictions but now wished to bring it back owing to relaxation of same . . . would be making further such deposits . . . Wanted cash left in a/c . . . considering investing in jewelry . . . large sums to be immediately available.*

2. *May 15.*   *Mme Stemkos deposited £3,000 in £5 notes . . .*

3. *May 19.*   *Mme Stemkos deposited . . .*

Good gracious, thought Miss Seeton, what a lot of money these people had.

4. *May 22.*   *Mme Stemkos, with Librecksin (husband's secretary) depos . . . Lodged package (contents unknown) in joint Stemkos safe in vault.*

5. *May 29.*   *Librecksin dep . . .*

. . . .

10. *July 8.*   *M. Stemkos, with Librecksin, d . . . (various currencies & denominations).*

With a sigh Miss Seeton pushed the papers to one side. Really, it was very difficult. And, she conceded with a wry smile, considering the amount of money involved, not what she was accustomed to, forged or not. She had tried very hard to understand the background which Mr. Telmark had been so insistent upon, but it wasn't, she feared, very clear. To her. However, it did appear, although the figures always came out different, that, since Mrs. Stemkos had withdrawn a sum in French francs with a great many naughts about two weeks ago, that Mr. and Mrs. Stemkos' account was now overdrawn. Which seemed odd for very rich people. Or, perhaps, that was how very rich people did it.

Tired of mathematical calculations, Miss Seeton began to jot down impressions of her visit to Switzerland. This exercise absorbed her and it wasn't until over an hour later when the floor waiter came to her room to remove her tea tray that she realized that she should hasten if she was to do her yoga drill and have a bath before going down to dinner. She glanced quickly through her jottings and felt ashamed. One should not do such slapdash work—really caricature. But, after all, they were quite private and only for one's own eyes. Really, the one of Mrs. Stemkos was, perhaps, unkind. A pair of nutcrackers angled to the front across the paper with the lady's face at the business end, her jaw forming the hinge. The one of Vee, too. Well, not exactly unkind. But odd. In removing all that blond hair, the eyelashes and the makeup, in an attempt to realize the character beneath, the result had the appearance of a young man. Miss Seeton put her sketchbook away, took off her coat and skirt, spread a rug and settled on the floor with her textbook *Yoga and Younger Every Day* open beside her.

Slowly, with careful counting of her breaths, she arched and bowed, she flexed and straightened and steadily, in progressive sequence, the postures became more complicated. Finally she prepared for her recent and greatest achievement, a full stretch of the spine and neck in a posture called The Noose. Before launching upon this endeavor she studied the book to confirm that she had got it correct. Of course, to say: *Lie down upon the floor. Then take one leg and, with no strain whatever, place it behind the head, lodging the foot at the back of the neck; then, still without the slightest strain, place the other leg behind the first, locking the ankles together. Now tighten the leg muscles to increase the bend and clasp the hands around the b . . .* was ridiculous. She did not see how any such maneuver could be performed with no strain whatever. By no stretch of the imagination—let alone the spine—could such a pose be termed natural. Really, so very like Mr. Kipling's armadillo, who loosened a notch each day and curled up tighter and tighter.

However, it was undoubtedly beneficial and Miss Seeton experienced a certain pride that in the few years she had been doing these exercises, she had progressed far enough to accomplish this strange and somewhat embarrassing position. Dutifully she lay back, raised one leg and grasped the foot.

Following normal hotel routine and intent upon turning down the bed, the chambermaid entered without knocking. She stared, unbelieving, at a bloomered bottom embraced by clasped hands, above which a small face gazed back at her in mild surprise. Legs in sensible stockings disappeared beneath the outstretched arms to reappear crossing behind the neck with the feet upraised like asses' ears above the head. For a moment the chambermaid wavered, with training and nature in precarious balance. At last:

"Pardon, madame," she managed. "I come back later."

"Mercy," replied Miss Seeton. Oh, dear. Really, how very awkward. For both of them. To be caught in such a posture was not, when one considered, in the normal way, quite easy to explain.

Returning from the adjoining bathroom, Miss Seeton halted in dismay behind the buttress wall which gave a semblance of division between bedroom and sitting room. A man with graying hair was seated on the edge of the bed and was using the telephone. She stood listening, though she would be the first to admit her French was far from fluent, in the hope that she might glean some explanation of his presence.

"*D'ac*," said the man. "*D'ac* . . . *D'ac* . . . *D'ac* . . . *D'ac*." He rang off.

Duck? wondered Miss Seeton. Not a word she knew. She must remember to look it up. She moved forward and the man sprang to his feet.

"Miss Seeton? A thousand pardons. The proprietor asked that I should call on you. The maid was a little disturbed. . . ." How in the name of tact did one say the woman had reported that the miss in 301 was having a fit? "I am," he continued, "a doctor, staying in the hotel, but evidently"—he smiled and indicated the yoga manual, which lay upon the coverlet—"you are your own physician, and all is resolved. Tell me"—professionally he was interested—"what made you commence and how long ago?"

Miss Seeton became pink and flustered. "Nearly five years. It was most unfortunate—my knees, you understand—there was no knock, you see—and they were becoming rather stiff. Then I saw an advertisement and decided to try it—but there was no time to explain, or even to uncurl. When she came in, I mean—with, I must admit, the most remarkable effect—and, in any case, one should not, it can be dangerous, from an advanced posture. Not quickly, that is. Uncurl," she added. She felt that she had not, perhaps, sufficiently exonerated the maid. "But I do understand how natural it would be for her not to."

The doctor looked at her in puzzlement, then bowed. "No, one sees that she did not quite understand. But allow me to congratulate you. Five years. It is remarkable, as you say, what the human body can achieve with perseverance. Completely remarkable." He opened the door, gave a final bow. "Your servant, Miss Seeton," and shut the door behind him.

At dinner Miss Seeton failed to notice that the service was that much more eager, the smiles were that much broader. Word had already circulated among the staff: here was one could do things they couldn't.

After dinner Miss Seeton, unaccustomed to idleness, still felt the urge to gather more impressions of Geneva; though now it was the city that was to be at her pencil's point rather than the people. A lovely evening, windless and warm; she could digest her meal sitting on the broad platform, near that copy of the Albert Memorial, which gave a wonderful view over this end of the lake. Later she would cross the bridge and explore the Old Town. On the drive up to Mr. Telmark's she had seen a sign, VIEILLE VILLE, so that it would be quite easy to find her way. It would be such a pity not to make the most of her time, not knowing how long she was to be here.

The view over the lake was indeed wonderful and the colors reflected in the dark water fascinated the artist in Miss Seeton. Ribbons, she thought—no, more like curtains of color—appeared to hang reflected in straight lines with sharp division, blurring only at their extremities, where they merged into the blackness of the water. It reminded her of the colored stones in the jewelry that appeared to be so fashionable here. But on the placid surface of the lake the brashness of the neon signs which blazed on the surrounding buildings was transmuted, acquiring a dreamlike quality. Geneva, city of colored dreams, thought Miss Seeton is unaccustomed poetic flight. *Geneva, city of colored stones,* wrote Miss Seeton in her sketchbook with habitual prosaism. Perhaps, if one listed the colors and then, by day, drew in the outlines, one would, from memory, be able to recapture the magic of the night. *Emerald, ruby, sapphire, topaz, aquamarine, amethyst,* jotted down Miss Seeton. But points of white jarred where the reflected street lights, like too-bright diamonds, overlayed the design, striking a false note. *Diamonds too bright, false,* she recorded.

"You come."

Miss Seeton started; she had heard no one. "I beg your pardon?"

"You come—wiz me," repeated Elio Mantoni impatiently.

Good gracious. It was that little man who'd been on the airplane. On all three, in fact. "No," replied Miss Seeton. "I do not."

"If you do not come, I fire." Looking down, she saw with astonishment that the hand in his open briefcase held a pistol with a funny bulbous end. "I wish to fire," he assured her, "but now they want first that you shall talk, so they discover what you know and what you have told."

Really. He must be making some mistake. But even so . . . Miss Seeton pushed the briefcase to one side; it gave a cough and jerked, emitting an acrid smell. A distant *ping,* followed by tinkling glass, testified that Mantoni was once more shooting up the Place des Alpes.

"You should not," said Miss Seeton severely, "point a thing like that. It could be dangerous."

Mantoni jumped back with fury. He leveled the briefcase again. Now he was indeed justified. He could say with truth the hellcat refused to come. His finger tightened on the trigger. Around him in the garden three more fingers tightened on three more triggers as Mme de Brillot and the agents from the Sûreté, concealed behind assorted shrubs, prepared for action.

"I say—" The impending barrage was checked when Thomas ffoley stepped between Mantoni and Miss Seeton. "You annoying this lady? Better push off, old chap."

Should he . . . ? Mantoni's finger itched as Tomfool stood in everyone's line of fire, unconscious that he might be riddled from all sides. No, the Italian realized, he would have to kill this one first and if he did the hellcat would kill him. Too much risk. He zipped his briefcase shut and bowed—"*Per favore, signore*"—flashed round Tomfool, grabbed for Miss Seeton's sketchbook and succeeded in snatching the top page before leaping the balustrade, to the ruin of the formal arrangement of lobelia and zinnia in the flower bed below, slithered to the pavement, crossed the Quai de Mont Blanc amid a stridence of protest from the traffic and was lost in the crowd that was wending its way across the bridge. Before he reached the bridge he stopped at the pedestrian crossing and, simmering with fury, waited for the lights to change. *Allora*, she had outwitted him and made of him a public fool. The night should not pass until she had paid for this. The little green man walking signaled to the pedestrians and Mantoni crossed with them to circle round the Place des Alpes and join his fellow watcher. If she would stay in the hotel, *allora*, upon some pretext he would enter it. He would . . . The door of the hotel revolved. He gripped his brother shadow's arm.

"*Ecco!*" he breathed.

Young Mr. ffoley was shaken. "I say," he quavered, "that chap had a gun. After all, I saw it—a g-gun. D-didn't you know?"

"Yes," said Miss Seeton. "Or no. Or rather, I don't think so. I mean, surely it can't have been. You see . . ." She gave the matter thought. No one could have cause to wish her ill. And, in any case, even if the whole affair was some mistake, no one would produce a real gun in such a public place. So very foolhardy. And besides . . . "It only went off with a sort of pop and made a smell. I think," she decided, "it must have been meant as some form of practical joke. Rather foolish and not, I'm afraid, in quite the best of taste."

"P-practical joke?"

"Yes. I remember now, I inadvertently caused him to drop his ticket and things at the airport and this, I imagine, is his idea of retaliation. But I don't think it can have been real—that seems so very unlikely. It must have been one of these newfangled toys and I expect he probably felt it would be amusing."

It was to be hoped that the owner of the pharmacy on the far side of the square who had lost the glass pane in his door would appreciate the jest next morning.

Thomas ffoley looked at Miss Seeton and scratched his

head. Did she really think he didn't know a gun with a silencer when he saw one? Quite bats. And to think he'd thought he was doing his career a bit of good by keeping an eye on her. He wouldn't be doing himself much good if he was dead. If she wanted to play hush-hush games with creeps with guns she could play 'em on her own. High time he got back to Bern.

A breeze had sprung up, introducing a chill into the air, and Miss Seeton returned to the hotel to fetch her coat. In the surrounding shrubbery silent prayers of thankfulness were offered: she was retiring for the night and the Sûreté men decided that they could go off duty.

Thrudd Banner, arriving at the hotel after a snatched meal, saw ffoley getting into his car. "Seen MissEss?" he asked.

Tomfool eyed him pityingly. "Rather missed the bus, haven't you, old man? She was having a run-in with some little creep with a gun over there by the monument, but I"—in retrospect he preened himself—"I—er—put a stop to it."

"You . . . ?"

The car began to move. "Sorry, old chap, can't wait—needed back at the embassy. And your Miss Seeton," he called back through the window, "has toddled off to bed."

To bed? Thrudd wondered. From what they'd told him of her, once she'd started something she followed through with the pace getting hotter all the time. He went to the reception desk and inquired. While they were confirming that the lady had gone up to her room, one of the lifts behind him opened and turning he saw Miss Seeton heading for the revolving door. He waited for a second to give her time to get ahead and was interested to note that a raised newspaper on a sofa in the corner of the hall was lowered, thrust aside and Vee Galam sauntered out of the hotel. Thrudd grinned. So here they all went again. He hurried after them. So much for Tomfool's "toddled off to bed."

In the darkness of the television lounge Mme de Brillot frowned. Then she had been right to believe that the fracas by the monument was not an end—rather a beginning. And evidently this evening everyone would promenade on foot. Hence she, in case of necessity, would take her car.

"She's on to the jewelry game."

At the other end of the line Librecksin interrupted: "Wait."

He shut the door of his office in the Stemkos chateau and returned to the telephone. "How do you know?"

Tolla explained. "Mantoni caught her alone by the Brunswick Monument. She refused to go with him and attacked him, trying to knock the gun out of his hand. He would have shot her then but some man walked in on them and Mantoni had to run for it, but he managed to snatch the top sheet of her notes and it's all there—a list of stones, and even mentions the diamonds are false."

Librecksin frowned. How could she know that? "What are her exact words?"

"Hang on, I took it down when Elio phoned in; I've got it here." He found the paper. "Here we are: 'emerald, ruby, sapphire,' et cetera; then 'diamonds too bright, false.'"

Librecksin was startled. "But when could she have seen them—and how does she know they are zircons?"

"She doesn't say zircons."

"But implies it," snapped the secretary. "Zircons are cut with more facets and are brighter."

Tolla laughed. "Well, we don't have to worry about her—she's handed herself to us on a plate. Mantoni circled round and joined my other man keeping watch in the Place des Alpes. She got her coat from the hotel and's gone for a walk. The second man seized an opportunity to phone his report a few minutes ago. He and Elio are on her tail and she's headed up this way toward the Old Town. I've got a couple of men in a car keeping an eye on things, and I'm only waiting for another call to be sure which route she's taking and I'll go down to join the fun myself. Whatever she does, or whoever tries to interfere, we've got 'em cold. She hasn't a chance."

It was stop-go up the Rue Verdaine. Every time Miss Seeton paused to admire antiques in some shopwindow her ill-assorted convoy had to halt, light cigarettes, tie shoelaces, examine guide maps, anything to preserve the fiction of their noninvolvement.

On the opposite side of the street Miss Seeton marked an intriguing doorway with above it in large letters the words PASSAGE INTERDIT. So sensible to have things clearly named. And so easy to remember should one lose one's way. She crossed the road. The beginning of the passage was roofed over and very dark, but farther on she could see that it came out into the open and there were lighted windows of buildings on the left which seemed to be below the passage level. It reminded her of something. Oh, yes, of course. Edinburgh. Those narrow, steep alleys called wynds near the castle which she'd explored once when on a schoolteachers' coach tour. Yes, this would be genuine old Geneva—and exactly what she'd set out to find. She felt in her bag for the flashlight which had become a regulation since living in the country.

The flashlight beam showed a wide, deep hole with a narrow plank across it. Really, if they were excavating here they should, surely, have put up some sort of notice. If one hadn't had one's torch one could easily have fallen. She trod with care and, as her weight pressed on the far end where the board rested on rounded cobbles, it upended and clattered down the hole. Oh, dear. Should she try to hook it out with her umbrella? She peered down. No, it was too deep. She would just have to hope that no one else would come this way till daylight.

When Miss Seeton disappeared Mantoni quickened his pace. At the entrance to the passage the warning on the board above it gave him pause. *Allora,* if the passage was forbidden she must then know that she was being followed and had laid a trap. He edged into the darkness, waiting until his eyes became accustomed to the change in light. No, no one ahead of him. He ran forward, floundered in space and crashed into the hole. Cut, bruised and shaken, he swore to be avenged. *Allora,* she had caught him in her trap, but he would catch her and she then should die, not once but twice, should die three times, would be so glad to die before he'd finished with her. For an instant a wavering flame lighted the pit. Good; his fellow follower had arrived. As the flame went out he threw his briefcase up, reached, gripped the cobbles, braced himself and sprang.

Vee began to run. Thrudd Banner sprinted after her, catching her at the passage mouth.

"No," he panted, "not you—I'll deal with him. You carry on up and guard the other end in case I miss out or she needs help up there."

Vee weighed the pros and cons, nodded and ran to the top of the Rue Verdaine, skirted the flower-filled fountain in the Place du Bourg de Four, past the old police headquarters—causing one or two of the students milling around the café on the opposite corner to raise an indulgent eyebrow over such antics in someone who must be well past twenty. She chased up the

Rue des Chaudronniers, turned left at the Promenade Saint Antoine and sped along to the Rue Théodore de Bèze, where she stationed herself at the head of the Passage Mathurin-Cordier.

Thrudd glanced at the notice above the entrance. What the hell was MissEss playing at cavorting up places clearly marked "Forbidden"? Or had she some trick up her umbrella? He went forward with caution and flicked on his lighter. "Forbidden" probably meant . . . Too right—it meant a bloody great hole. One foot smacked into the head of the upspringing Mantoni and sent Thrudd sprawling, concussing the Italian, who subsided again to the bottom of the pit. Unaware of what had tripped him, the reporter picked himself up, collecting the briefcase on which he had fallen. Fair enough—the little squirt had dropped his luggage in his hurry. Well, possession was nine points . . . Briefcase in hand, Thrudd bounded up the passage.

Coming into the Place du Bourg de Four from the opposite side, Xerxes Tolla narrowly missed a head-on encounter with Vee Galam. Outside the passage he had a brief report from Mantoni's second string, told the man to stay where he was on guard for about five minutes and then to join Mantoni in case he was needed. At the bottom of the street he found his other two operatives, with their car parked at right angles to the Rue Verdaine, arguing their next move. He jumped in the back.

"All right," he rapped. "Since you are headed this way, carry on, take your first right and come up round the Théodore de Bèze, where we can keep a watch at the top."

From the end of the street Mme de Brillot had witnessed the proceedings in the Rue Verdaine. Evidently the enemy was mounting an operation and everyone was out in force tonight. She assessed the probabilities, unaware from where she sat that the Passage Mathurin-Cordier was officially, if temporarily, out of bounds. The press man, Banner, after a word with Vee, had followed Mantoni and Vee must be intending to contain the Italian in a pincer movement from above. The other man—she had seen Tolla speak to him—still loitered, so apparently he had orders to remain where he was. More serious, she had been correct in her suspicions of the two men in the car ahead of her.

Tolla had joined them and now they were headed . . . almost certainly up to the Saint Antoine via the Théodore de Bèze. Vee might need help. She slipped a pistol from her bag, laid it on the seat beside her for quick action and started after them.

Really, Miss Seeton congratulated herself, how very wise she had been to come this way. A single lamp hung on a cable above, ill-lighting the cobbled way. On her right a stretch of low wall held back a flower bed which rose sharply to a small dwelling. On her left railings protected her from falling to the ground floor of what looked like the back of a tenement building. The railing ended and she mounted steep steps between rough stone walls. Unquestionably this would be one of the oldest parts of the city. She must come here by day and settle down to sketch. More Cobbles. A stepped low doorway on her right, then a high plain wall. An old building to her left. More steps; more railings which finished at the entrance to the building; above the door the single word COLLÈGE. A college? Could this be, she wondered, Calvin's original school?

It was. It was also to be wondered whether the spirit of M. Cordier, its first headmaster, was abroad that night to watch over the well-being of this latter-day ex-colleague, herself so very much abroad.

At the top of one more flight of steps there was a final slope. Better lighting ahead showed Miss Seeton a wall, on the farther side of a road, with rising ground above and statuary. Goodness, how satisfactory. Now she knew where she was. Quite near where Mr. Telmark lived. She stepped onto the pavement and gave a jump.

"Vee. How you startled me. What are you doing here?"

"Waiting for you—what else?" Vee Galam was on edge. "Couldn't you just for once stay home at night and give us all a break?"

"Waiting for me? Stay at home? I don't understand."

"No, I guess you don't at that." Vee realized she had overstepped. "Forget it. It was just that when I saw you quit the hotel I thought I'd best tag along. You never know what may break in strange cities after dark."

Miss Seeton was touched. Really. The young. Such an amazing sense of responsibility. And so kind. But not, perhaps, appreciating that a young attractive woman, or someone rich, might well be at peril in such circumstances. When one was old and not, she feared, attractive, not rich, one at least gained this advantage, that these same dangers passed one by. That Vee should have worried about her . . . She put her hand on the other's arm.

"Thank you, my dear."

Her words were almost drowned by the sound of an engine as a car roared up the bend on the corner. Vee stiffened and her hand went to her bag. The car appeared and shot toward them, coming to a halt with a scream of tires. Two men in front; a dark-skinned man in the back. Vee freed her pistol, but the front passenger was already out; his right hand, with a glint of steel, had flashed forward. She whirled, pinning Miss Seeton against the wall. Vee jerked and, still keeping her charge behind her, half turned. Her pistol arm was heavy; disinclined to move. Slowly she forced the muzzle up and, as the knife thrower scrambled back into the car, she shot him through the head. The driver hauled the body in, slammed the door, gunned the motor and streaked down the promenade.

Hearing the shot, Banner charged up the last slope past the college, skidding to a stop in time to see the speeding car. He looked at the pistol in Vee's hand. "Got one of 'em?"

"Yeah." Vee's low voice had deepened, was lagging. "We leveled off. I got the one got me."

"You?"

"Forget it." She leaned one shoulder against the wall. "Take the gun—and run for it."

"But you . . . ?"

The heavy eyelashes lifted. "Grab her and go, but take—the—gun."

Still he hesitated. "I never fired one."

Vee smiled her sad grimace. "Point, pull and pray."

"But what about you?"

She made the effort. "Gotta stay here."

"Right." Thrudd passed the briefcase to Miss Seeton. "Hold this." Then he bent and took the pistol from Vee's slack hand. "Come on." He grasped Miss Seeton's arm, saluted Vee: "Be seeing you," and dragging his reluctant prisoner, began to run.

Another engine revving; another change of gears. Vee tried to straighten, to prepare, but all she achieved was to open unwilling eyes. Scarlet paint gleamed under the street light. Habit rather than brain accepted who it was.

"Vee." Mme de Brillot sprang from her car and ran to her.

Explanations, exhortations jostled in Vee's head. "After them," she muttered.

Looking down the promenade, Mme de Brillot saw the running figures. "In the car," she ordered.

A slight headshake. For the last time the forlorn distortion of a smile. "Remember me to . . ." Her mind was clouding. Anyway did it matter? She tried again. "Remember me . . ." No—didn't matter. Tired. She coughed and blood sluiced down her dress. Her legs buckled, she slumped and Mme de Brillot saw the knife handle protruding from her back. Tight-lipped, she traced a cross with her forefinger, jumped into her car and hurled it down the promenade.

Miss Seeton was finding running difficult. Encumbered by her handbag, her umbrella, a heavy briefcase and Thrudd's grip upon her arm, she was off balance and out of step.

"Please, Mr. Banner," she panted, "if you would let go my arm, it would be easier. And can I put my handbag in the case? Less things to carry."

Thrudd released her. "Go ahead," he puffed. "Not my case. Found it in the passage. I'll take it."

Oh. Miss Seeton slowed to a stop, wedged her umbrella under one arm and knew before she pulled the zipper what it would hold. She stared helplessly at Mantoni's pistol.

"Good God." Thrudd pulled up sharply. "More guns? What the hell goes on?"

"It's all right, Mr. Banner." Miss Seeton pushed her handbag below the pistol. "It's only a sort of trick one that makes a smell."

Thrudd's jaw dropped. Trust her to know. "Fair enough. You'd better keep it then since I've got this"—he hefted Vee's weapon—"but if we meet trouble, wave your trick at 'em, smells or not."

Less hampered now, Miss Seeton forged ahead and Thrudd was put to it to keep up with her. At the Rue des Chaudron-niers—

"Right wheel," he gasped, but headlights were leaping up the street toward them. "Hold it—" he began.

A red car flashed across in front of them and pulled up dead, blocking the side street. Mme de Brillot leaned from her window.

"Run on," she called.

They sprinted forward as the other car, its horn blaring, neared the Lancia. The woman held her place, intent upon who was driving. The car changed down, mounted the pavement and, screaming its wings against the corner house, whipped into the promenade. Seeing Tolla in the back, Mme de Brillot fired for a wheel, a tire exploded and the car lurched across the promenade to crash into a tree. The driver and Tolla leaped out, saw Thrudd disappearing after Miss Seeton down the curve of the Rue Beauregard and gave chase.

Thrudd heard the pounding footsteps drawing closer and realized he was blown.

"You carry on," he wheezed. How did she do it? "Turn right at the main road. I'll hold 'em up." He swung round at bay.

Miss Seeton ran a few more steps, then stopped. She recognized the precipitous cobbled slope and the side street beyond, which Vee Galam had used to cut back through the Old Town. Vee. Miss Seeton still felt disturbed. She hadn't liked to leave her. The girl had sounded . . . Something had been wrong. But both she and Mr. Banner had been so insistent they'd given her no chance to . . . All this running and people with guns. Vee had fired at someone in that car, she was almost sure—although pressed against the wall she couldn't see. What was it all about? And now she was told to run again. Why? She wouldn't. Besides, if Mr. Banner was right and there was trouble, he might need help.

Two men came racing down the Rue Beauregard and diverged. Tolla headed for Miss Seeton and the driver prepared to tackle Thrudd. Thrudd saw the knife in the man's hand and obeying Vee's instructions pointed the pistol, pulled and prayed. There was a loud report and the kick nearly made him drop it. The driver laughed and ran in close, his knife held low, and Thrudd jumped aside as it swept upward. Both snatched for the other's fighting hand. With arms outstretched, each clutching the other's wrist, they swayed and swiveled and, with foot aimed at shin and knee at crotch, they danced an ungainly polka across the Rue de la Croix Rouge until they smacked into the balustrade beside the steps leading to the road below. Thrudd's luck was in, it was his opponent's back which took the blow, making him break his hold. Although the reporter was new in fighting, he reacted like a veteran. He thrust his

arm behind the other's knees, heaved and the driver hurried
down the odd thirty feet to the Rue Saint Leger without benefit
of steps.

Tolla reached Miss Seeton as the red Lancia raced down
toward them, right-angled and braked to a stop. Seeing the
pistol pointing from the car window, he crouched behind Miss
Seeton, thrust forward and raised his automatic.

"Stop that, at once," Miss Seeton ordered. She swung her
umbrella as he fired, sending the automatic and the bullet
skyward. He knocked the umbrella from her hand and,
balancing himself on the steep cobbles, held her as a shield in
front of him. He advanced on Mme de Brillot as she darted
from her car and flung Miss Seeton at her, knocking both
women to the ground. Jumping at Mme de Brillot, he hooked
his arm around her throat, forcing her head back to break her
neck.

"*If we meet trouble, wave your trick at 'em, smells or not.*"
Memory and instinct helped Miss Seeton to unzip the briefcase
and raise Mantoni's gun and, instinct failing her, memory
dragged up from some forgotten film or book:

"Halt, or I fire"—since neither memory nor instinct had
suggested "Stop, or I'll make a smell."

The words and tone caught his attention and Tolla saw the
pistol's silencer a bare foot from his face. He reared in alarm
and springing backward to get clear, he landed on the
umbrella's ferrule. Thus abused, the umbrella raised its crook
as though in protest and caught the ankle of his other leg, still
flailing for a foothold, and overturned him in a neat parabola.
In a series of backward somersaults he hurtled down the slope
and at the bottom crashed head on into a stone trough with
flowers, arched slowly and ungracefully over it and sprawled
into the Rue Saint Leger a little farther down than his late and
unlamented driver.

Thrudd, racing back across the road to take on the next
comer, lost his stride and nearly fell on seeing MissEss, her
hat over one ear, kneeling beside a prostrate Mme de Brillot,
holding a gun with some whacking great tube on the muzzle in
both hands and shooting the living daylights out of a black
man. And she'd said it only made a smell. Some pong. He'd
let her fool him again with her pretended innocence. Well, this
was it. The end. Next time he'd get behind her skirt and let her
call the deal. Reaction hit him now the affray was over. He'd

never killed a man before—never even thought in terms of killing. Weak-kneed, he tottered over.

"Congratulations, ma'am—nice marksmanship. You trained at Bisley?"

"But I didn't fire it," Miss Seeton protested. "I only waved it at him as you told me and he fell. It's dreadful. I'm very much afraid he broke his neck."

Mme de Brillot, on her feet, massaged her throat. "More quickly and more kind than what he tried to do to me."

"You all right?" Thrudd asked.

She nodded. "Yes, and thank you for what you did."

"Think nothing of it." The reporter was beginning to recover his aplomb. "Anytime—anytime at all; just call on me." He addressed Miss Seeton. "And you, MissEss, you thought I thought you shot him? Perish the thought. Never crossed my mind. I know the gun just jumped out of the case, then grabbed your hand and fired. Nothing to do with you. Just blind luck it knew which way to aim." He looked down the slope, past the passive umbrella, to where the remains of Tolla lay. "But between us, one way—and of course another—we've rather littered up the Rue Saint Leger." He glanced around. "Lucky there's nobody about up here at night—nor traffic down there. Still, with your permission"—he bowed—"maybe we'd best call the cops and get this place tidied up."

"Leave that to me, Mr. Banner." Mme de Brillot took command. "There is a crashed automobile on the Promenade Saint Antoine and"—her expression was bleak—"other matters to be what you call tidied up. I will inform the proper authorities and make arrangements. Where is your car?"

"By the hotel."

"Good. Then we will put Miss Seeton in the back and I will take you down to the Richesse." She pulled her seat forward to allow Miss Seeton, her handbag, her umbrella—none the worse for its adventure—and the briefcase with the pistol to squeeze into the narrow space behind, while Thrudd went around and opened the passenger door. "And please, Mr. Banner," she continued, "there must be no reporting of tonight's affair—unless you have permission from the police. You may find that they will prefer that the whole matter should be forgotten. Including," she added, "the fact that you have killed a man." Thrudd settled in his seat and for once in his professional life forbore to argue. Mme de Brillot's fingers lingered on the ignition key. "What happened to Mantoni?"

"Mantoni? That the little half-pint that was following MissEss? No idea, though I found his case in the passage. There's where our MissEss got her cannon. Maybe this Mantoni of yours was down the hole; the case was on the edge of it. Come to think of it, I kicked something when I jumped. Maybe it was him."

"Hole?"

"Yes, the passage is closed, with a whacking great hole in the fairway."

Miss Seeton was straightening her hat. "Yes," she agreed. "There was a board over it but when I crossed it, it tilted and fell in."

Oh, it did, did it? thought Thrudd, still under the influence of renewed skepticism. So that was why she'd hopped in there when she saw it was forbidden, pitched the board down the hole, laid in wait, then conked the little squirt and chucked him down as well. In God's name, why, he wondered, did everybody feel bound to protect MissEss? Protect? Talk about teaching your grandmother . . . "I expect," he suggested, "your Master Mantoni's down the pit still wondering"—he jerked a thumb toward the back seat—"who hit him."

Mantoni was not wondering who hit him. He knew. That wicked, terrible woman had ensnared him into a grave she had prepared, then, striking a match to gloat on what she had done, seeing him try to save himself, in cowardice, had hit him on the head with a stone, had traitorously stolen his case, his pistol, and had left him there for dead. He should have known—he should have recognized . . . Native superstition now held the Italian in thrall. Who but one with the evil eye could follow him as she had done? Know his every move as she had done? See through a painting as she had done? Mock him as she had done? Who but a sorceress would push aside a loaded pistol in contempt as she had done, knowing it could not harm her? *Allora,* now that he knew from where she derived her power, never, never would he come within her influence again. Whatever the man on the telephone in future might command, whatever he might say, he, Elio, would refute. Mantoni was not to learn until next day that the man on the telephone would say no more; and that the same grapevine of the underworld would inform him that single-handed this same sorceress had wrecked a car and then destroyed three men. All this and more he tried to explain through the muzziness of headache and a slight concussion to his fellow follower who had helped him out of the pit. Take care, he insisted, put yourself on guard, avoid her, for she is one of those who do not sleep in bed but fly by night.

Miss Seeton was preparing for bed. The events of the evening, which even she was forced to admit were unusual—for her, that was to say—had tired her a little. All that running. Thank heaven she had done her exercises earlier, or she would have been very stiff tomorrow morning. Also there was no denying that her habitual equanimity was disturbed. It would be some weeks before she would dismiss the affair, if by then she remembered it at all, as a manifestation of the instability of the foreign temperament. Meanwhile she had to face it and could not ignore, or not entirely, that she herself was in some measure involved, personally. Which did not suit her conception of her personality. Why should she, a modest, retired and retiring art teacher, become caught up in an immodest and vulgar brawl? Her natural resilience came to her rescue and produced the answer. She had not. It was, of course, nothing to do with her personally. Obviously it concerned those papers from the bank. Mr. Telmark had been most emphatic on the question of their privacy and someone must have discovered that they were, temporarily, in her possession and was determined to lay hands on them. She must make sure to get the papers back to Mr. Telmark first thing in the morning. She left the briefcase with the pistol on the occasional table, then taking her handbag with her, she knelt and pushed it under the bed. She straightened in confusion when the door behind her opened without warning.

"Madam der Bree-oh," she exclaimed. "I—I wasn't expecting you."

"Evidently." Mme de Brillot closed the door and crossed to the armchair by the table. "It is time to talk," she continued in a flat voice, "for the two of us." Under the light from the floor lamp her expression was somber. She looked—Miss Seeton sought for the adjective and found it—she looked implacable. So very like, in fact, that sketch that one had done of her as Lady Macbeth.

Although she had said that it was time to talk, Mme de
Brillot appeared to be in no hurry and Miss Seeton tried to
make conversation.

"Tell me, did you by any chance see Vee—I mean Miss
Galam? We left her by that alley. I didn't like to, but she said
that she must stay there, but that we shouldn't. Stay, I mean.
And Mr. Banner was insistent, too."

The Frenchwoman roused herself and cut in. "Yes, I saw
Vee. I am afraid that she has gone."

"Gone? Oh, I'm sorry," Miss Seeton regretted. "I should
like to have said good-bye and thank you. Such a kind person.
And that lovely voice. I did wonder if she had left when she
wasn't there at dinner. But later, at the top of that alley, when
she was—there, I mean—I imagined . . ."

Mme de Brillot's mouth twisted. "For once your imagination is at fault; she has gone. And now will you please tell me
what it is you know—what you have discovered that makes
them attack you."

"Why, yes, I . . ." Miss Seeton stopped. "You are a friend
of Mr. Telmark's, aren't you? You were with him in the picture
gallery."

Mme de Brillot rose, picked up the telephone receiver, asked
for a number and, after a moment:

"Karl?" She spoke rapidly in French, then, after another
pause: "*D'ac . . . D'ac . . . D'accord.*" She handed over
the receiver.

Distantly, metallically, Karl Telmark's voice told Miss
Seeton that she was to treat Mme de Brillot as himself, to tell
her anything, to discuss anything, with no reservations, none at
all. Miss Seeton knelt beside the bed, groped under it and
retrieved her handbag, took out the papers referring to the
deposits and withdrawals in the joint Stemkos account and
handed them to her visitor.

"It is these," she explained. "Mr. Telmark told me that they
were private, and, even though I don't entirely understand
them, I can see that they would be, and clearly someone is
trying to get hold of them."

Mme de Brillot flicked through the papers. "And you are
convinced that these are the sole reason for tonight's trouble?"

"Why, yes. What other reason could there be?"

Putting the papers on the table, Mme de Brillot noticed the
briefcase, opened it and extracted the pistol. "Do you always

hide your handbag beneath the bed and leave pistols lying on the table for anyone to take?"

Miss Seeton was indignant. "It has nothing to do with me. Mr. Banner told you he gave it me and that it belonged to that man you called Mantoni."

The Frenchwoman tipped the rest of the contents onto the table. A crumpled piece of paper caught her attention and she smoothed it out. "Is this the paper he snatched from you earlier this evening?"

Miss Seeton looked at it. "Oh, how very fortunate. It will save me having to write it out again."

"To whom do these jewels belong?"

"Jewels?" Miss Seeton floundered, then laughed. "It has nothing to do with jewelry. It's only a list of colors—rather fancifully put, perhaps, but a reminder, as it were, for when I try to work from memory after I've made a sketch of it by day. The lake, that is. Just one of my impressions of Geneva."

"One?" Mme de Brillot sat up. "There are others?"

"No," Miss Seeton answered quickly, then wilted under an accusing glance and ended lamely, "that is to say, no." Mme de Brillot held out her hand. "But I assure you," Miss Seeton protested, "that they are not impressions—not of the city, that is—but merely notes on people." The hand remained outstretched, reminding her of Chief Superintendent Delphick and the way in which he made her surrender any sketch that she made, however private, insisting that, since she was on a retainer to the Yard, he had the right to view all work she did during the course of an inquiry in case it should have some bearing. The reminder was so strong that she obediently fetched her sketchbook, unhappily aware of the likeness of her interlocutor as Lady Macbeth, which, like the list of colors, now appeared to her as "rather fancifully put, perhaps."

Mme de Brillot studied the drawings for a long time; so long indeed that Miss Seeton felt that some justification on her part was necessary.

"I think, perhaps—" she began.

"*J'vous en prie.*" The other waved her to silence.

Could this woman be the innocent she would appear, or was she an intrigant? The caricatures were clever—some, like the one of Natalie Stemkos as a pair of nutcrackers, wickedly so; all ruthlessly exposed character. She reexamined the sketch of the overpainted Gainsborough—another type of exposure. But was it possible that so much revelation could derive from nothing but intuition? Or was it based on knowledge? She raised her head, her eyes accusing.

"My reputation is to be gay, superficial and amusing, and I flatter myself I play the part well. You depict me as *une femme fatale*, with cloak and dagger. Why?"

"I . . ." Miss Seeton was at a loss. "It just came out like that. I didn't mean it to. It was meant to be a study of the bones. But I did wonder afterward if, perhaps, at one time, you'd been upon the stage. Lady Macbeth, you see."

A flicker of amusement at the lips. "No, I have never acted—on the stage. You draw Vee Galam as a boy and surround the head with wig, false eyelashes, et cetera, in mockery. Why?"

Miss Seeton was roused. "I did nothing of the kind. In mockery, I mean. It's only that the hair and lashes were so very extreme that I tried, by taking them off, to see what was beneath."

The lips twisted wryly. "You succeeded." Mme de Brillot examined again the head of the boy she had once known as Vincent Gardnor—one of the most promising, bravest and most reliable of their younger operatives. Vincent, who, after a more bitter and prolonged struggle with his own nature and his inclinations than ever he had waged against his country's adversaries, had undergone an operation, changed his sex, but had remained with them as Vee—for Vivienne, Ventura, Veronica, always V—and, using fantastical makeup as disguise, had still remained their best, their bravest and their most reliable operative. "So be it." She handed back the sketchbook. "Though, if I may, I will borrow this later to take photostats. I will take a risk and will rely entirely on your judgment of these characters and we will act on the assumption that you know these people better than they know themselves."

"But I don't," expostulated Miss Seeton. "I don't know them at all. Those are only private notes of how they seem to me."

The Frenchwoman's expression lightened and the blue eyes began to sparkle. "In regard to Natalie Stemkos as a nutcracker—she seems so to me too. That one I know is true. Elio Mantoni skiing toward a precipice on paintbrushes for skis—likely to be true. Librecksin as the Devil spearing a litter of paper money with a two-pronged fork—I believe to be true.

nd Heracles Stemkos as your jolly English King Cole—that
e will now pray to be true."

Her decision made, she moved quickly to the bed, sat and
.ed the telephone. After the number had been obtained Miss
:eton concentrated on the rapid flow of French, of which all
le caught was "Monsieur Stemkos? . . . Mme de Brillot
•mething . . . Miss Seeton . . . Hôtel de la Riches-
. . ." then a lot which she failed to understand, followed
' the inevitable "duck . . . duck," which she now recog-
zed must be a shortened version of *d'accord*—that was to
y, "It is agreed"—and finally "something . . . some-
ing . . . *En dix minutes*."

Mme de Brillot put down the receiver, lifted it again and
•oke to room service. "*Trois cafés en dix minutes, avec*"—
le considered—"*avec alors du paté de fois, des friandises,
    également,*" she supplemented, "*du cognac et du
hisky. . . . Entendu, en dix minutes.*"

She returned to her chair, shuffled Miss Seeton's sketches
to order, laid on top of them the reports from the Banque du
ac, then, on a thought, searched in her bag and found a
:wspaper cutting from the previous week which read:

MME STEMKOS ROBBED IN PARIS

At the Hotel Ritz-Palais, the beautiful Mme Stemkos,
fifth wife of Heracles Stemkos, the Greek shipping
millionaire, was attacked and robbed of thousands of
pounds' worth of jewels. A chambermaid discovered
Mme Stemkos bound and gagged in a chair and the room
rifled.

Last night Mme Stemkos was still too shocked to
comment, but it is believed that the value of the jewels
stolen runs into hundreds of thousands of pounds. The
police have a full description of the stolen items, some
only recently purchased and all fortunately insured.

She placed the cutting among the bank papers, glanced
•und the room, fetched an upright chair from the writing
ible, ousted Miss Seeton's clothes from another, grouped the
hairs round the table and sat down again, satisfied with her
rrangements.

"*B'en,*" she remarked. "We are now in the hands of God, or

rather"—her eyes twinkled at Miss Seeton—"in yours—
though we will pray that the good God takes over the business
If He does not, my career will be cooked to a point and yo
will return to your village to do whatever it is you do i
villages—always provided that we live."

Miss Seeton smiled in sympathy. It was so pleasant to se
her visitor animated again after the sad embittered woman wh
had entered the room.

"You," said Mme de Brillot, pointing, "will place yourse
there, I here and we will put M. Stemkos in the armchair t
improve his mood."

"Mr. Stemkos?"

"Oh, la-la, I forgot to translate. M. Stemkos will be here i
a few minutes and I have ordered coffee, brandy, whiskey an
some bagatelles to eat, all for the sake of improving his moo
and, let us hope, increasing his understanding."

"But why—" Miss Seeton began, then, looking dowr
"Good gracious, I must dress." Did people abroad, sh
wondered, always arrange meals in other people's bedroon
late at night? So like what one had read of bohemian Paris i
the olden days—Trilby, and things like that.

"You cannot dress now," Mme de Brillot informed her. "W
do not want to waste time when he arrives. And better"—sh
laughed for the first time that evening—"much better to b
caught in a very proper dressing gown than in imprope
déshabillé, and we shall give him so much to think of that h
will have no opportunity to imagine that either of us is trying t
seduce him. *Tiens*—" She put the silenced pistol on top of th
briefcase. "There, that will add a touch of drama and len
weight to our story." Miss Seeton opened her mouth to say—
What could one say? In the event she was forestalled by
knock upon the door. Mme de Brillot rose. "*Entrez,*" sh
called.

A waiter entered and announced, "M. Stemkos, me:
dames."

Heracles Stemkos bustled in, followed by the waite
wheeling a laden trolley. While greetings were exchanged th
waiter arranged the trolley and put cups and plates upon th
table. His eyes widened when he saw the pistol. Finished, h
bowed and murmured, " 'Sieur et 'dames," and withdrew, h
eyes still wide and shining with anticipatory joy. What a mis:
this English one. Such a one introduced a flavor into the life c

hotel. First she ties herself in knots and now she entertains at midnight in her night attire the *beau monde* and the opulent with coffee for three and guns for one. What a miss.

There was no jollity in the attitude of Heracles Stemkos. By a narrow margin he remained polite and, in deference to Miss Seeton, the conversation was conducted in English, but he made it clear that he resented being called out late at night however important the matter and, although he was prepared to acknowledge that Mme de Brillot would not have arranged this somewhat unconventional meeting had there not been a question of urgency, he implied that he would prefer the urgency and the importance to take precedence over social niceties, including food and drink.

To match his mood Mme de Brillot put on a pair of horn-rimmed glasses and became the brisk business executive and Miss Seeton began to appreciate the pause the Frenchwoman had made when saying she had never acted—upon the stage.

Stemkos heard the summary of the bank statements in silence, skimmed through the papers, frowned and remarked:

"These are private matters between the bank and myself. How did you get hold of them?"

"They were given to Miss Seeton."

"Who by?"

"The director of the bank, Karl Telmark."

"I see." He turned to glare at Miss Seeton. "And who are you that Telmark makes so free of my affairs?"

"Why, nobody," said Miss Seeton. "It's just that Mr. Telmark sent for me, or so I understood, to draw something, or somebody, though he hasn't yet told me what. Or whom," she added in the interest of grammar. "But he insisted, first, that I should understand the background and this—these—or rather those"—she indicated the papers—"are it. The background, that is. Though, actually, I didn't. Understand it, I mean."

"You won't need to—nor will Telmark. I'll stop his handling of my affairs tomorrow morning."

"That," said Mme de Brillot, "is your privilege; just as it is your privilege to commit professional and social suicide, since it is your privilege to be a fool and to pass judgment without knowledge of the facts, relying quite entirely on your own prejudices." She gathered up the papers and the drawings.

Not since his divorce from his first wife had Heracles Stemkos had to endure plain speaking and he empurpled under

the whiplash. He got to his feet and made to take the bank
statements. "Leave those," he rapped. "They're mine."

"Then collect them from Karl Telmark in the morning. I am
not entitled to return them to you. They have been entrusted to
an agent of Scotland Yard, with the knowledge and approval of
the police and the Sûreté here, by arrangement with the Bank
of England and the sanction of the British government in
conjunction with the Crédit Suisse, the Swiss Bank Corporation and the Banque du Lac."

Stemkos was dumbfounded. "Agent? For . . . ?"

"You wished to know who Miss Seeton was. Now you do."

Paying no heed to Miss Seeton's disclaimer, "But I assure
you . . ." Stemkos sat down heavily.

"Explain."

Unknowing, his hand strayed toward the napkin-wrapped
toast. Mme de Brillot casually pushed butter and foie gras
nearer, went to the trolley, poured coffee, handed it to Miss
Seeton with the salver of *friandises,* gave her a wink and traced
a gesture of finger on lip, poured a strong whiskey for their
guest and a weak one for herself, settled on her chair, adjusted
her glasses and proceeded to expound.

Stemkos listened tight-lipped, tallying amounts and dates in
the lists and making notes. He did not relish the juxtaposition
of the newspaper cutting, nor the implication that he had been
cuckolded by his secretary both maritally and professionally,
but the inference was unavoidable and he accepted it.

"How much," he asked, "of this forged English money am
I held responsible for?"

"None," said Mme de Brillot, "since we, in this room, are
assuming that you knew nothing of it."

"And the British government and the Bank, do they agree
with you?"

"No." She was frank. "They have not made up their
minds."

"Why have you?"

"Because of that." She held out Miss Seeton's cartoon of
him. He looked at the black minstrel version of himself, seated
spread-legged on a throne, the ermine-trimmed cloak corded
loosely across his chest, the paper crown set at a jaunty angle
over one eye, and was forced to grin, making the likeness to
the caricature complete. "That is Miss Seeton's assessment of

your character and on that assessment alone we decided to risk this meeting.

He bowed toward Miss Seeton. "I am honored."

Miss Seeton smiled but said nothing. Not for anything would she speak. Mme de Brillot had cautioned her to silence and she was fascinated to watch the way in which this very, very clever woman played her cards. And was playing Mr. Stemkos too. At the beginning, when he had been so angry, he had looked such a dangerous man. But now the atmosphere was changing. And if Mme de Brillot was twisting the truth and facts a little here and there—especially with regard to oneself—to suit her own purpose, that purpose was still, one was convinced, a good one. And if keeping silent helped, then silent she would be.

The millionaire returned to Mme de Brillot. "And had the assessment of my character been wrong, was this"—he waved at the pistol—"your next line of persuasion—or defense?"

The Frenchwoman removed her glasses and her blue eyes flashed with laughter. "No, that belongs to the next chapter of this history. *Figurez-vous* . . ." Slipping into French, she described Miss Seeton's journeyings, her escapades and their sequels, leaving him to draw his own conclusions. She showed him the sketch of the overpainted Gainsborough, adding that x rays had proved Miss Seeton right and that owing to her the stolen paintings had been recovered. Then she let him see their hostess' appraisement of the various characters involved, with the exception of her own and Vee's, and left the sketches to speak for themselves.

Stemkos viewed Miss Seeton with a new respect. So this meek little mouse had penetrated to the center of a web; her air of simplicity must be assumed. For his own part he would have a session with Telmark in the morning, contact the Paris office and set some inquiries in train. He could . . . "What is this tune you mentioned which was repeated?"

"The 'Song of India,' from *Sadko.*"

He could . . . short notice, but by applying some pressure in the right quarters, he could give a dinner party tomorrow—he noticed the time—no, tonight, have some music and watch the effect of Miss Seeton's appearance on his wife and secretary. Stemkos got to his feet.

"You will both dine with me tonight—informal—a snack, at such short notice. What," he asked Miss Seeton, "is your choice?'' She rose but was too surprised to speak. "There must be some dish you have missed since you left England. Name it.''

She thought of the overindulgence, the overabundance of rich food that she had suffered recently. Something that she had missed? How kind of Mr. Stemkos. Well, actually, there was. One would so enjoy plain . . .

"Scrambled eggs," said Miss Seeton.

Sir Hubert Everleigh surveyed his crowded office. If any more departments wished to be represented at these conferences—or as he privately thought of them, these Seeton Sessions—they'd need to be held in the board room. He would be intrigued to know what had brought Duncan Oblon over from the Foreign and Commonwealth Office with some urgent query that had to be settled by midday. So far Oblon had contributed nothing to the discussion, but presumably time would tell, and it would have been a waste of their time to have proposed that his problem should have been dealt with first on the agenda. The F.C.O. gentry were not to be hurried. They liked to weigh pros with the same deliberation with which they balanced cons, and they preferred to brood over everybody else's estimate of a situation before coming to some such momentous decision as that final judgment should be deferred until some later date.

Fenn, he thought, was looking tired. Hadn't uttered so far, and indeed appeared to be asleep.

"Then we can take it," he asked Inspector Borden, "that the case against Estevel is going satisfactorily?"

"He's badly rattled, sir. We saw him again at his flat and he blew his top. He's running scared and it shouldn't take long now. It's his wife and kids I'm sorry for. I don't think she's a clue what he's been up to."

Sir Hubert made a grimace of distaste. "Typical. Like all traitors—they want to occupy first, second and third place. Family and friends aren't entered in the race—but nothing we can do there to help, that I can see. Is there," he inquired, "any further business, or should I say development, any of you gentlemen wish to treat of?"

Commander Conway cleared his throat. "One development, sir, but it's still a bit soon yet to do more than guess at what it means. The stream of forgeries pouring into the Bank of England is less—"

"Down to a trickle," corroborated Jonathan Feldman.

"Also there is a rumor, unconfirmed, that Tolla's dead."

"Rumor confirmed," stated Fenn without opening his eyes. There was a general movement of surprise. "And can we take that as official?" queried Sir Hubert.

Fenn's eyes opened. "Not official, A.C., in the sense that you can send a wreath or congratulations, but, yes, you can take it as read."

Commander Conway smiled. "You're not telling us that he came up against MissEss and that she settled his hash?"

"He trod on her umbrella and it bit him and he died of it. But since he'd established residence in Switzerland and was working for, and against, half the countries in the U.N., they thought it best to let him disappear without trace."

"So," remarked the A.C., "there's been a death. Let us hope that that's the end of it. But in these affairs, or I should say in my experience of these matters, one death—"

"Four." Sir Hubert straightened. "Three of theirs, one of ours," amplified Fenn. "Theirs didn't matter—ours did."

In view of Fenn's grim mien, no one liked to break the silence. Inspector Borden tried to switch the subject.

"The Duke of Belton's pictures are back in the Abbey. The official story goes that he'd forgotten he'd taken them down for cleaning. The story doesn't go with us, as the Swiss asked us to meet 'em at the airport and escort 'em home. They said nothing about the where, why or what have you, but the word I got was that MissEss breezed into some gallery or other, gave the pictures the once-over, wagged her brolly, said, 'That, that, that and that,' and breezed out again." He glanced at Fenn. "I always thought that Tolla was behind the stolen-picture racket."

"He was," agreed Fenn, "and Miss Seeton blew it—at the art museum. But since"—he turned to Jonathan Feldman—"your friend Telmark is a director of the museum as well as the Banque du Lac, and is also her official employer, pro tem, that story was sat on."

Oblon coughed. "I—er—we at the F.O. need a spot of advice." All eyes turned to him. "Is the ambassador to dine with Stemkos tonight, or not? I mean," he supplemented, on seeing their blank expressions, "the dinner's in honor of this woman, this Miss—er—Seeton. I believe Belgium's going, but do we? What we need to know is, is Stemkos in the clear? Invitation only came this morning, so easy enough to plead prior do. But could be a spot unwise, as Stemkos usually rates a spot of priority. Puts us in a bit of a—er—spot."

Sir Hubert hid a smile. It wasn't often that the police were asked to adjudicate on the priorities of entertainment at ambassadorial level. "Your province, Mr. Fenn, I think."

Fenn accepted the pass. "No proof either way. His secretary's bent, and I'd say so's his wife."

Oblon was aghast. "In that case, definitely, we'd better—"

"You'd better," interrupted Fenn, "rely on Miss Seeton like the rest of us. She considers Stemkos is jolly. And since she, and others, are risking their lives on that assumption I don't see why your ambassador can't risk," he mimicked acidly, "a spot of indigestion."

The chef had tried.

Scrumbledeggs Miss Seeton

·

Riz de Veau Emilie

·

Bœuf en croute Dorothée

·

Pommes Nouvelles • Haricots Verts

·

Bombe Miss Seeton en Surprise

Reading her individual menu, Miss Seeton's appetite shrank. If this was Mr. Stemkos' idea of a snack, what, she wondered, must be his idea of a full-course meal. Also his little joke of putting her name to the different courses. So embarrassing.

However, she comforted herself that few of the guests, some twenty in all were likely to detect the teasing.

Mr. Stemkos himself, on her left, although punctilious, appeared preoccupied. She was not to know that the conference with Karl Telmark that morning had given him reason for preoccupation. Apart from confirmation of all he had learned the night before, he had discovered that his wife had forestalled him, visiting the bank immediately upon its opening, and had had access to their joint deposit box. He and Telmark had repaired to the vaults, taken the box to one of the cubicles outside the grille for examination and found that it contained two parcels. One had proved to be a wad of new English five-pound notes which, by lunchtime, were confirmed to be forgeries, the other had held the full complement of the "stolen" jewelry on which his wife was claiming insurance in Paris. With Miss Seeton's list of colors before him, he had examined the stones and sent for a lapidarist. The list had been exact: the colored stones were real; the diamonds false.

On the opposite side of the table Belgium's representative noticed his host's absorption. He asked Miss Seeton if she spoke French and, on her admission of "Tray per," said that with the permission of the princess—he bowed to the lady on his right—he would be grateful for the opportunity to practice his English. Princess Lefardi, elderly, with darting eyes and snapping jaws which gave her a vulpine look, raised bony shoulders; red-tipped claws spread languages in the air before her—of five she had no preference. On Miss Seeton's other side the British ambassador, who had been dreading some overearnest arty female and was delighted with this quaint reincarnation of a favorite aunt, black lace and all, laid himself out to entertain and to amuse.

Gold plates? One had read about such things, but never had one thought to see them. Did one, Miss Seeton wondered, eat off them? Might it not scratch the surface? She was relieved when exquisite Paris china was laid atop and she was offered an iced dish of yellow paste surmounted by what looked like grayish tapioca. She helped herself with caution, added the trappings of minced onion and a wedge of lemon and accepted two small hot rounds like pancakes. Scrambled eggs? The yellow paste proved to be quite simply that. For the rest, although caviar is reputed to be an acquired taste, Miss Seeton took to it at once and also took, unusual in her case, a second helping.

She ate delicious food, sipped wines and chatted with ambassadors and the only break in the pleasant flow, bringing her back to the reason behind this party, was when the string trio providing background music began the soft evocative plaint of the "Song of India." The nostalgic mood of the melody was unexpectedly torn as Anatole Librecksin, toward the far end of the table, jerked and snapped his wineglass stem.

Tension had been building in Librecksin. The fiasco of the previous night's attempt upon Miss Seeton, ending in Tolla's death, had tumbled his plans and he had spent the day trying to pick up and rejoin the threads of the black man's organization insofar as they affected his own projects. Never before had he had to appear in person on the darker side of the moon, interviewing and instructing men who later would be able to identify him. He had dispatched the panic-stricken Mantoni to Paris with orders to get in touch with a contact of his own, a girl called Lilianne, one of the *figurantes* who was rehearsing for a new revue at the Casino de Paris. She would arrange for a studio and provide him with paintings, stolen in France, which the Italian was to disguise.

Librecksin rated his position. The two men concerned with the theft of the paintings; the man who had staged the theft of the jewelry in Paris; Mantoni; Lilianne herself—all could be directly linked or traced back to him. The question of Miss Seeton's removal he would now have to deal with personally—and soon—since his employer's unexplained departure in the middle of the previous night, followed by this hastily arranged dinner in her honor, had added to his anxieties. Also this playing of the "Song of India" could not be chance and if, as he suspected, it was a ruse engendered by Stemkos to test his reaction, it was a test which he had failed to pass. It rang the knell to his original aim: with his employer discredited, he himself would be the logical candidate to hold the reins of the Stemkos empire or, failing that, to become the manipulator of whatever puppet the shareholders should elect. Owing to this woman's machinations, his carefully nurtured, jealousy guarded image as the power behind the Stemkos throne was endangered. His alternative, his insurance policy against failure—flight—was being forced upon him.

Natalie had collected the diamonds from the bank this morning and he was keeping them on his person in case of such an enforced departure. He wished that he had told her to take

out the last remaining packet of forged notes at the same time.
However, except in the unlikely event of Stemkos having
occasion to open the box, there was no possibility of their
being discovered until he himself was safely out of the country.
He had already warned Natalie of the threat that Miss Seeton
constituted to their schemes and that in consequence there
might be little time left to them. But if this Seeton female was
eliminated, there might still be a chance to recover his
position.

In apologizing to his hostess for maladroitness, his eyes
flashed her a warning: time had run out.

Time. Natalie Stemkos pressed on the accelerator. Anatole
had insisted that it was essential to get the timing right;
imperative, too, to keep an eye on her driving mirror as she
neared the Italian frontier; vital that he should be directly
behind her when they entered the tunnel.

Miss Seeton was grateful that her companion had spoken
little during the long drive. The changing scenery, especially
on nearing Mont Blanc, engrossed her.

Mme Stemkos had arrived soon after ten o'clock at the
Richesse with a letter signed *Heracles Stemkos* which stated
that he would expect Miss Seeton for lunch at Filippo's, the
famous hors d'œuvre restaurant just over the border in Italy on
the far side of the Mont Blanc tunnel. He reckoned that both
Filippo's and the tunnel were experiences which she should not
miss during her visit to Switzerland. He, the letter had said,
was impelled to be in northern Italy on business and his wife
would drive her to the rendezvous.

Miss Seeton was in no position to refuse such an invitation,
which was, in any case, clearly, so very well meant. Certainly
to see the famous tunnel would be interesting, and a restaurant
which only served hors d'œuvre would be a relief after the
enormous meals which appeared to be the rule abroad.

Being lunchtime, there was not the habitual queue of cars at
the tunnel's entrance and the man in charge, after a brief
question, passed them straight through and turned to the only
other car in view behind them. Miss Seeton had been intrigued
to notice two men busy over a large wall map in the
background. They, Mme Stemkos told her, followed the course
of each car through the tunnel, checking its speed and its
position, particularly in relation to other cars. The tunnel

impressed Miss Seeton: its seemingly interminable length; its
signs, in figures, which her *chauffeuse* explained, gave the
prescribed speed for different sections and would flash a
warning if the speed was not adhered to, or too close an
approach was made to the vehicle in front; the different-sized
lay-bys, for maintenance, for lorries and for cars; but above
all, as they proceeded, the tunnel's endlessly diminishing point
of distance, which produced the hypnotic impression that they
needed to drive ever faster in order to stay still. What she had
not expected were the occassional patches of damp where
seepage running down the walls made short stretches of the
road glisten like glass under the lights.

Before one such patch the car began to falter. Mme Stemkos
exclaimed impatiently in French. The engine stopped and the
car braked to a halt. A few feet ahead to their right was a lay-by
and, beyond it, the round sign on the wall, marked 100, began
to flash its warning. Headlights were bearing down on them
from behind and Natalie Stemkos jabbed helplessly at the
starter.

"Quick," she gasped, "an accident. I will guide and you
push from behind."

Miss Seeton ran to the back of the car, but as she leaned her
weight against it the engine caught and the car sprang forward
into the shelter of the lay-by, throwing Miss Seeton to her
knees.

The insistent flicker of the signs, the blaze of the nearing
headlights, the blare of the car's horn; behind it again yet
brighter lights, a more strident horn; the double roar of engines
at full throttle, and in the distance the beginning rise and fall of
police sirens, combined to hold her in thrall and for a space
Miss Seeton knelt there petrified. She jumped to her feet,
prepared to run. But where? A lorry was thundering toward her
from the opposite direction. She was trapped. With bare inches
to spare from the lorry's bonnet, a flash of red flicked round the
car bearing down on her and, with its tires shrieking in a
controlled skid, rocked to a stop beside her. The door swung
open.

"In," cried Mme de Brillot.

Miss Seeton sprawled obedience and the Lancia spurted
forward as Librecksin, swerving to avoid a collision, lost
control on the wet surface and crashed into the lay-by. One
thin, high scream rose above the cacophony of tearing metal

and splintering glass, and the lorry driver leaped from his cab to help, thankful for the first time in his driving life to hear the pulsating wail of police cars racing toward him.

Two police cars followed by a small white ambulance, their blue roof lights winking, forced their way past the occasional traffic in the opposite lane and whipped by them. Miss Seeton sat shocked. It had been so very near. If it hadn't been for Mme de Brillot . . . Vaguely she remembered hearing the sound of a smash as they fled the scene. Oughtn't they to have stayed? One did so hope that no one had been . . . hurt? If it hadn't been for Mme de Brillot, Miss Seeton was beginning to realize, she herself would have been killed. The car was making a whining noise which seemed familiar. Oh, yes—her mind was clearing—so very like the noise the airplanes made before they left the ground. A pointer of a large dial on the dashboard touched 180. One knew that this would not be miles because abroad they had kilometers. And were they more—or less? One did trust they wouldn't leave the ground, though, frankly, at this speed it wouldn't be surprising. A stationary car loomed ahead of them and the Lancia cut round it illegally, to the continuing and futile protests from the speed indicators on the wall, which now read 80. It wasn't until they were actually abreast that she realized that the "stationary" car was moving. A slight curve, a half circle of daylight in the distance, and the end of the tunnel rushed at them. The whine of the Lancia deepened, to become the normal sound of a car engine as it slowed, and Mme de Brillot brought it to a halt at a barricade set across the entrance. Men in uniform surrounded them, the doors were snatched open, they were ordered out and marched into a building on their left.

Miss Seeton understood little of the ensuing interrogation. Mme de Brillot talked, produced papers. The officer who appeared to be in charge spoke on the telephone; then Mme de Brillot spoke, handed back the receiver; the officer spoke again, and Miss Seeton did notice that the atmosphere was becoming warmer. Even friendly.

"What," Mme de Brillot asked her, "induced you to set out on this expedition?" Miss Seeton quoted the letter. Did she have it? No, Mrs. Stemkos had it. Mme de Brillot exchanged looks and shrugs with the officer. *"Soit,"* she exclaimed. "You were offered a lunch at La Maison de Filippo. This charming gentleman and his *confrères*"—a wave of the hand indicated

the other officers around them—"wish us to remain a little, in
case we can be of assistance. So we will attend them at
Filippo's and you shall have your promised lunch."

They shook hands all around, were ushered back to the car
with much circumstance and drove the few yards to the Italian
customs post armed with a temporary pass for Miss Seeton and
an assurance that her handbag with her passport and her
umbrella should be searched for immediately and returned to
her.

By way of firred slopes, the mottled gray and brown of
rocks, with snow-capped peaks towering over them, they
wound their way up past the clustering rough stone dwellings,
with their unequal slated roofs, of the tiny village, until the
Lancia stopped before a large chalet which, although its fabric
was more stone than timber, still gave Miss Seeton the
impression that a cuckoo on a wire spring might launch itself
from an upper window at any moment.

They were shown to a table on a balcony and tray after tray
of plates were served. Miss Seeton eyed the twenty-odd
platters of hors d'œuvre with misgiving. So many varieties to
choose from. But then, after all, it was not necessary to sample
everything. But, then again, so difficult to make one's choice.
All looked delicious. She looked down over the carved rail of
the balcony to the courtyard below. What an attractive place.
The pink-and-white-checked tablecloths, the rough wooden
benches, the tall tree, circled by a wooden platform, on which
stood bowls of fruit and the inevitable stone troughs filled with
flowers. Back of the tree, a small aviary and coffee tables. At
one of these . . . Miss Seeton frowned.

"What is it?" asked Mme de Brillot.

Miss Seeton started. "Nothing. It's just that I . . . No—
nothing." She came back to the matter in hand. The choice.
She began to help herself.

"Do you like pasta?" Surprised, Miss Seeton admitted that
she did. "Then take very little of this course," advised her
mentor, "omit altogether the next course of hot hors d'œuvre,
which are ham, beef and lamb, and concentrate on the pasta
hors d'œuvre which follow and are delicious, and finish with
the ice cream hors d'œuvre, which is superb." She might have
known it, Miss Seeton reflected. No meal abroad would be as
simple as it sounded.

Between courses Miss Seeton continued to puzzle over the man having coffee at a table by the tree. Mme de Brillot watched her. With the help of new surroundings, an adroit turn of conversation and the help of the police, the Sûreté and the customs officers, she had succeeded in relegating the attempted murder in the tunnel to the back of her guest's mind. It would be raised again. They had yet to learn the result of the crash behind them. Inevitably there would be more questioning; depositions. But meanwhile, what was it that MissEss had seen down there? She had learned that it was to treat any aberration on Miss Seeton's part with due respect. So she smiled at the debonair young Filippo, who had come to inquire if the meal had been to their satisfaction, and told him that they would take their coffee down below.

On the way down the wooden planks which served as a railless staircase, Miss Seeton stopped suddenly beside one of the baskets of mixed fruits which bordered the outer edge. Of course. She remembered now. "The wrong pajamas."

"The—the what?"

Hastily Miss Seeton explained. "Oh, I don't mean pajamas. It's just that—well, that's how I remember him. More likely, papers. And, possibly, a toothbrush. Which would have been wrong, too. Not his, I mean."

Mme de Brillot began to worry. This funny little woman—so simple; so imperturbable in crises—it was easy to forget she was no longer young. Had that terrifying experience in the tunnel affected her more than one had realized?

Miss Seeton continued to expound. She described the incident at Heathrow when the gentleman at her table had been humming that tune by Tchaikovsky—Rimsky-Korsakov, mentally corrected her companion—and this other gentleman had come to borrow sugar, and the mix-up over the briefcases, although the first gentleman—the one who she knew was called Mantoni—had denied it, but she was still quite sure that she was right, and the second gentleman—the one who'd wanted sugar—"is here"—she pointed downward—"having coffee."

Mme de Brillot unraveled the skein. "Good," she announced. "Then this sugar borrower shall be diverted. We will entertain him with a song and see what arrives."

The Frenchman was nearing the point of desparation. His instructions had been clear: lunch in the yard at Filippo's,

where contact and exchange of cases would be made. He had
been pleased. Filippo's: a good choice; a busy restaurant; and,
for himself, no frontier to cross; no customs to question him;
both would be the contact's responsibility. And after this, his
last assignment with the forged notes, he would be free to
return to France and food cooked in butter instead of oil.

But no contact had been made. No one had so much as
whistled the "Song of India." This was the third day running
on which he had overindulged in Filippo's interpretation of
hors d'œuvre, and his stomach was by now as troubled as his
mind. He had tried, repeatedly he had tried, to telephone the
only number he knew in Geneva. The first day—no answer.
The second day—an answer, but instinct had warned him that
the answering voice was wrong. He had operated too long on
the other side of the sticks not to recognize the official, the
police, voice when he heard it. This morning again had been
the same and he had replaced the receiver without speaking.
Something had gone wrong. He had combed the newspapers to
no avail; he could find nothing in them to give him a clue as to
what might have happened; though even had Tolla's death been
reported, the name would have meant nothing to him. The
trouble of running a business in watertight compartments is
that, should the main spring a leak, the other compartments
must dry out through lack of supply. Apart from the telephone
number he had no means of communication, so there was
nothing he could do except continue to overeat and hope.

He glanced up as an attractive fair woman—mentally he
dubbed her *une jolie laide*—and an older woman came through
the doorway and seated themselves at a table near him. An
older . . . He looked again. But—he remembered her. That
older woman had been at London Airport. Hope began to
burgeon—or could it be some form of trap?

As they sat themselves, it dawned on Mme de Brillot that
Miss Seeton was for once unarmed—both her handbag and her
umbrella had been in Natalie Stemkos' car. She therefore put
her own bag on the ground beside her chair and hoped that it
would suffice.

A girl came and set a wooden bowl with a carved lid on the
table. Miss Seeton was intrigued. Around the rim of the bowl
were holes. No, really more like stubby spouts. It resembled a
bowl such as one might see in a florist's with some clever

flower arrangement; except that in this case wisps of steam were escaping from the spouts, together with a pungent aroma of coffee. She waited for the girl to bring cups.

"Now," murmured Mme de Brillot. "Hum the tune."

Miss Seeton blushed. No, really. The morning's events, plus too much delicious food and a slightly sparkling wine, to which she was not accustomed, were combining to take effect. But even so—no, really, she did not think she could.

"I'm afraid," she apologized, "that I'm not very musical. I—I don't think I could."

Her companion lifted the bowl and drank from one of the spouts. Miss Seeton watched, astonished, and, receiving the bowl in her turn, approached her mouth tentatively to another spout. Her eyes watered and she blinked.

"It's much too hot," she protested.

No, not too hot, she was assured. "Try it." Miss Seeton sipped. Fire coursed down her and she nearly dropped the bowl. "It's called," Mme de Brillot told her, "*le café de l'amitié*—the coffee of friendship. It's an old Valdostani custom. Try it again."

Miss Seeton imbibed more hot brandy flavored with coffee, sugar and orange peel. With concentration and care she lowered the bowl to the table. The facade of the chalet with its balconies wavered slightly: there seemed to be more tables in the courtyard—more, and they shimmered; in fact everything was shimmering, just a little.

"Now," commanded Mme de Brillot. "Hum."

Hum? Well, one did, one would be the first to admit, owe Mme de Brillot a great deal . . . And if, as she seemed to think—as Mme de Brillot seemed to think—it was important, one must, of course, try. Slowly, flatly, gathering Dutch courage and changing from different to indifferent key, Miss Seeton began to hum.

In a sweet clear soprano, Mme de Brillot took up the second half of the melody:

"Ho-ors de-es flo-ots ti-i-è-è-è-des
U-un ru-u-bi-is s'é-é-lè-lè-è-ve."

Clever—very clever. The Frenchman listened in admiration. It was evident, in fact, that something had gone wrong, and that this was the old woman's way of putting the thing right.

And he, too, had been right in continuing to come here. He felt a surge of relief. At last he would get rid of these accursed, these dangerous notes. He would receive his money and he could go home. That little woman must be of the front rank, and at London Airport she had been there to watch, to make a check. He scrutinized Miss Seeton again. Never, never would he have suspected her. So clever. And to sing the song between them as though discussing and reminding each other of the tune—so natural, and so clever. And then, since ladies do not carry briefcases, to arrange for only one of them to have a handbag so that he should know what to take. But so very, very clever.

He signaled for his bill, pocketed his change, took his receipt and, moving forward, allowed it to slip from his fingers.

"Pardon, mesdames." He stopped, put down his briefcase, retrieved the piece of paper and picked up Mme de Brillot's bag.

Its owner laid her hand upon his wrist. With a grimace of pain he froze in position, unable even to relax his fingers and drop the bag.

Three cars drew up before the low stone wall that divided the courtyard from the road. From the first sprang three officers, one of them bearing in triumph Miss Seeton's handbag and umbrella, and with smiles of recognition they hurried to the table.

The remaining two vehicles were the tag of Miss Seeton's retinue. A Sûreté man hurried from one of them, took stock of the position in the yard, and disappeared into Filippo's determined upon sustenance for himself and his partner while they had the chance.

Thrudd Banner sauntered from the last car and sat down on the wall. Uhuh. Quite a headline morning. Natalie Stemkos calls for MissEss and heads for Italy. Odd. Librecksin follows in another car. Odder. The Stemkos frail killed in the tunnel in a mix-up with Librecksin's car. Oddest yet—especially in view of current gossip. No trace of Librecksin in or out of the wreckage. Definitely odd—and fretting the police somewhat. And then, trust MissEss to come up with her own particular brand of oddity. Goes into the tunnel in one car and, ignoring trifles like wrecked cars and a body, sails out in another to guzzle lunch and brandy here. He'd nearly missed this end of it at that. By the time the traffic was unsnarled and on its way again he'd lost the track. But a policeman carrying a lady's umbrella, circa 1910, had clued him and . . .

Thrudd brought his camera up and took pictures as two of the officers marched the Frenchman to their waiting car.

When the third officer left carrying a briefcase, Mme de Brillot paid the bill. Thrudd intercepted the women as they reached the Lancia.

"Just a little thing. I've got the tunnel stuff, with pictures, but this follow-up—the man you've just had pinched. Can I have the story, or is it another hush?"

Mme de Brillot's blue eyes shone with mischief. "But no, Mr. Banner, it is not hush. It is all quite simple and you are welcome to it. We were sitting there"—she indicated—"he there"—she pointed—"and—this can happen in the Val d'Aosta—Miss Seeton seduced him—with a song."

"One more shot—and back up against the glass, so that we get the odd plane or two in the background." Thrudd leveled, took two angles, then snapped the disk over the lens and let the camera dangle from the strap around his neck. "Bet you're glad to be going home; must be wanting a rest after your 'holiday.'"

Miss Seeton flushed slightly. It had been particularly impressed on her that she was to insist that this visit to Geneva was purely a holiday, but one did so dislike having to prevaricate. It complicated things.

Thrudd, the only press representative who had gained access on this occasion to the V.I.P. lounge at the airport, took stock of those present: Mme de Brillot, looking svelte; Telmark, the banker, looking stuffed; a police inspector from headquarters, looking sour; two men in raincoats and felt hats, looking blank; some odd police bods in uniform, looking out of place; a hostess looking brisk while she handed round coffee and drinks; and MissEss, looking, as usual, a bit lost and rather pathetic. He brought her back, sat her down and fetched coffee.

"Your village must be agog to hear what you've been up to."

Miss Seeton considered. "Why, no, Mr. Banner. They

wouldn't be interested. And, besides, no one knows I'm away."

Thrudd tried to picture any community, large or small, which could remain unaware of MissEss' presence—or absence—and failed. The village, he guessed—if not she—was probably enjoying a well-earned holiday. "No one?" he queried.

"Except the milkman," she allowed, "who brings the papers. And, naturally, Stan and Martha, who help to look after the cottage. And Mr. Treeves, the vicar, and his sister. And Sir George and Lady Colveden and their son, Nigel. And, of course, Dr. Knight and his family." She stopped and smiled. "One doesn't realize how many, until one thinks. But none of them know where I am. Except Martha. For forwarding Letters, I mean. And, of course, Ann Knight—that's the daughter—because she's engaged to Bob—that is to say Sergeant Ranger—who works with Chief Superintendent Delphick. And . . . Oh, dear."

"Dear what?"

"It's next week. Their wedding. And I'd meant to get something while I was here. But somehow there seems to have been so little time."

"Somehow" was good. He kept a straight face. The odd murder here and there did tend to take up time. "Never mind, you'll still have a chance to look around when you get back.'

She was dubious. "Ye-es. But I had thought that something from abroad would make a change."

For an instant Thrudd saw Miss Seeton as she saw herself: the ex-schoolmistress, the English gentlewoman, where anything from abroad held glamour against the minutiae of English village life. He could also visualize the popping eyes, could they see their schoolmarm being given the treatment at an international airport. Only Stemkos was missing to complete the galaxy.

"Mizeetong?" piped a treble voice. At the entrance appeared a vast bouquet of flowers. "Mizeetong?" The bouquet advanced on tiny feet below plum-colored trousers which clashed with the enormous pink and silver bow that held the cellophaned confection together. Receiving direction from Karl Telmark, the offering settled down beside Miss Seeton's chair revealing a small boy in a bum-freezer jacket and pillbox hat. The cherub beamed, chirped, "Mizeetong," bowed and backed away. Miss Seeton fumbled in her bag, but he waved the gesture aside.

"Oh, mercy," she said, "mercy beaucoop."

"Plaisir, miz." He departed.

Thrudd chuckled. Stemkos, he guessed, was represented after all. Miss Seeton took the envelope which nestled in the bow, opened it, read the contents; she frowned. Really, it was, of course, very kind of Mr. Stemkos. But . . . *wishing you to finish your assignment, am taking over your employment from Telmark . . . have fixed your hotel accommodation . . . you will call at my Paris offices on the Boulevard Haussmann where you may draw on such funds as you require . . . Mme de Brillot will explain in detail . . .* Paris? But—she didn't understand. There was some mistake. She was leaving almost at once for London. She glanced in appeal at Mme de Brillot, who failed to catch her eye.

The hostess appeared at her side, collected the flowers— "Eet ees time we starrt"—and led the way.

Miss Seeton shook hands with Thrudd, thanked him, said good-bye and followed, accompanied by Mélie de Brillot, trailed by the two raincoats and felt hats, with the odd bods in uniform bringing up the rear.

It wasn't raining, though the usual gale which afflicts all passengers walking to their aircraft had sprung from nowhere. Thrudd, sheltered behind the glass wall of the lounge, watched with amusement as the hostess who led the party with a white scarf tied over her uniform cap tacked and went about when the wind caught the polythene round that overdone bunch of vegetation; MissEss had one hand for protection on that godawful hat; the Sûreté men's raincoats huffed and puffed until they looked like Tweedledum and Tweedledee; and the police bods merely looked unhappy. Only Mme de Brillot, immaculate as always, might have been lacquered against the elements. His eyes widened. What the . . .? The lying jade. The little twister. Going home? "Oh, yes, Mr. Banner, believe me, Mr. Banner, straight back to my itsy-bitsy village." Like hell. Believe her? She'd had him fooled again. Anybody who believed a word that bent umbrella said should be certified. The party had veered left from the London plane which they

had been approaching and the hostess, the bouquet, Mme de
Brillot and Miss Seeton climbed the steps of the direct flight to
Paris while their retinue stood on guard below.

Thrudd swung about, to be met by the outstretched arm and
acid expression of the police inspector. The newspaperman
dived a hand into a pocket and waved his press card.

"Out of the way. I've got to phone and make arrangments."

The inspector was unmoved. "No, M. Banner, you will not
telephone, but if you will conduct yourself with discretion I
might then assist with your 'arrangments.' It is my responsibility to see that no word of this Miss Seeton's actual destination
escapes in advance; but once she is arrived"—he shrugged—
"it is no longer our affair and"—remembering with displea-
sure his vain attempt to obtain information from Miss Seeton at
their abortive interview—"once she is there the French are
most welcome to make what they can of her. There is a flight
on KLM to Paris within an hour."

Thrudd turned to the banker. "Do you know where she'll
be?"

Karl Telmark raised his shoulders, shook his head. "Then
how the devil," snapped the reporter, "am I supposed to find
her once she's disappeared in Paris?"

"Disappeared? That one?" The inspector almost smiled. "It
will be necessary only to listen for the loudest noise, to
discover the greatest trouble, and there, at the center, she will
be."

The assistant commissioner looked down the table of the
board room next to his office.

The trickiest yet of the Seeton Sessions and it was to be
hoped the last. The Treasury had turned out in force and, in
their parlance, they were disturbed and distressed, which, in
anybody else's vocabulary, would read "fighting mad." Of the
four, Ian Pledder as senior official they could have expected to
suffer, but why inflict on them a makeweight—except that he
made none—like Horace Bence, who was simply a yes-man,
more accurately a yes-indeed-man, a phrase which Bence
repeated with monotonous regularity whenever one of his

colleagues spoke. He could appreciate, Sir Hubert allowed, that the two investigators—again, why two when one was ample?—held themselves to be slighted, or perhaps more correctly felt that their competence had been called in question, but he had reckoned on more sense, or at all events more realism, from Pledder. But no. Ian Pledder had complained—it would be truer to say he had dilated—on behalf of himself and his department. Why had they not been allowed to deal with the question of the counterfeit notes themselves in accordance with normal procedure? Why had not the Bank of England approached them in the first place? Why had one of his staff been hounded to his death by the police when a quiet word in season could have led to a resignation "for personal reasons"?

"Hounded?" Sir Hubert looked interrogatively at Conway. "Did you hound Estevel, Commander?"

"Hound? Why, no, Assistant Commissioner. Considering he'd turned commie for gain and was due to be arrested for treason, I think we drew it pretty mild. You never hounded him, did you, Borden?"

The inspector was shocked. "Certainly not, sir. We had to interview him, of course, several times in his office and at home and the last time, when we had the warrant for his arrest, we thought it best to go to his flat. But we didn't even see him. He—er—fell out of the window while we were still talking to his wife at the door."

Pledder was not satisfied and continued to demand "Why this . . . ?" and "Why not that . . . ?" and a plethora of other "Whys" until Lord Gatwood, on Sir Hubert's right, who had become increasingly restive, cleared his throat and leaned forward.

"Mr.—um—Pledder, I—ah—approached the police because I couldn't be sure at—the—time"—he spaced the words as he stared deliberately at each of the Treasury men in turn— "who in your setup was pinching the damn paper."

And if, Sir Hubert put in smoothly, it was the comparatively unobtrusive suicide of their colleague which was their main objection, he could easily arrange to leak the truth behind Estevel's death and the scandal, including the necessity for more efficient screening at the Treasury, would then be aired in full in the press, provided, he finished caustically, that was genuinely what they preferred. Whether or not this appeased

Pledder, it silenced him. Sir Hubert addressed the governor of the Bank of England.

"Can I take it, Lord Gatwood, that you are satisfied now from the Bank's point of view?"

His lordship smiled at Jonathan Feldman before replying. "Satisfied? Um—yes indeed. Odd dribble'll still come in. Nothin' to worry about. Been expensive, but cheaper than devaluation by a few hundred million or so. Came here meself to say woman's done a damn good job. So've you. Damn good job all round."

Oblon from the Foreign and Commonwealth Office was restless, clearly pregnant with speech. What, wondered the assistant commissioner, had they sent him along for this time? Not more advice? What was the man's name? He couldn't remember. If he tried to check it now from the lists in front of him it would show, so he injected rather more warmth than usual into his smile.

"I trust his excellency enjoyed his dinner."

"The dinner?" Oblon pursed his lips. "Oh, yes, there was nothing wrong with the dinner—in itself—but this woman's not the sort who should be allowed to attend functions which include two ambassadors and many of the best continental society. Her behavior reflects on us; it's—it's bad for relations." Sir Hubert rested his elbows on the table. It would seem that the F.O. was upset—it was going to be a long accouchement. "She may be very good at her work"—Oblon bowed stiffly to Lord Gatwood—"and we're not presuming to criticize her on that score, but in every other respect she appears to be totally irresponsible."

"Irresponsible? Miss Seeton?" echoed Chief Superintendent Delphick.

"We've just learned she was a passenger in the car which crashed, killing Mme Stemkos, yet, within an hour of the tragedy, Miss Seeton was seen at some trattoria in Italy drinking brandy and actually singing. We're not happy about the situation at the F.O.—not happy." Beside Delphick, Sergeant Ranger gave an indignant snort. Oblon looked accusingly up and down the table. "It was understood she was to be discrete, instead of which she has courted publicity throughout, and it's only a spot of luck that she hasn't so far been involved in an Incident. After all, the minister personally intervened at your request"—he glanced at Jonathan Feldman—"to get this woman sent out there, so it's only natural the minister should feel a parental responsibility."

"I can see—" The trouble for Sir Hubert was that he could. The words "parental responsibility" evoked a mind picture which flickered and jerked like a silent film in which the minister, harsh-faced as a Victorian father, pointed an adamant finger while Miss Seeton, her hat bowed in shame over the shawl-wrapped bundle in her arms, stumbled forth into the snow. He bit his lip. "I can see," he repeated, "the minister's dilemma; can see it the more clearly when I recollect that the police were utterly opposed—I myself protested strongly—to Miss Seeton becoming involved in this affair, and that it was your minister who overruled us by making an issue of the matter."

"If that's your attitude, Assistant Commissioner"—the Foreign Office representative rose—"I'll report back. But since"—he smiled thinly—"I gather the woman's work is now finished, and I presume you are recalling her, I will inform the minister that at least we needn't anticipate any further spots of trouble." He stalked to the door and closed it sharply behind him.

There was a general easement down the table after Oblon's departure.

"It's nice to know," remarked Delphick, "that the F.O. can now sleep o' nights."

Sir Hubert spoke through the laugh that followed. "Sergeant Ranger is to meet Miss Seeton at the airport, thus obviating, or so we trust, any danger of her finishing up in Cornwall or the Outer Hebrides. But before she goes back to Plummergen I thought it best to make sure that none of you wish to see her, though I doubt there is any way in which she could help you further and I doubt even more that there are any points that she could clear up." No one appeared anxious to avail themselves of the offer. "You know her best, Chief Superintendent; what's your view?"

"Frankly, sir," replied Delphick, "I too doubt—one, if she fully realizes why she was ever sent to Switzerland; and two, if anyone questioned her on what she's been up to, by the time she'd finished explaining and then backstitching over the explanation to make quite sure she'd been completely accurate, I'd doubt they'd know either. But I should think"—he grinned at the head of the Special Branch—"that in this case Mr. Fenn could give you a better answer than I could. After all, it's he who's had a man keeping an eye on her."

All turned to Fenn, who was doodling on a piece of paper. He looked up. "Actually, A.C., I've been waiting for the chance to tell you, but I didn't want Oblon climbing further up the wall. She's not coming back—yet."

"Not . . ." Sir Hubert let it hang, and Bob Ranger, who was already on his feet preparatory to setting out for Heathrow, sat down again, hard. He might've known. She never did what she was expected to do—supposed to do. Never had—never would. But—his imagination boggled—what the devil could she be up to now?

"Stemkos," continued Fenn, "has decided to take her over from Telmark and is footing the bill. It's riding a bit roughshod perhaps, but difficult to aruge with, and I gather she's convinced him—or he's convinced himself—that she can pull any sized rabbit out of her hat. Granted there are a few loose ends still lying around, but they're not strictly our concern. Librecksin's gone missing—so's a parcel of diamonds. At a guess I'd say Librecksin probably hid in the back of a lorry in the tunnel in the general confusion and returned to Switzerland. It's rumored he's reached Paris and Stemkos is out to get him and get the diamonds back. Incidentally the picture game's been hotting up the last few weeks: three canvases from Brussels; couple from Florence; and now the French are leaping over two Bouchers, a Watteau and a Fragonard pinched in Fontaineblue, and as Elio Mantoni's turned up in Paris—he's been seen—there may be a connection. Don't see myself how your MissEss can help, but my man out there swears by her and thinks with a little guidance she might blow the whole thing wide apart."

"How could she?" demanded Delphick. "She knows nobody in Paris, no contact, and her French is of the Voulez-vous un cup de tea? order. Or have you"—he regarded Fenn quizzically—"or Stemkos, some bright idea—somebody in mind you think she'll scare into the open?"

"Well, yes," admitted Fenn. "Librecksin's had a bit of fluff on the side for the last year or two—one of the nudes at the Casino de Paris—and we thought if Miss Seeton was put alongside her it might liven things up a bit."

For those who knew Miss Seeton, even for those who only knew of her, it was a moment of awe: Miss Seeton alongside a nude at the Casino de Paris. Delphick had a vision of MissEss, scantily attired in ostrich plumes but with her inevitable hat, her handbag and umbrella, tripping down a flight of *diamanté* stairs.

"Don't worry," Fenn reassured them. "Your lady'll be well looked after and morally we haven't got a leg to stand on. They've been pretty cooperative one way and another, particularly Switzerland and Italy, over the counterfeiting, over the Belton Abbey pictures, over MissEss herself, and over hushing up the odd incident or three like Tolla's death. Stemkos is sold on her in a big way, and if the general feeling is that she could be helpful, I don't see how we can whisk her back just because we don't agree. And if it should wind up with Stemkos getting his baubles back, and the French are saved a few paintings, it'd be what Oblon'd call good for relations. If not, no harm done." He laughed. "It boils down to Hobson's choice—unless we're prepared to fight it out with Stemkos."

"Quite." Sir Hubert placed the tips of his fingers together and communed with the ceiling. "But can we," he asked of it, "for the sake of peace with Stemkos, afford a war with France?"

Paris

FRANCE? Paris? But why?

Miss Seeton surveyed her suite at the Ritz-Palace with a feeling akin to despair. As an artist retained on the fringe of police work Miss Seeton was prepared to accept that she might find herself, upon occassion, in situations which she did not understand and which, as an artist, were not her concern. But now a sense of becoming a shuttlecock, airborne in a game the rules of which had not been explained, worried her. She appealed to Mme de Brillot.

"You see, I had a letter from the sergeant—Sergeant Ranger, that is—who said that he would be meeting me at London Airport when I arrived. But if he can't, because I won't—arrive, I mean—what will he think?"

Mme de Brillot comforted her. "The sergeant will have been informed of the change of plan."

Miss Seeton was not comforted. "And I told Mr. Banner that I was going straight to London."

"Good." Mme de Brillot was pleased. "The less the newspapers know of our activities, the better."

Miss Seeton was not pleased. "But he will imagine that I deliberately misled him." Even her goodwill and sense of duty

153

had a saturation point and Miss Seeton, in her own vernacular, was beginning to feel a little frippy.

The root of her present state of mind was homesickness. Launched for this past week into an environment of wealth for which nothing in a hard working life had prepared her, she lacked orientation. She longed for the simplicity and peace of her cottage in Plummergen where she could potter through the daily trivia in surroundings to which she was accustomed and among people whom she knew; where scrambled eggs remained scrambled eggs and were not translated into caviar, however delicious. The fact that she seldom pottered and that violence had erupted in the village on three occasions since her arrival there and that she herself had been in the forefront of the troubles, she was able to forget or to ignore, drawing the atmosphere of her home around her like a protective shawl. Now she was denied this comfort since the atmosphere of luxury hotels, however agreeable, is not the material of which protective shawls are made. She missed the presence of Chief Superintendent Delphick, who, although he might sometimes bully her, had become a directive force in her life and someone upon whom she could rely for counsel and understanding when working for the police landed her into predicaments which were beyond her experience. A predicament such as that posed by a letter which she had received that morning at the hotel in Switzerland, in which the Coveral Assurance Company informed her that their representative would call on her shortly to discuss the reward for the return of the Belton Abbey pictures.

A reward? Surely that couldn't be right. They must be made to realize that the whole thing had been purely by chance. And it seemed very wrong to accept money just because . . . Failing the chief superintendent, it would have been a relief to have shown the letter to Bob Ranger; or, even better, to Anne Knight and ask their . . . And she mustn't forget to remember their wedding present. Perhaps in Paris? Perhaps Mme de Brillot might help. Miss Seeton sighed. It was all so difficult. And to find that she was not going home, as she had thought, had been such a sharp disappointment. Not, of course, that Mme de Brillot wasn't kind. She was. And those lovely face bones. And Mr. Stemkos, too. Though not, in his case, of course, the bones. But . . . she sighed again. It really was very difficult. Especially when one did not know quite where one was. Or why?

```
*********** *************************************
*         *                                     *
*    N     * CASINO DE PARIS                     *
*   AI     *                                     *
*  H      *  La Nouvelle Revenue                 *
* C  O     *                                     *
*  R  R    * LES FEMMES DU MONDE                 *
*   P  C   *                                     *
*    D  A  *      avec                           *
*     I  M *                                     *
*      R  * Les Cyrcil Twins                     *
*       A  *                                     *
*        M * GRAND SPECTACLE NU                  *
*          *                                     *
*********** *************************************
```

As their taxi drew up in the Rue de Clichy Miss Seeton read the posters with indulgence, doing her best to translate. *Les femmes du monde:* The woman of the world. Elizabeth the first, of course. Catherine the Great, certainly. Boadicea? Cleopatra? Surely there must be some French ones. Ah, yes. Joan of Arc—but not in the sense of a worldly woman. Catherine de Medici—except, of course, that she was Italian. Mme de Pompadour. Marie Antoinette—but there again, she was Austrian, and, in any case, hardly qualified; such a silly woman. It all sounded most interesting.

Miss Seeton was feeling better. Mme de Brillot had explained everything. There was no question of a protracted stay in Paris. One would be going home tomorrow. Or, possibly, the day after; it all depended. All one was being asked to do was draw some girl called Lilianne in this revue. She had ventured to suggest that, surely, there must be photographs, but Mme de Brillot had pointed out that these would be studio portraits and touched up, which was not quite what was wanted. Also there was, apparently, some possibility that that little Italian, Mr. Mantoni, and Mr. Stemkos' secretary. Mr. Libercksin, might be here. Disguised. And they—Mme de Brillot and Mr. Stemkos, that was—felt that, as an artist, one might find it easier to penetrate any such change in appearance than they—Mme de Brillot and Mr. Stemkos—would.

At last Miss Seeton felt that she was being asked to undertake work of which she was capable. Also Mme de Brillot had been most helpful over Bob and Anne's wedding present. Such a clever idea. And not one, one must admit, that one would have thought of. A long, narrow, stainless steel

platter for serving food, either hot or cold. The shop, too, had
been very kind and had insisted on writing her name and
address on the parcel, saying they would send it to the Ritz-
Palace. But she had felt that with the possibility of going home
tomorrow it would be safer to carry it with her. And so she
was. Carrying it with her—although it was a little heavy. But it
was such a comfort to know that it was done.

Mme de Brillot paid off the taxi and led Miss Seeton to an
inconspicuous door at one side of the theater. The stage-door
keeper shouted, the front-of-the-house manager arrived, read a
note that Mme de Brillot handed to him, took the ladies up
stone steps and through a heavy door into the bedlam of the
wings. He glanced again at Mme de Brillot's note.

"En v'la Lilianne," he murmured, indicating a statuesque
young woman who was approaching them. The first half of the
revue, he explained, was to end in a spectacle showing the
resurgence of the spirit of different countries arising from the
grave and Lilianne was to portray the spirit of England. Mme
de Brillot translated.

The young woman was simply dressed in a spangled *cache-
sexe*, with a transparent cloak across her back fastened to her
hands by finger rings. The cloak when spread purported to
represent the Union Jack, but, Miss Seeton noticed with
disapproval, displayed it upside down. Lilianne, unconscious
of their scrutiny, sauntered toward the side wall. The manager
turned and, clearing a path through an assortment of over-
dressed men and underdressed women, led the way to the pass
door into the auditorium. Mme de Brillot followed him.

Miss Seeton was gazing around her with interest. So like—
so very like—in some respects, a life class in anatomy. Except
that here, of course, these were better looking. She made to
follow Mme de Brillot only to be confronted by a basket of
improbable blue roses painted on canvas. She moved to one
side; the basket followed her. She sidestepped again, but
basket after basket in a seemingly endless procession blocked
her path. Finally the stagehand carrying the end of the ground
row passed her and she found herself against the side wall by a
circular iron staircase leading downward.

Downward? Oh, yes, of course. One had forgotten that the
audience was below the level of the stage.

· · ·

Anatole Librecksin was consumed by resentment.

Mixed blood is a gamble and the odds depend upon the
dividual's acceptance or rejection of the converging streams.
brecksin had rejected both his main arteries, Arab and
ugoslav, and had never bothered to explore the contributing
butaries. Born a bastard, he had graduated in bastardy,
cking the depth of character to speculate whether softer
notions in conflict with prejudices and difficulties of environ-
ent might not have formed the root of his being. From street
rab in Tangier at the age of eight years old to pimp for
numerable "sisters" at the age of twelve, he had fought his
ay upward to a position of credit as the trusted social
cretary of a multimillionaire. Now that the position and
wer for which he had striven had crumbled through a flaw in
s character which denied faith in others, he was prepared to
ame anyone and everyone except himself.

A moment of panic engendered by the guilt of his and
atalie's attempt to kill Miss Seeton had driven him to worm
s way beneath the tarpaulin covering the lorry's load rather
an remain to bluff out the accident with the police. The
xtreme discomfort of the ride; his flight to France with only
e money he had on him and the packet of diamonds in his
ocket as potential capital; the jolt he had received on his
rival in Paris when, telephoning Lilianne, he had learned that
ue had been visited by the police and was afraid that her
partment might be under surveillance—for all he held
temkos, Natalie, Mme de Brillot, even Lilianne herself, in
art responsible, but principally he blamed the English agent,
us Miss Seeton.

Lilianne was nervous; nervous of the flics; nervous of
natole. A visit by the police, alerted by Interpol to check on
l Librecksin's contacts in Paris, had unsettled her. A second
all, of which she had not told Librecksin, had intrigued her. A
rigadier from the *préfecture de police*, arriving unofficially
nd alone, had pointed out that the insurance company would
e prepared to pay a substantial reward for the diamonds
ostracted from the stolen Stemkos jewelry.

Lilianne was typically French, which is to say she was
ssentially practical. She had no intention of coming to bad
rms with the police—unless of course it was made worth her

while. Until now Anatole had done so, but if he was on the r
there might be more profit in selling than in aiding him. F
safety's sake she had taken the stolen canvases which had bee
brought to her apartment for delivery to Elio and hidden the
in the theater, where, even should they be discovered by son
unlucky chance, no connection with herself could be prove
Also she had no desire to risk Anatole's presence in h
apartment at this juncture until a meeting had given her a
opportunity to assess his present and her own future prospec
She had arranged, therefore, to meet both Librecksin a
Mantoni at the theater, choosing the day of the dress rehearsa
when the traditional confusion would make it simple for the
to slip in unnoticed and find their way below the stage. Th
murky cavern of the *sous-scène*, where old props are stor
and small pieces of scenery are stacked, provided plenty
opportunities for concealment.

Lilianne herself could have a valid reason for being the
and she decided that her best moment would be to go dow
early during the two scenes which preceded the finale of th
first half. If questioned she would claim that the lining to h
coffin was uncomfortable and she wished to adjust the paddin
The other girls and their dresser, who disliked the dusty gloo
of the "celler," would not come down to take their positio
until the last moment. And the stagehand responsible f
working the mechanism was never sent below until short
before his cue to operate the complication of levers whi
trundled each coffin onto the lift which in turn sent the
through a trap to the height of the staircase set upstage, tippin
them upright, before sinking down to collect the next.

By the side wall, behind the stage manager's back, an
unchallenged, Lilianne hurried down the perforated iron tread
of the circular stairs. The undercroft by any building is apt
be a limbo. In a theater an errie quality is added by the ghos
of past productions awaiting their resurrection. Lilianne a
knowledged the atmosphere of the place with a shiver. Th
only illumination was a pilot light above the row of gilde
boxes destined to take aloft the reviving "spirits of th
nations." Although prepared, Lilianne started when the sma
figure of Elio Mantoni edged from behind a flat. She went
the third sarcophagus, lifted the lid, took from it a seale
cardboard cylinder and held it out. In the shadows behind the

Anatole Librecksin watched and waited. He had no wish to be seen by the Italian if it could be avoided. Mantoni's extended hand fell to his side at the sound of footsteps on the iron stairs. He turned, his eyes dilated, his jaw dropped and he emitted a thin whinny of terror. He bolted, roughly shouldered aside the figure at the bottom of the stairs, sprang, grabbed the handrail, scrambled upward and disappeared.

Good gracious. Miss Seeton recovered her balance. That, surely—yes, certainly—had been Mr. Mantoni. She looked up, but the Italian was already out of sight. Mme de Brillot had been quite right. She must tell her at once. And he was not, after all, as one had been led to expect, wearing a disguise. Now, where . . . ? Perhaps the young woman over there . . . Oh. It was the one they had pointed out as Lilianne. The one they wanted her to draw. Doubtless she would know which way Mme de Brillot had gone. Miss Seeton approached.

"Excusez-moi—" Lilianne stood petrified, still holding out the cardboard cylinder which contained the stolen paintings. How very odd, thought Miss Seeton, that an actress, if that was the correct term, should not have bothered to conceal that small pear-shaped birthmark on the inside of the upper arm. Perhaps, under the strong lights of the stage, it did not show. "Voulez-vous," she asked—now what was "tell me" in French?—"direr moi oo est gone—that is to say . . ." But Miss Seeton's quandary as to whether "partie" or "allée" would be the best translation was unexpectedly resolved. She had not noticed that Lilianne was looking past her; had not heard Librecksin's silent advance in her rear. A piece of timber wrested from the back of the "old monument" behind which he had been concealed thwacked into the back of her head. A black explosion: pinpoints of light like falling meteorites, twisting, diminishing, and Miss Seeton spiraled with them, diminishing, until only the black remained.

Librecksin knelt, hoisted the inert form and thrust it into the empty coffin, throwing her handbag and umbrella after her. But four into one would not go and the parcel which she had dropped failed to fit. A quick consultation with Lilianne and the girl pulled off her veiling, which they spread atop Miss Seeton, then they smacked down the ventilated lid. There was little time to spare. They looked around. Coveralls on a wall

hook solved Lilianne's problem and, while she zipped them on
the length of the trouser legs concealing her silver sandal
Librecksin, who had found the cardboard cylinder and Mi.
Seeton's parcel to be of a length, forced the roll under th
string, then gave his hat to Lilianne, who pulled it low over he
forehead. Above them the intermittent thump of changin
scenery had ceased. There was a muffled clash of cor
followed by a drum roll from the orchestra. Lilianne gaspec
    "Le finale."

Feet, accompanied by giggles and girlish twitter, sounded c
the stairs. A hoarse voice shouted:
    "En scène p'r l'finale."

Lilianne darted into the gloom at the side of the motor for th
revolving stage, dragged open a narrow door leading to th
deserted scene dock. Librecksin eased the door shut behin
them and, picking their way through the litter of woode
frames, cutouts and paintpots, they climbed a ladder, pushe
the safety bar on a side door and gained the Rue Blanch
which left them only a few minutes' walk to Lilianne
apartment near the Place Pigalle.

Six girls, a dresser and a stagehand clattered down the la
steps into the cellar.
    "Mais où donc est Lilianne?" the dresser snapped. The gir
looked at each other; one of them raised expressive eye:
"Mais merde alors qu'est-c'qu'elle fait, cette vache-là?"
demanded the dresser. Indicative fingers followed the upwar
trend of the expressive eyes in a rude suggestion.

The stagehand pushed an indifferent path through the nake
torsos, slouched across to coffin number three, raised the li
saw the Union Jack, shrugged, said, "Déjà en place," an
slammed it down again.

Amid squeals and protests the dresser got the girls dispose
in their respective caskets.
    "En place—en place," the voice from above yelled wit
increasing urgency.

A red light blinked, the stagehand pulled a lever and th
dresser pushed the last, expressive, still expostulating "spirit
flat, banging the lid on her as the rollers began to turn and th
line of coffins wavered toward the lift.

The director strode back and forth in the aisles between th
rows of almost empty stalls; back and forth across the orchestr

pit; leaped up the improvised ramp onto the stage to fulminate, to demand and to implore in a fury of—the backers lolled in their seats in a gloom of—despair.

Front-of-house personnel, theater cleaners, occasionally stagehands, dressers and members of the press watched with apathetic or cynical indifference while bare bosoms came, bare bottoms went and sketch followed song in monotone broken by mildly diverting hitches from the scenery and lights, and the dress rehearsal of the much publicized new revue at the Casino de Paris, *Les Femmes du Monde,* proceeded to take no shape.

Mme de Brillot was not, to speak the truth, troubled—as yet; but she recognized the first pinpricks of disquiet. Nothing—but assuredly nothing—could have happened among such a crowd. And, among such a crowd back there and such confusion, it was easy to lose one's way. She half rose from her seat in the stalls, then sat back. No. No, better to leave it to the manager. He had promised that he would find her friend and escort her here. And besides, as he had pointed out, alone he would be quicker and it would cause less distraction to the rehearsal. Evidently, that was true. And since she had used much influence to gain permission to attend this rehearsal, she had no desire to abuse her position. All the same, it must be . . . She consulted her watch. No, barely five minutes. Hardly time for him to have found Miss Seeton. Mme de Brillot relaxed. A series of crashing chords from the orchestra, a roll of drums and the curtain swept up for the finale of the first part. The boredom of such a revue as this without one new idea—one spark of originality.

An overflowing contralto sang of countries, of their origins, their revival, while the cast, singly or in groups according to their status, descended or posed on the glittering staircase. The sulky nudes jostled each other for the best positions. The chorus, one of whom had remembered to wear an eager smile, tripped down out of step and out of time. The music was flat, the contralto sharp. Lights flashing on the backcloth read JAPON. Another roll of drums heralded the appearance, high up at the back, of a large gilt coffin which, after a preliminary bump, lurched upright. A clash of cymbals nearly coincided with the opening of its lid and a slant-eyed beauty, her hands folded modestly across her breasts, stepped forward. Les Cyrcil Twins, two fairhaired boys in frilled white shirts, white clinging trousers and gold cummerbunds, ran lightly up the stairs in unison. Each took a hand and immodestly spread the beauty's arms so that the diaphanous cloak behind her naked body displayed the Red Sun of Japan. The contralto, inappropriately, sang "La Petite Tonkinoise" while they led down Miss Japan, escorted her to one side and then ran back to repeat the treatment for Miss Norway to the refrain of "Solveig's Song."

A third coffin teetered upright. The cymbals clashed. There was a pause. The lights were flashing ANGLETERRE. The cymbals clashed again. Another pause. The twins ran up and one swung wide the coffin lid. The cymbals rushed in with another clash. Still nothing happened. Then slowly an umbrella leaned from the coffin to clatter, handle downward, on the stairs. A handbag toppled after it.

There were muffled snorts from among the press; the backers sat up in surprise; the director stood transfixed.

"Mais non," breathed Mme de Brillot. "Ah non, ça—pas possible."

Thrudd Banner put his hands on the back of her seat. "Oh, yes it is," he whispered. "With that congenital little liar all things are possible."

Les Cyrcil Twins went forward. Each took a finger ring of the transparent covering, spreading wide the almost Union Jack. They looked behind it; they exchanged a glance. Where did they go from here?

"O-o-h." Miss Seeton moaned gently. Oh, her head did hurt. And she felt, she was afraid, a little sick. She opened her eyes: light blazed and blinded her, making her headache worse. She tried to move but found there was no floor in front of her. Strong hands gripped hers, supporting her. She looked down. She was on steps. But everything shone so. And there was some colored material in front of her. She couldn't see. Where was she? What had happened? The sustaining hands eased her down two steps, then stopped her.

"Stay there, ducky," said a voice.

"Just for a sec," said another.

"We'll be back," said the first.

Cecil and Cyril let go Miss Seeton's hands, leaned backward, ripping the Gossamer Union Jack in half, crumpled the pieces and flung them over their shoulders behind the girls grouped on the stairs. As one they sprang two steps up; Cecil collected the handbag, Cyril the umbrella, and Les Cyrcil

Twins were back, kneeling in devotional attitudes one step below their charge.

The orchestra had completed the first three bars of "Rule Britannia" and the contralto had informed the company in execrable English that Britannia ruled the waves, when the Union Jack was swept aside. After the old-fashioned umbrella and the practical handbag, the revelation of Miss England as the apt if incongruous little figure in a shapeless hat, a serviceable suit and sensible shoes, surprised guffaws from the press, laughs from the backers and chuckles from the theater personnel. The director collapsed into a seat.

The musical conductor glared at the stage and smacked his baton down, halting the orchestra. If the producer could make last-minute changes and introduce farce without warning him, then so in the name of the good God could he. He tore the sheet music of "Rule Britannia" and flung it from him; bent forward and eyed the musicians venomously.

" 'Heureux tous les deux,' " he hissed, raised his baton and swung them into "I Want to Be Happy."

Miss Seeton, left alone, saw the staircase as a tinsel precipice; vertigo assailed her and she swayed, pitching forward. Reassuring hands caught her again, held her, closing her fingers round the handle of her own umbrella, the strap of her own handbag. The stairs were lined with young women with next to nothing—some with nothing—on. Memory stirred. Of course. She had been following Mme de Brillot behind the scenes . . . and a lot of nude models . . . and some iron stairs . . . and one of them—the models, that was—had been called . . . ? Lilianne. That was it. And had been wearing a sort of wrapper like a Union Jack. That would account for the material she'd thought she'd seen in front of her. Yes, that explained everything. The steps, the naked women and the Union Jack. This was some silly, stupid dream, and . . . Oh, her head did hurt.

Had she slipped on those stairs and hit her head? And yet . . . And yet—that didn't seem quite right. Surely she'd been at the bottom of the stairs and seen something—or someone—important and Mme de Brillot must be told. Yes, that was it, and she'd asked the young woman by some gold boxes like coffins—such a morbid idea—yes, Lilianne . . . and . . . she couldn't remember any more.

The Cyril Twins had not missed the laughter from the

"house." They were sensitive by training to audience reaction, and the rehearsal had already told them that the revue would fail. Explanations could wait, but meanwhile they were determined to take advantage of the situation and play this new angle, this chance for its survival, to the hilt. In triumph and slow tempo they led the dazed "Miss England" down, to raucous appreciation from the front of the house.

Cecil's eyes slid to his right. "Join in and sing, you dilly cows," he ordered the girls.

Cyril's eyes slid left. *"Chantez, belles bêtes,"* he commanded the chorus near him. The girl with the eager smile grasped the idea.

"Tous ensemble," directed Cecil.

Falteringly, then with gathering enthusiasm, the company straggled into song. Owing to numerous revivals, many of them actually knew the English words.

"Ay von tew *bee* yappy . . . ," they chanted.

Even the contralto in the corner, who had considered the interruption of her scene as a direct insult, caught the infection, threw offended dignity to the winds and boomed in, stamping to the rhythm in a personalized version of Knees-up Mother Brown.

"Miss England" reached the bottom of the stairs. Still holding her hands, the twins swung round and knelt facing her, blond heads thrown back in seeming adoration.

"Ducky, do something," begged Cecil.

"Something funny," pleaded Cyril.

"We don't know who you are—"

"Or why you're here—"

"But you've wowed 'em."

"The angels are in front—"

"And so's the press—"

"And this dead duck of a show—"

"Might lay a golden egg."

"Whatever you do—"

"We'll play along—"

"Until someone has the sense—"

"To wake up—"

"And ring down on us."

"So meanwhile—"

"Please do—"

"Please, please do—"

"Something funny."

Something funny . . . ? She didn't understand. It was dawning on Miss Seeton that this was no dream but that somehow, in some dreadful fashion, she was, in fact, upon the stage. If only she didn't feel so muzzy—and if only her head . . . Something in the kindness in those supporting hands, something of the message in those imploring eyes penetrated. She would help, if she could. . . . But, there was nothing. . . . The insistent melody carried her back to her childhood, when her aunt had taken her for a birthday treat to see a musical production called *No, No, Nanette*. She remembered so well that clever Miss Hale twisting her legs around each other and how, in her bedroom later, she had tried to do the same and had fallen down. So curious that now one knew the movement as part of a yoga balance posture called the Eagle and did it frequently. In automatic reflex, without thought, Miss Seeton crossed her legs and locked one foot behind the other ankle.

From the stalls two or three shouts of approval greeted this achievement. The twins surged forward, gathered Miss Seeton up, hoisted her in jubilation and sat her on their shoulders. For a moment she stayed there, her arms waving to keep a precarious balance and inadvertently belaboring first one twin and then the other with her handbag and umbrella. A glance of communication between the two young men: their eyes rolled up and, legs widening into splits, they slithered to the floor in feigned unconsciousness. Miss Seeton, her legs still interlocked, subsided with them and the stage manager, aroused at last, rang down the curtain.

There was a splatter of applause from different parts of the theater; some members of the press catcalled or wolf-whistled and among the backers one angel wiped his eyes. The director, ignoring the fulminating conductor, gained the stage in three bounds and disappeared through the tabs. Mme de Brillot sprang to her feet.

"Going round to congratulate the new star?" asked Thrudd. "I'll tag along."

"You will not." She edged quickly between the seats and reached the aisle. "I do not know how you have followed us here . . ."

"Easy. You told the porter at the Ritz-Palace the address to give the taxi and"—he rubbed a thumb and forefinger together—"he told me."

Backstage was pandemonium. The cast, the stage manager and the staff demanded explanations. The stagehand from below, expecting to be blamed, loudly denied responsibility, accusing the girls' dresser of switching the body in his box. The dresser counterattacked inveighing against Lilianne. And if it wasn't a deliberate prank or plot, then where was Lilianne? No one knew, though the nude with the expressive eyes was ready with suggestions.

The director, bursting through the curtains and shouting louder then the rest, quelled the tumult. The front-of-house manager, catching sight of Mme de Brillot, rushed forward, seized both her hands and pumped them. Her friend, her friend, her friend, he enthused, superb, superb, superb.

Mme de Brillot reclaimed her hand and eyed him stonily. Where was Miss Seeton?

He looked about him, made inquiries. Everyone looked around, asked questions, but all denied any idea of Miss Seeton's whereabouts. Where were the Cyrcil Twins? But, evidently, where would one expect them to be but in their dressing room? And there, evidently, was the answer. The lady they were seeking must be there too.

Cecil turned an artless face toward his visitors. Miss Seeton? Was that her name? Really he couldn't say. She'd popped up on stage like a fairy godmother with an umbrella for a wand and then when the tabs came down she'd vanished—probably in a puff of smoke.

"But," insisted Mme de Brillot, "you must have seen her." Cecil giggled. "Didn't we all? Lovely sense of timing, but"— he frowned, mock serious—"do you really think she's got the stamina for a run?"

"The question does not arise."

Cecil's eyes gleamed. "Oh, but it will. You'll see. With this dead duck of a show and then that little ducky suddenly gaying it up d'you think the angels'll sit back and let all their lovely lolly go flushing down the loo? They'll sign her up—you'll see."

Mme de Brillot examined the dressing room. "What is in there?" She pointed to a door behind a rack of costumes to one side of the mirrored makeup bench with its two stools.

"Cyril," replied Cecil. He reached into the air and pulled an imaginary chain. "Having a shower," he explained. He went and banged on the door. "Cyril, ducky, come out—it's my turn."

There was the sound of running water, much splashing, and a light tenor began to sing:

> "If you were the only man in the world
> And I was the only boy . . ."

Cecil hammered again. the singing stopped. The door opened a few inches and a face half covered with dripping blond hair peered round.

"Oops," cried Cyril, "company." The head vanished, to reappear a moment later swathed in toweling. Pulling his dressing gown cord tighter, Cyril apologized. "Sorry, duckies, didn't know anybody was here." He perched among the makeup and waved to an overstuffed chair and a stool. "Won't you park?"

Thrudd Banner felt that the twins were overplaying it—covering up. "Hang on," he called. "Mind if I look in there?"

Cecil ogled him and held the bathroom door invitingly. "Of course, ducky—come in and scrub my back. Such a thrill."

Thrudd took a step forward, hesitated; he could see most of the small room from here. "All right, forget it."

Cecil pouted. "How could I, ducky—ever?" He gave Thrudd a last languishing look, skipped into the bathroom and closed the door. More water ran and his voice took up the song:

> ". . . was the only boy,
> Nothing much could happen in this world today;
> The population problem would be solved that way . . ."

Questioned, Cyril was professing to know no more than Cecil, when they were interrupted by the stage manager with a message: there was to be an hour's break in the rehearsal for a conference, after which a company call; everybody on stage, please. Cyril turned to Mme de Brillot.

"There you are, ducky; there's your answer. You'll find your friend swilling champers and discussing terms with the management."

The twins' dresser, Gustave, an elderly man, gray-haired, minced in with a loaded tray. He set it on a low table by the armchair and looked around in surprise. He opened his mouth

to speak but Cyril cut in quickly and dismissed him, explaining
that their friends weren't staying and that Cecil would arrive in
a second because though the coffee might keep, the omelets
wouldn't. Would he conduct their friends to where the
conference was taking place since they, in their turn, were in
search of a friend who would undoubtedly be there. And then
to come back.

Mme de Brillot and Thrudd Banner found themselves
ushered out and escorted down the corridor before they had
time to think of further questions.

The twins were delighted with themselves. They surveyed
Miss Seeton, who lay back deeply asleep in an overstuffed
armchair behind the bathroom door.

"We didn't give her too much?"

"Only one tablet," said Cyril. "Give her a lovely kip for an
hour or so—and give us time to think."

They closed and locked the bathroom door, then settled to
their meal.

Mme de Brillot was in a quandary. She did not wish to enlist
the aid of the police. There was little she could adduce but
intangibles to support her present worry. Miss Seeton had
appeared upon the stage—by accident, it must have been by
accident—she then had disappeared. But the police would
argue understandably that in such a crowd it could not have
been by force and that having, as she must have done, left of
her own free will, she would in her own time return to the
hotel. If Miss Seeton proved not to be in the theater—and by
now she had the impression that this hope was doomed—she
would probably do better to return to the hotel herself and
direct the search from there. Mr. Banner had thought that there
was something bizarre about the behavior of Les Cyrcil Twins;
she had sensed the same, but it was something—something
about the dressing room itself that bothered her; something that
for all her recapitulation of the scene she could not indicate
exactly; something about the room itself . . . No, it would
not come. Meanwhile she could justifiably alert the police in
regard to Lilianne's disappearance—there must be some
connection—and the undoubted connection between Lilianne
and Librecksin would stir them into action.

• • •

Lilianne went ahead to reconnoiter. There was no occupied parked car near the building, no loitering figure, no—unlikely at this hour—road sweeper or repair van for electricity or gas. This was not to say that her apartment was unobserved from some window opposite the front or from the back, but it reassured her and would give confidence to Anatole. She signaled; he joined her and they climbed the stairs.

Lilianne thrust Librecksin's hat on a peg in the three-by-four-foot space which the landlords termed the vestibule, opened the door of the living room and switched on the top light instead of the muted roseate glow of lamps, as was her wont.

This was a business deal, not an assignation. The harsh glare was unkind to the surroundings, showing wear on the tawdry furniture; brutal to her, stressing the disarray of her elaborate coiffure, her heavy makeup, the soiled coveralls and the ridiculous glints from the silver sandals with their encrusted paste heels below the trousers. She drew unfortunate comparison to an overcooked tart with wilted garnishing served on a chipped plate.

Lilianne was jolted to lear that Libercksin wished to borrow money; it was usurping her prerogative. Money, in cash or kind, was an asset she was accustomed to receive for favors bestowed rather than to dispense, however good the collateral. She was risking her job, would probably be sacked and for that she must be compensated. That Paris was dangerous for Anatole at this juncture she allowed and agreed to raise what wind she could next morning if he would leave the diamonds, or some of them, in her safekeeping. He refused and the argument grew acrimonious. That he proposed to send Mantoni to work in England, where he himself could follow and negotiate in safety for the canvases with the Arab buyers who had already agreed on terms with Tolla; that from England it would be simple for him to cross to Antwerp and dispose of sufficient diamonds for his immediate needs; that he would then be in a position to reimburse her tenfold—did not impress Lilianne. England and Holland were far away. She was in Paris, where Anatole was afraid—and once the hunt was on would be still more afraid—to show his face. In sum, to her mind, she was likely to be bilked. She grew shrill and Librecksin, conscious of the neighbors, gave in, admitting the force of her arguments, produced the diamonds, sorted them and handed her one-third. She decided not to press her advantage further. He was holed up at the Hôtel de l'Europe et de la Rose, small and cheap, in a courtyard behind the Boulevard des Italiens. She promised to come there on the following day with what money she could muster before he was due to leave for the airport to catch the evening flight to London, the bargain was sealed with a perfunctory kiss and while Lilianne fingered the stones in rapt contemplation Librecksin crossed the room, retrieved his hat in the vestibule and banged the outer door.

The girl reflected: Anatole was—and would be—of no further use to her. She slipped the diamonds into an envelope. These she could keep; need never acknowledge. But—if she sold him, and the rest of the stones were recovered, she would finish in good odor with the police and gain the reward from the insurance. She reached for the telephone. Slowly, silently the handle turned and the door to the sitting room was eased ajar. Librecksin stood listening, heard the dialing, a pause, then:

"*Le Préfecture? M. l'Inspecteur Chiffard, s'il vous plaît.*"

Another wait. Quickly, soundlessly Librecksin moved.

"*Allo?*" asked the instrument.

Lilianne took a nervous breath, but hard fingers closed on her windpipue, cutting her communication with the police; Librecksin's left hand caught the falling receiver and replaced it, then joined the other to encircle her neck—cutting all communication.

Librecksin humped the body to the bathroom, stripped it and dumped it in the bathtub. Lilianne must disappear: should she be found the police were likely to connect him with the killing; if she disappeared the police might well presume that she—and maybe he—had quitted France. He repaired to the kitchenette. As he remembered: a gift unit of a meat chopper with its complement of kitchen knives including the wicked blade of a frozen food saw. He set to work.

A weighted hatbox held the head, the glittering *cache-sexe* and the coveralls—that for the river Seine. The rest of the dismemberment, wrapped in polythene and stuffed in suitcases, could be distributed between the different points of the railway's compass. Crossing the living room with one of the cases, his eye lighted on Miss Seeton's parcel. He studied it. He began to laugh.

Luck was running Librecksin's way. He had been surprised to find how little time his amateur butchery had taken him. The longest part of his self-appointed task had proved to be the cleaning of the bathtub and the wiping of all surfaces in the flat that he had touched.

He had planned his itinerary carefully: first the one long leg, the most tricky, southeast across the city to the Gare de Lyon, the only sizable station near the river. It was as his taxi approached the Bastille that they met the first traces of a river mist and by the time they reached the station it swirled and eddied, transforming people into phantoms. He dismissed the taxi, stacked his luggage for plausibility close to a porter's barrow against the wall and, taking the hatbox with him, set out for the nearest bridge.

Beside the river he had to pick his way and on the Pont d'Austerlitz visibility was down to feet. He saw no one on the bridge and no outcry accompanied the splash when the hatbox fell.

Back at the station he found his luggage untouched and deposited the heaviest of the cases at the left luggage office; then with growing confidence he piled the remainder into a taxi. The worst risk, that of leaving the luggage unattended, was over, but the fog which had helped him was now a hindrance and he chafed as the cab crawled up the Rue de Lyon, hugging the curb, with the driver grumbling incessantly that people who wished to travel in such conditions must be mad or criminal or both and that for himself he had no idea but to quit the streets and take the Métro home.

As they went north the mist thinned and the Boulevard de Magenta was clear. He got rid of another case at the Gare de l'Est, the short trip to the Gare du Nord relieved him of another and a final taxi took him west to the Gare Saint-Lazare, where he left the station encumbered only by Miss Seeton's parcel and but a short distance from the Casino.

Librecksin stood at the corner of the Rue d'Athènes, opposite the theater. His financial position had improved. Having known where Lilianne hid her valuables, he was now the richer by several thousand francs and some pawnable trinkets. Close by, the essence of Parisian night life ululated from a basement, where an accordion screaked and mewled an old favorite, "Si Tous les Cocus."

The front of the casino was dark except for a dim glow at the back of the foyer. He looked at his watch: half-past ten. It was unlikely that the dress rehearsal would be over yet. He had no idea what had brought Miss Seeton to the theater, nor any assurance that she was still there. It was a possibility, no more, but a chance worth taking on a night when fortune appeared ready to favor him. He realized that unless he dealt with her, Mantoni would refuse to go to England. The fool was hysterical about her and credited her with the evil eye. The other point he had to consider was had she seen him? He thought not—was almost sure not. She had certainly seen Mantoni and she had seen the cardboard roll containing the canvases, although it was arguable that she might not have grasped its significance. She had been speaking to Lilianne when he had come up behind her and although she had twisted in falling after the blow, could she have seen his face before losing consciousness? The glimpse must have been too brief and too confused for recognition; of that he was virtually certain. Still, virtual certainty was but two-thirds of a guarantee. Safety lay in her riddance.

He looked down toward La Trinité. The top of the church had disappeared and fog was already clouding the square in front of it. If she was still in the theater, transport would be difficult and the conditions ideal for him. If not, he would use her parcel as an excuse and make an opportunity at her hotel in the morning.

Shouts, stamping and cries of "*bis*" from the *boîte de nuit* greeted the final chorus of "Si Tous les Cocus," making him turn his head, and when he looked back the theater facade was shrouded in mist. He moved forward into the Rue de Clichy. Behind him the accordian started again and an inept understudy to Jean Sablon began to lament "Vous Qui Passez Sans Me Voir."

On cue the side door opened and a figure emerged. Librecksin felt a surge of triumph. Unmistakable; those clothes, that hat, that umbrella questing its way forward in the murk. Allowing a few seconds for his quarry to get clear of the theater, he started in pursuit. Underneath the street light by the church he caught up, raised a knife and stabbed. Alerted by a sense of danger, his prey wheeled suddenly, swinging the umbrella in defense so that the knife, missing the vulnerable triangle between the collarbone and shoulder, was deflected by the rib cage and sliced down to the waist. Librecksin dropped the parcel and stooped over the tumbled form to strike again but was halted by shouts and the thud of feet as two indistinct trousered shapes loomed close. Librecksin jumped clear of the body, groped his way down the thick darkness of the Rue de la Trinité above the church and into the Rue Blanche. If not dead, he congratulated himself, at least disabled, and this time alone—for long enough—with no Mme de Brillot to effect a last-minute rescue.

Mme de Brillot disliked Paris. She found its reputation as ill-founded as its Eiffel Tower: a city where a spurious warmth and gaiety, like a waxed veneer, overlay the grim business of living in an essentially gray metropolis where generosity was at a premium and the violence of the apache and of the barricades smoldered beneath the surface. She sat in the hall of the Ritz-Palace with an untasted drink in front of her, ignoring Thrudd Banner's conversational gambits.

At last. Of a sudden she knew what had been wrong with the dressing room. Two men, two stools—but one armchair. She rose and hurried to the line of telephone kiosks at the back and asked the swtichboard for the stage door of the Casino. There was an appreciable wait before the call was answered and a morose voice demanded her business.

The director? Not there. No one was there. The rehearsal was over and the theater closed. A dressing room? No, he would not. It was not his affair to search dressing rooms. As if he had not enough to do with guarding the theater and answering questions from the police. The police? Why, about the attack, of course, what else? Where? But evidently down by the Trinité, where else, and not, God be blessed, one of the company. Who? How should he know? Some old woman, or so he understood from what the police had said. No, he had not seen her. It was not his affair to leave the theater and set foot on the streets with murderers about. No, he did not know. One of the twins had returned excited and had used the phone—without permission or paying, which would have to be regulated—to call for an ambulance and the police, and had then departed precipitately. And to what good, with all the delay before the police and ambulance could arrive thanks to the fog. What hospital? How should he know? It was not his affair. The receiver clicked.

Mme de Brillot looked through the glass door of the booth at the hotel clock. Nearly midnight. Her best contact at the préfecture would be . . . Thrudd Banner was on his feet,

staring. Her glance followed his to the revolving doors. In the
name of God . . . Two slim boyish figures stood, uncertain,
by the entrance. One, bareheaded, held a long narrow parcel
and the other, sporting a visored cap, carried a handbag and
umbrella. A brief consultation between the two and Cecil ran
forward.

"Duckies."

The long nose down which the night receptionist had been
looking twitched. Affronted by this vulgar invasion of the Ritz-
Palace by such—such types, he had been upon the point of
signaling to one of the bellboys to remove them. Now he
waited. If Mme de Brillot recognized these—these deplor-
ables, then he and the hotel must do the same. Overhearing the
greetings and the exclamations, he sniffed. Ah, all explained
itself; English, and everyone knew the English did not know
how to conduct themselves. He watched with disdain as the
strangely assorted group settled round the table. The frightful
cap was removed, the ill-fitting yellow wig under it was lifted
to reveal a bandage around gray hair. Death of God, it was the
English miss, the one whose suite had been booked by M.
Stemkos, no less, with precise instructions that everything
possible should be done to give her pleasure. He hastened to
them. With a smile as artificial as the teeth that it displayed, he
bowed.

"Mademoiselle has had an accident?" Was there anything
that he could do? Any way in which he could be of service?

Miss Seeton began to shake her head, then stopped.
Although feeling so very much better, it was brought home to
her that her head was not yet in a condition to be abused.

"Ducky," said Cecil—the receptionist flinched—"if you
could give birth to some sandwiches? Miss Seeton's had no
dinner and I've only had a teensy omelet since brekker." He
looked a query at Mme de Brillot and Thrudd: relief allowed
both to realize that they too had not dined and that curiosity
could wait on appetite.

Sandwiches? The receptionist winced. For a protégée of M.
Stemkos? Unheard of. The improbable teeth flashed again.
Unfortunately the dining room was closed, the chef off duty,
but if he might suggest—some crème de vichyssoise, pâté de
maison aux truffles, a specialty, a salmon mayonnaise with
salad and, it went without saying, some champagne. He eyed
Miss Seeton's borrowed jacket and trousers. Perhaps mademoiselle would prefer that the repast should be served in her suite?

"No." Miss Seeton was firm. It was such a relief to be sitting down after all that had happened. That quite shocking business of the stabbing in the street—thank heaven that it had proved to be not too serious. The fog. And then the police. The questions. The ambulance. The hospital. She was feeling almost light-headed and did not wish to move. Cecil was right. For the first time since she'd been abroad she was really hungry. But she was still determined to stop this foreign habit of serving late-night meals in bedrooms.

Cecil gazed at the receptionist with ardor. "Ducky, you're inspired—I could kiss you."

The man retreated hastily to get matters under way.

Mme de Brillot's present feelings would have been Chief Superintendent Delphick's sympathy: the mixture of relief and exasperation that made her want to smack Miss Seeton to assuage the hours of worry. How dared she return thus from the grave, or at least from hospital, with nothing to show for it except one small bandage and disguised in trousers, with that ridiculous wig and cap.

". . . so you do see, duckies, don't you," Cecil was apologizing, "that we simply dared not risk it? For all we knew you were the ones that slugged her and there was nothing we could do till we got out of the theater so we bandaged her, filled her up with headache powders and half a sleeping tablet and hid her in our loo. Then Cyl got this stupe idea of dressing up as her and we tossed for it but Cyl won—though I think he cheated because he loves a bit of drag—and off he went looking the spit an' image and we followed. Then by the church this bastard jumped him with a knife"—fleetingly the hard core of anger showed through the affectation—"and we dashed up shouting and he slid off somewhere in the fog and we told the police," he protested, "over and over again we never really saw him—just a shape—and there was Cyl bleeding all over the pavement and ducky, here, insisted on staying with him though Mack the Knife could've been back at any moment—so brave—while I went to telephone and everything took simply ages because nobody could see a yard, but here we are and do you wonder"—he grinned warmly at Miss Seeton—"she's still feeling a bit woozy? But she'll strut her stuff as soon as she's had some food, you'll see."

As if in answer to a summons, waiters appeared, flicked tablecloths, laid cutlery, wheeled in the meal and served it. All four set to with appetite.

"Your brother—" began Thrudd with soup spoon raised.

"Brother?" Cecil was pained. "Oh, no, ducks, no relation." He giggled. "Just good friends. And neighbors," he amplified. "Me, I'm from Lancashire and Cyl's from a dreary little place next door called Yorkshire—so inferior."

Thrudd smiled. "You had me fooled there with the color of the hair."

"I should hope so, ducky; it's out of the same bottle."

The reporter persevered. "But seriously—anything we can do? Is your—is Cyril all right?"

"Yes." Cecil was curt, anger and concern showing again. Quickly he masked them. "They doped Cyl, stitched him up and tucked him into bed with a lovely bit of tatting down his side. And the doctor—beige-colored and so good-looking. Cyl'll be thrilled when he wakes up, and—"

"You think"—Mme de Brillot roused herself from thought—"that this man with the knife was the same one who attacked Miss Seeton in the theater?"

"Oh, yes." Miss Seeton was definite. "He was." With every mouthful she was feeling better. "Or rather, he must have been. Because of the parcel."

"The . . . ?"

"This." Cecil retrieved the sergeant's and Anne's wedding present from the floor beside his chair.

"You see," Miss Seeton explained. "I had it with me. And then, later, it wasn't there. But it was there afterward—on the pavement, that is. So it must have been. The same man, I mean." The paper was a little crumpled and the box was dented at one end. She had wondered whether, perhaps, she ought to ask the shop to do it up again. But, no. There was the label with her name and the hotel's address, quite unsuitable, so, really, it would be better to leave it as it was and then rewrap it properly when she got home.

Home. This morning home seemed to Miss Seeton to be so very far away. Fog had clamped down on Paris and Mme de Brillot had told her that all flights were canceled until it lifted.

They had been lucky. The doorman at the Ritz-Palace had persuaded a taxi to drive them to the vast pile of La Lariboisière, which had been the nearest hospital for the previous night's emergency, and there they had loaded a cheerful Cyril with fruit, flowers and gratitude, thankful to

earn that, apart from being stiff and sore and that his stitches
tched, he was not in serious condition. Cyril was in fact
engaged in battle with the nurses over his immediate discharge,
since the opening at the Casino had been postponed for two
days until Thursday for a rewrite and he wanted to rehearse,
ridiculing the doctor's dictum that there could be no question of
his working for a fortnight.

Now on leaving the hospital, the two ladies found that the
sparse traffic had come to a standstill to all intents and
purposes, only an occasional bus creeping past the cars
abandoned by the curbside. The scene reminded Miss Seeton
of the London pea-soupers of her childhood. Mme de Brillot
shrugged; nothing to do save walk. They strayed erratically
down the Rue du Faubourg Poissonnière, since the sole means
of distinguishing between the pavement and the road was by
identifying the obstacles into which they bumped or over
which they tripped. At the Place La Fayette Mme de Brillot,
realizing that they would be late, decided to risk the crowded
Métro, but kept her arm firmly linked in that of her companion
until the train arrived at the Chaussée-d'Antin: experience was
teaching her that Miss Seeton, once mislaid, was as likely to
eventuate in Spain as Timbuctoo. They surfaced on the
Boulevard Haussmann but a few doors from the Stemkos
offices and no more than three minutes late for the ex-
schoolteacher's appointment with the multimillionaire.

When the lift door had closed behind her charge Mme de
Brillot relaxed. Nothing untoward had occurred but the journey
through the fog had stretched trained sensibility to snapping
point; now for half an hour she could shelve responsibility. She
gave explicit instructions to the receptionist: in no case, for
whatever might be the reason, was Miss Seeton to leave the
building until her return. For her part she would be at Étienne's
on the Capucines, close to the Opéra, if anything should arise.

She found the anonymity of the darkened streets welcome
now that she was alone, and on reaching the café she settled
automatically in a corner on a banquette against the wall since
the weather had emptied the sidewalk tables, ordered a
Campari, marshaled her thoughts and began to prepare a
report. It was a tribute to her personality that, although every
eye had followed her progress, no man approached her.

A pest that, on such a morning, Stemkos should want to see
Miss Seeton; no doubt he too wanted a report. Well, he would

learn at least that Mantoni was in Paris, but as to the rest, Miss Seeton's strongly individual style was likely to obscure the narrative and defeat any conclusion. To her mind the inevitable conclusion was that Librecksin was in Paris. No one else except Mantoni had reason for the attack and, since the Italian had fled before the assault in the theater, Librecksin was the only logical suspect, and for Lilianne to disappear at the same time supported the idea. Meanwhile, how to trace Librecksin? The police were already looking both for him and for the girl. Almost certainly he would attempt to leave the country. The police must have mounted guard at ports and airports, but Librecksin was clever; would probably be disguised; would have obtained false papers. She sipped her Campari thoughtfully. More to the purpose, where was he now?

A hundred yards away along the Grands Boulevards Librecksin, now gray-haired and mustached, with credentials as false as his English drawl, was trying to extract a firm promise from the girl behind the counter at the Agence Cook in the Place de la Madeleine that he and his friend would have reserved seats on the first flight to England when the fog dispersed. Once in England, he and Mantoni would be in small danger of a chance identification by Miss Seeton. Besides, when that wretched woman discovered the trick they had played on her last night—the delayed-action bomb that he had planted—as a precaution in case he had failed to put her out of commission, she would find herself too busy with police inquiries over here to give her attention to him. Never, in thirty-five years of resentment against all authority, had he hated anybody as he hated her. She had killed Tolla, disrupted his organization, reduced Mantoni to gibbering idiocy and forced him, Anatole Librecksin, to kill Natalie by mistake and to fly for his life. She would find now—his sudden wolf's grin disturbed the girl who was attending him—that in him she had met her match. He was ahead of her—always supposing that she recovered from the knife.

Miss Seeton was recovering from surprise. She was surprised to find that Mr. Stemkos seemed actually pleased about that quite dreadful business last night and the fact that Cyril was in hospital.

It was no wonder, Stemkos decided the English police

thought highly of this little woman who knew so precisely what she was doing. Within an hour of her arrival in Paris she had traced Anatole—it could only have been he—and this Italian artist to the Casino and had succeeded in enlisting the aid of members of the cast. How?

"Why," he asked, "did you go to the theater?"

"To make a sketch of this girl, Lilianne," began Miss Seeton, "because, you see . . ."

"And you did?"

Well, no. It dawned upon her that she hadn't. So much had happened. Really, there'd been very little time.

"Do so now."

Obediently she rummaged in her handbag, found crayons, opened her sketchbook and stared helplessly at the paper. Really. She couldn't remember. After all, one had only glimpsed the young woman twice.

Stemkos watched her for a moment, then turned to the papers on his desk. With Anatole out, the accountants were in and a number of irregularities had come to light. A curious pattern had emerged. On every occasion that the social secretary had been in a position to make a killing he had failed to follow through and no serious loss had been incurred. Whether Librecksin had lost his nerve at the last moment, or whether a fortuitous change in personnel had balked him, it was impossible to judge without more data, but it was a fact that the engagement of a new assistant, the sacking of an employee, the promotion of an executive, or a switch of staff between Paris and Geneva had coincided with each questionable deal. He marked a query beside a paragraph, reached for the telephone and demanded the head accountant.

"*Sur ce compte—l'article numéro dix-huit . . .*"

With the French flowing smoothly past her understanding, Miss Seeton concentrated, reliving, re-viewing the people and events of the previous night. Of course . . . Now she began to see. . . . Her crayon made a tentative stroke; another. She picked a different color from the carton—another—working quickly, absorbed.

The shipowner finished his conversation, pushed the papers from him and leaned back, drumming his fingers on the desk. So the accountants had not noticed the coincidence; he must discover if there was any connection between Anatole's failure to do any severe damage and this shift of personnel.

Anatole . . . His jaw muscles tightened. Natalie had paid.
Anatole would pay—on that he was determined. In common
with all controllers of an empire, Heracles Stemkos could not
afford to lose face. To look ridiculous was one thing, but to be
made to look ridiculous was another, and years of experience
had taught him that the one way to fight publicity was with
publicity; never to allow the world to jeer that you had retired
to lick your wounds. The ideal course would be to remarry
immediately . . . but no; he was cured of beddable beauties
not worth their weight in alimony. What he needed . . . what
he needed was someone more like himself—someone who
understood him—someone like Mousha. He smiles slightly,
remembering how angry he had been when his first wife, at the
time of their divorce, had refused a settlement, insisting that if
he wanted to be free of her she preferred to be equally
affranchised. Mousha . . . Raising his eyes he saw Miss
Seeton huddled in the tan leather armchair drawing as if her life
depended on it—which by all accounts it might. Physical
attributes apart, she reminded him of Mousha: something of
the same uncompromising spirit; and independence and an
honesty. What would Mousha—what would any woman of that
type . . . ? For instance:

"What would you," he asked Miss Seeton, "say if I
suggested that we married?"

So deep was she in the throes of composition, the question
barely impinged upon her consciousness. "I should say no,"
replied Miss Seeton and continued working.

The mere hint of opposition automatically aroused the
fighter in him. "Then you would be the first woman who hasn't
jumped at the chance."

She did wish Mr. Stemkos wouldn't keep interrupting just
when she'd nearly finished. "It says little for the women you
have known. Or, perhaps, for your choice of them," she
answered abstractedly. There—she drew a final line—that was
done. She held the sketch from her and examined it. Oh, dear.
How very vulgar.

His smile broadened. He'd been right; she was like Mousha.
"Well?" He held out his hand.

She gave him the sketchbook apologetically. "It looks—
well, rather vulgar, I'm afraid."

"And marriage?"

Marriage? Well—yes, that, too. Really, the foreign sense of
umor. She laughed dutifully.

"You find the idea amusing?"

Well, no, frankly she didn't. But naturally one couldn't say
. "Well, no, frankly I don't," said Miss Seeton. She
astened to make amends. "That is to say, I'm sure it's very
unny, but these things are really a question of taste." Not,
erhaps, she decided, quite the happiest choice of word. She
ied to soften the effect. "Or, of course, lack of it," she
dded.

His smile faded and his jaw set. What had started as a trivial
emark was developing into a contest of wills. He was
eginning to visualize a partnership with this woman as a
ound business proposition. The other side of marriage could
e kept—on the side. His expression struck Miss Seeton as that
f a spoiled boy in class who on being told he could not have
is way was hardening in determination to be intractable. To
eep control one must deflect his thoughts.

"What," she demanded, "put this ridiculous idea into your
ead?"

It might have been Mousha speaking. "You happen to
emind me of my first wife."

"Then I suggest," said Miss Seeton briskly—knowing
othing of the original Mme Stemkos, she saw no compli-
ent—"you'd better remarry her. If, that is to say, she happens
o be free. Or would consider you."

He glowered, then throwing back his head, he laughed and
ressed the button of the intercom.

"Yes, sir?"

"Find my first wife."

"Your . . . ? Yes, sir."

He gazed at Miss Seeton with respect. "So, you undertake
o solve all problems. Then come, let us pursue your problem
a vulgarity." He placed the sketchbook under the desk lamp.

There was a knock upon the door. Stemkos growled
nintelligibly and his secretary entered, pert, trim and with a
ecret smile.

"The director of personnel to see you, sir."

"Not now," snapped the financier. He bounced to his feet,
trode across the thick-pile carpet to the window, where he
tood staring into the obscurity. "Wait," he barked. This must
ean that the accountants had uncovered the connection

concerning Anatole that he'd been looking for. "I'll see hi
for a minute, but after that I'm not to be disturbed—for a
reason."

"Very good, sir." With her secret smile trembling towa
giggles, the secretary fled.

There was a feeling—an atmosphere. Miss Seeton w
intrigued. A dumpy yet attractive woman, severe in black, h
gray hair drawn to a neat bun, closed the door behind t
secretary and stood waiting.

Stemkos flung away from the window toward his des
"Well?"

"You desired to see me, sir?"

The woman's voice halted him in midstride. He stoo
lowering, his head slung from one to the other of the tw
women like a bull uncertain at which target to charge. A plo
No, it was clear they did not know each other. He ignored Mi
Seeton and concentrated upon the figure by the door.

"What brought you here?"

"Your secretary. She has telephoned my office—it is but
few steps."

"You, then—you are the director of personnel?"

"Yes, sir."

He returned to his desk and waved her to the upright cha
opposite him. "For how long?"

She sat, feet together, lips pursed, calculating on her finger
"Let us see. It is fifteen years that I have worked here and
yes, there are ten years that I am director of personnel—sir.

He banged the desk with his fist. "Don't call me 'sir.'

Her eyelids dropped demurely. "No—Hero."

No one but Mousha had ever called him that. It was—th
shock jolted him—nearly twenty years. His effort to suppress
grin resulted in a scowl.

"The staff know who you are?"

"But naturally."

"And they have helped to conceal your presence from me.
has been a conspiracy."

"But yes," she granted, "a conspiracy—of kindness."

He regarded her shrewdly. "So then it has been you wh
were responsible for thwarting Anatole?"

"Twortin?" Her mind fumbled the translation. *Traverser
Bloquer?* She beamed in triumph. "Ah, yes, for blocki
Anatole. There is a type that I have never trusted from the fir

time I have seen him. And from some while I have suspected . . . So—a little movement of personnel here—a
change there—and he is become nervous. One did what one
could.''

"Why?''

"Why?'' Her limpid gaze questioned his sanity. "But is it
not the obligation of a wife to guard her husband's interests?''

Despite himself the grin broke through; his shoulders shook.
"No one but you, Mousha, could take that attitude.''

"Attitude?'' She rounded on him in indignation. "It is not
an attitude. It is what I believe.''

For the first time in all those nearly twenty years the wing of
a genuine emotion brushed him: how had he ever come to
throw away the substance for the shadow? He leaned across the
desk and touched her arm. "That was what I meant.'' The
gesture rather than the words mollified her. "It is the opinion of
Miss Seeton''—a pass of the hand served for an introduction—
"and it would appear that she is always right—that you and I
should remarry. That is''—he searched his memory for the
exact words—"if you should happen to be free—or would
consider me.''

Mousha Stemkos was off her chair and clasping both Miss
Seeton's hands. "This gives me great pleasure. I have read of
you—the Umbrella of the English police.'' The practical
woman of affairs was yielding to natural ebullience. "What is
it that you do for Hero? You trace Anatole? You recover the
diamonds he has stole?''

Miss Seeton, fascinated—it was like watching two iron
filings flashed together by a magnetic current—had no time to
reply before Stemoks intervened.

"Miss Seeton has set us a vulgar puzzle.''

"Puzzle? *Une énigme?*'' Delighted, Mousha hurried back to
the desk and studied Miss Seeton's drawing. An over-made-up,
sandal-shod, but otherwise naked girl, her knees crossed the
better to display remarkable legs, sat on a suitcase with other
cases round her. Below, on her left, was water; behind her, the
light tracing of a bridge; on her right, railway lines in steep
perspective showed the rear end of a disappearing train. With
joy Mousha raised her eyes, shoulders, hands and crowed.
"Feelthy peectures. My poor Hero,'' she commiserated. "You
find that the virility escapes you—that the hour has arrived for
pornography?''

They discussed Miss Seeton's experiences at the theater in
relation to her impression of Lilianne and decided that the
inference to be drawn from the sketch was palpable: Librecksin
and the girl had left Paris and intended to cross the Channel.

Stemkos glanced toward the window with satisfaction. "In
this fog they will not have gone far."

For Mousha an outstanding and, as yet, unremedied feature
of the story was: "But this poor Miss Seeton—she has lost her
clothes. They must be replaced."

Overriding the ex-schoolteacher's protests, Stemkos un-
locked a drawer. Miss Seeton without clothes was not an image
that he wished to contemplate. He tossed a thick wad of notes
to his ex-wife. "Arrange it."

Mousha clapped her hands in delight and caught Miss
Seeton's arm. "Come, we will go at once and have a shopping
bombe."

"Mousha."

She looked back. "*Hein?*"

"You have not answered."

"Not . . . ? Ah, that . . ." Shoulders began to lift and
hands to spread until a shyness arrested them. "If you desire
it."

"Your English has improved."

"It was necessary for business." The long years in Paris had
made French come more easily than her native Greek. "I have
worked with an English dictionary, but the idiom—that still
escapes me. I—" Her whole personality had become muted.
"I will lose my position here?"

"It would not be fitting for my wife to be the director of
personnel."

Despondent, she agreed. "*Non, ça ce voit—pas conven-
able.*"

"But I would be grateful, if you wish it, that you should
continue to run the Paris office—but officially and as a
partner."

They regarded each other in silence, yet Miss Seeton
recognized that they were engrossed in a conversation which
had no need of words. She gave a small sigh of pleasure. So
romantic. And, of course, so right. The upsurge of feeling
sweeping through Mousha shone in her face.

Stemkos grunted. "Arrange that too, then—with my secretary. She will see to the details and inform me of the time and

place for the ceremony, and ask her to send in the head accountant.''

Restored, bright-eyed, Mousha gave him a mock salute. ''Very good—sir.'' She seized Miss Seeton's shoulders and squeezed them. ''Come, *ma p'tite*, we will carry out our orders and then we will commence our shopping *bombe*.''

The shopping *bombe* began modestly on the Boulevard des Italiens, where they bought a hat. Mme de Brillot and Mousha Stemkos were enthusiastic, but Miss Seeton had reservations. However, with an addition here and there, and worn straight, and not at the angle that her two friends and the saleslady insisted on, it would, she felt, eventually do. Through the fog they worked their way carefully down the Avenue de l'Opéra and up the financial *échelon* to Victor's, where they bought a coat. Again Miss Seeton was dubious, but was quelled. The large red-and-black wool check seemed so very—flamboyant. But, on the other hand, she had to admit the coat was practical since it reversed, for wet weather, to a fawn-gray gabardine.

Emerging onto the Rue de Rivoli, mousha, with the bit between her teeth, headed for Bamiel's, where they bought a suit—so suitable, she explained with glee—and, at Mme de Brillot's suggestion, remembering the black lace, a semi-cocktail-evening in gray with purple, pearl and black embroidery. Neither needed much in the way of alteration—a little arrangement to this; a nothing to that—and both would be delivered to the hotel during the afternoon. Miss Seeton was shocked: quite lovely, of course, but, really, quite wickedly extravagant. She was overruled and, filled with pride in their accomplishment, they repaired round the corner to the Ritz-Palace for lunch.

Lunch was gay. They toasted Mousha's re-engagements both marital and professional; they celebrated what they insisted on describing as Miss Seeton's flair for clothes, and Mousha, abubble with happiness, gave an account of the ''feelthy peecture.'' Mme de Brillot held out her hand and Miss Seeton was forced to smile: so like, really so very like, Chief Superintendent Delphick. She produced the sketchbook with the warning:

''I'm afraid it's rather like one of those holiday postcards at the seaside with the rude punning titles.''

"Punning?" Mousha seized on the new word. "What is that?"

"A sort of play on words," Miss Seeton clarified.

"Ah, understood—like suit and suitable. And what rude punning"—she pointed to the drawing—"you are going to put on this?"

Miss Seeton thought. "I fear they would call it something like *Abandoned Baggage*."

Mme de Brillot was withdrawn, concentrating on the drawing. She looked up. "Abandoned . . . ?" she repeated slowly. She went still, her gaze fixed upon a concept developing in her mind. She rose, saying that she must telephone but would be back. The reception clerk approached the table. He was sorry, he apologized, he had not seen the ladies come in—had only just heard. M. Eigord, the manager of the Casino de Paris, had telephoned three times. At last M. Eigord had left a message: with Miss Seeton's permission he proposed to call upon her after lunch.

Mousha was enchanted. "So," she chortled, "you too have choices of profession. You can rest a detective, draw feelthy peectures for much money, or go to the Casino to become *une grande vedette*—a star."

M. Eigord, his associates, the *artistes*, the staff, even the musicians at the Casino de Paris were jubilant. They felt that two unremitting days and nights of drudgery were being rewarded, for during the afternoon a light breeze had sprung up, shifting the fog, and by six o'clock, although the conditions still prevailed in the Channel and over England, Paris was comparatively clear and, in festive mood after its incarceration, was beseiging the Casino box office.

The altered version of the original finale to the first act had been set forward to scene three as a grand opening for the full ensemble. The gilded coffins, all but Miss England's, had been scrapped and the girls' cloaks redesigned to represent the flags of European countries. Cecil, resplendent in white, led the girls down the stairs in turn and relinquished them to two stalwart youths who danced them and maneuvered them into place.

A fanfare: the lights flashed ANGLETERRE; a bump upstage and the opening bars of "Rule Britannia" heralded the entrance of the new star, Missesse. In a concerted, if unsynchronized, movement the entire cast pivoted and pointed

```
************** *************************    CE*****
*                                                *
* JEUDI PROCHAIN      CASINO DE PARIS          SOIR *
*                                                *
*                        MISSESSE                *
*                                                *
*                   dans la nouvelle revue       *
*                     MISS-EN-SCÈNE              *
*                          avec                   *
*                      CECIL CYRCIL              *
*                                                *
*  CE SOIR    GRAND SPECTACLE NU ET SATIRIQUE  CE SOIR *
***** *********************************    *****
```

to the coffin. Even the nudes were inspired to turn their
attention from the gentlemen in the stage boxes and front stalls
and raised languid hands in approximately the right direction.
The gold coffin for Miss England, with its suggestion of the
Sleeping Beauty to be aroused at last by the young prince in
white, brought anticipatory chuckles from the spectators. Cecil
swung the coffin lid open: the umbrella fell, the handbag
tumbled and the audience after a startled silence caught the gist
and roared. With the rending of England's veil to reveal the
dowdy little figure with its old-fashioned hat, the theater
shouted its approval. At the foot of the steps, with the whole
company vocalizing their insistence that they would not be
happy until they made "yew 'appy tew-ew," Cecil was joined
by the two stalwarts in an acrobatic dance while Miss England,
wild-eyed with fright, fought them off at the point of an
umbrella. When the ferrule landed on their toes they hopped,
they clutched their feet and then returned to the attack, and the
undertheme of political satire convulsed the house. Finally
Missesse, muddled, legs intertwined and locked through trying
to escape first this way and then that, was held aloft by Cecil
with a firm grip round the waist: but when, belabored, he
subsided in a split, his grip slipped for a moment and he
tightened it.

"Ee—mind my bloody stitches," gasped Missesse, and the
curtain swept down to tumultuous applause.

London

OVATION FOR NEW STAR

MISSESSE WOWS THEM AT THE CASINO

from Thrudd Banner in Paris

Chief Superintendent Delphick lowered the paper and
addressed his sergeant. "Hop over, Bob, and see if any of the
French dailies have come in."

"I don't think they can have, sir. Miss Seeton's plane will be
the first out of Paris since the fog."

"There are still the cross-Channel boats. Go and see."

Sergeant Ranger left the office at London Airport in which
they were waiting, passed the counters of the banks and travel
agencies, reached a news stall and returned triumphant.

"Just this one, sir. *Paris Midi*."

Delphick exchanged papers with him. "You did say 'Miss
Seeton's plane,'" he observed. "Make what you can of that."
He pointed to the banner notice. In *Paris Midi* he found what
he wanted on the front page.

UNE NOUVELLE MISTINGUETT?

MISSESSE AU CASINO DE PARIS

Hier soir on a vue ici le début de . . .

He skimmed down the review. It told him little more th
had Thrudd Banner's report.

Reading the English paper, Bob Ranger's jaw dropped. "B
she couldn't've, sir—I mean she wouldn't've." Miss Seeton-
Aunt Em, as he and Anne now called her—in a nudie show
Granted she never did what you expected and always what yo
didn't, still this . . . No. "She couldn't. Well, I mean sh
wouldn't—would she, sir?" It was a plea for reassurance

"I imagine not." Yet Delphick was reminded that h
imagination had conjured precisely such a vision at the last o
the A.C.'s conferences. "But I find the coincidence of th
names Missesse and MissEss a little hard to take; our versio
must be mixed up in it somewhere. After all, we knew she w
likely to go to that theater. Obviously, as usual, she's gon
farther than was meant; but that she's gone so far as to becom
their leading lady I doubt."

The loudspeaker announced the flight from Paris and the
descended to customs. Delphick had arranged with the airpo
authorities to be on hand for Miss Seeton's arrival
case . . . No—no likelihood of trouble that he could forese
but he would still prefer to be there—just in case. He and Bo
watched the porters bring forward trolleys when the revolvir
volcano which ejects the luggage started to turn and th
passengers began to filter through from passports. First cla
first.

A chic, fair-haired, attractive woman won Delphick's appr
ciation. She had secured a porter and was standing beside a
equally smart older woman wearing a stylish hat and a blac
and-red-check coat. The older woman was cluttered with
long parcel, a large handbag and, incongruously, an ol
fashioned umbrel— Good God. He stared in disbelief: the
Miss Seeton—metamorphosed. If it hadn't been for th
umbrella he'd never have . . . Quickly he showed his pa
and, followed by Bob, went across to greet her.

• • •

Miss Seeton was happy; to be back at last; to see the chief superintendent and Bob; and to introduce them to her friend Mme de Brillot, who had been so kind and had arranged everything. A further cause for happiness had been the notices of the revue in the morning papers, which Mme de Brillot had translated during the journey. It was so gratifying to know that the twins had had a great success. Such nice, kind boys. They deserved it. Though how that poor Cyril had managed all those acrobatics and that fooling with his strapping and his stitches she couldn't think. Her heart had been in her mouth quite half the time. It had been rather a shock, and embarrassing at first— although she had given Mr. Eigord permission to use the name Missesse and what he had repeatedly referred to as her "act"— to see her own clothes—mended? or were they copies?—on the stage. But after a while one had realized how amusing it appeared. And Mr. Eigord, so generous, after giving them his box at the theater, had taken them to supper, Mme de Brillot, herself, the twins and Mr. and Mousha Stemkos, and they'd all been so gay. And all that other, unpleasant, and quite dreadful, business was finished. Left behind. And now she was nearly home. Miss Seeton was happy.

Mme de Brillot was disappointed. It had appeared a good idea to take Miss Seeton to Paris but, professionally, it had not succeeded. In truth, they had established that Mantoni was in the city—and, by inference, Librecksin—but there was no proof. Her telephone call to the police at lunch yesterday had been useful to a point and she had gained a certain satisfaction from a small paragraph in the papers this morning to the effect that the remains of an unidentified woman—the head and an arm were missing—had been discovered in suitcases at various left-luggage offices. However, although she and the police might presume the body to be that of Lilianne, again there was no proof. As an indirect bonus Miss Seeton had reunited Heracles and Mousha Stemkos, had transformed the Cyrcil Twins into stars and had turned a revue from bad to good—but these were the fringe benefits of a fairy godmother; no part of the case; nor sufficient restitution for Vee's death. But then— she shrugged—it was not reasonable to hope to win every trick, nor to count on Miss Seeton to establish every detail.

She indicated their luggage as it rotated and the porter asked had they anything to declare? She shook her head.

Miss Seeton promptly contradicted, saying, "This." With

an effort she held up the parcel, which appeared to grow
heavier the longer she carried it.

With Miss Seeton heading for a customs officer, their paths
diverged. Mme de Brillot stopped on her way to the farther
exit.

"Do not forget," she reminded, "to pass word"—she
stressed both syllables—"to your friend of that song you have
so often heard." She gave a wave of the hand and walked out
of Miss Seeton's life with the same apparent casualness with
which she had entered it.

Delphick, who had done no more than smile and say How do
you do, was surprised to experience a sense of loss and was
perceptive enough to realize that Miss Seeton also felt
deserted. He watched the elegant, somehow lonely figure
follow the porter, whom Bob had relieved of Miss Seeton's
luggage, and then it struck him. "Pass word," "so kind,"
"arranged everything." She must've been—must be—Fenn's
"man." Give the Special Branch its due—to guard a woman
it'd take a woman. He turned to Miss Seeton, who was
explaining to the customs officer: no, not the two cases, both of
which were now open; it was really this. She handed over the
parcel.

"You see," she confided, "I'd rather that tall young man
behind me didn't know what's in it. It's for his wedding next
week."

The officer smiled. "Did it cost more than ten pounds?"

"Good gracious, no. At least, that is to say, I shouldn't think
so. It was French—the money, I mean—which isn't quite the
same thing. Though," she admitted, "it did take rather a lot of
it."

He propped the parcel on the open suitcase so that their lids
would conceal it from Bob Ranger and began to undo the
string.

"Tell me," Delphick asked. "What was this password—this
song your friend spoke of?"

"Oh, something Russian, I think," she told him. "About
India, I believe."

Oblon complaining of Miss Seeton being drunk and singing.
"Did you sing it at some eating place in Italy?"

"Why, yes." She was surprised to learn that he should know
of it. "Or rather, I should say, Mme de Brillot did. I only
hummed."

"What happened?"

"The police arrested him."

"Him?"

It dawned upon her that Delphick was not versed in all the details and she hastened to supply them. "The man with the wrong briefcase, who took the other man's when he, the other one, was singing it. Not there, of course, but here. Originally. And he tried to take Mme de Brillot's handbag. The other one, I mean. The one in Italy."

Delphick shook his head to clear it. He'd get it out of her later if it was important. Meanwhile . . . Russian—India? "Do you mean Rimsky-Korsakov's 'Song of India'?"

"It may be," she accepted. "I'm afraid I'm not very knowledgeable about music."

In a pleasant baritone Delphick sang:

"Les diamants chez nous sont innombrables,
Les perles dans nos mers incalculables;
C'est l'Inde . . ."

Behind him there was an exclamation and a thud. He looked around. Miss Seeton turned.

In spite of the difficulty in obtaining seats, Librecksin recognized that the package flight had worked to his advantage. The police had been in evidence at Orly Airport, but a multitude of faces dulls the visual sense and both his and Mantoni's disguises and forged passports had passed through without comment.

Now, at Heathrow, wedged in the crowd around the luggage conveyor, he was feeling confident. He and Mantoni pressed forward in the crush toward the No Declaration exit. Abruptly the Italian halted, trembling.

"Polizia," he breathed.

Librecksin scanned the scene ahead of them: a middle-aged man and an enormous younger one were standing behind a woman at the customs desk. The trio had their backs to them and, police or not, neither man was showing the least interest in his surroundings. Librecksin reassured the jittering Italian. The elder of the men in front began to sing. Mantoni gave a stifled scream, dropping his case and the rug holdall which contained the canvases. Allora, he had been tricked. This

Librecksin had betrayed him. And now the English pig
derided him—sang at him in derision. The song stopped shor
and the man swung round. The woman turned.

"Good gracious," said Miss Seeton, "it's Mr. Mantoni."

Librecksin remained transfixed. Elio gaped at her, petrified
by this vision from the pit. Betrayed. . . . He gobbled or
rising notes. Betrayed. . . . He went berserk.

For an instant Delphick was thrown off balance. A little
man, emoting in Italian in which only such words as *diavolo*
strega and *tradimento* were distinguishable, had leaped at
gray-haired man beside him, knocking him to the ground, bu
Miss Seeton's mention of the name Mantoni had galvanized
both him and his sergeant into action and Bob Ranger plucked
the Italian from his victim and held him, shrieking and kicking
in midair while Delphick assisted the other to his feet.

"Know this one too?" he asked.

Miss Seeton studied the man. To an artist the trivia o
substitution or the color of hair must always be subordinate t
bone structure. "Why, yes. Yes, that's Mr. Librecksin." Sh
glanced about her in uncertainty: what a pity that Mme d'
Brillot wasn't here.

Two uniformed policemen, alerted by the noise, brok
through the cordon of passengers which had formed around th
combatants. Delphick showed his credentials.

"I suggest you hold both these men on suspicion and searc
them while we confirm identification." He addressed Mis
Seeton. "If you're ready, we'll have to go along too. Sorry,
he sympathized on seeing her expression, "but I'm afrai
you'll have to make a statement and sign it. Shouldn't tak
long."

Miss Seeton turned back to the customs officer to find that h
had been joined by an older man with a face like a granit
mask. The latter spoke.

"This parcel is yours, madam?"

"Yes." She leaned forward to whisper. "You see, as
explained, it's a wedding present for the tall young man behin
me. I wanted it to be a surprise."

"I've no doubt it would've been, madam."

His grim manner disturbed her. "Shouldn't I have brough
it?"

A flicker of expression threatened to crack the mask
"Frankly no, madam, I don't think you should." He stoo

ack as a young man approached. "This gentleman would like
ou to go with him and give an account of it."

Detective Constable Haley reached the desk. On a tip from
ae Sûreté, Fraud had sent him over to check all flights from
'aris in case Mantoni tried to reenter the country, also
upplying him with a photograph of Librecksin. And now here
vas customs chasing themselves up the wall about some
aurder they'd uncovered. He looked down at Miss Seeton's
aggage, flinched, hurriedly raised his eyes and swallowed.
"Where did you . . . ?" he began, then stopped.

"It's only fair to say the lady declared it herself," volun-
:ered the elder customs officer.

Haley wasn't listening. He stared: the Brolly—or he was a
lue-eyed baboon—all dressed to kill; then he winced at the
ptness of the metaphor. And, behind her, the Oracle himself;
vith his sergeant. Well, what the hell were customs up to,
ragging in a lowly D.C. when everything was already under
ontrol.

"Sorry, Chief Superintendent," he apologized, "for butting
1, it's all—er—yours."

"What is?"

"You haven't seen it, sir?"

"Not yet."

Haley hesitated. "I think, sir, you'd better come round. If
ve shut the case lids and the crowd get an eyeful half of 'em'll
aint and the rest'll leg it for the loo."

Delphick and Bob Ranger moved to stare down at a human
rm sealed in polythene lying on a long stainless steel platter.
Aiss Seeton joined them.

"Oh, no." She caught her breath. "Oh, dear," she gasped.
Oh, dear, how truly dreadful. That poor young woman."

"You know who this belongs to?" demanded Delphick.

"But of course." She indicated a birthmark on the upper
rm. "I remember noticing that particularly in the theater. It's
ae girl Lilianne, whom Mme de Brillot told me was a friend—
r rather, to be frank, I understood her to be a mistress of Mr.
.ibrecksin there." She pointed.

Librecksin made a convulsive movement, but hands tight-
ned on his arm and he closed his eyes. Nothing to be done.
he diamonds in his pocket would be found; the canvases in
Aantoni's holdall would be discovered; this devil-woman had
utwitted him and the trick he had played on her—the delayed-

action bomb that he had planted to keep her involved with
French police—had delayed too long and had exploded in
face.

On the whole he wouldn't, Bob decided, tell Anne about
arm—it might spoil her pleasure in the present. And yet—y
never knew. Suddenly he suspected that as a trained nu
Anne might even find it funny. Women were tougher over th
things than men. He regarded Miss Seeton with a grudging,
affectionate, respect. When he'd seen her coming fr
passports he'd thought at first she'd changed out of recog
tion. But no—it'd only been the hat and coat—Aunt Em had
changed. Nobody else in the world'd come trotting ho
clutching a dish with the joint already on it and then innocer
serve it up to customs.